STUMBLING STONES

BASED ON A TRUE STORY

BONNIE SUCHMAN

Black Rose Writing | Texas

The author grants the final approval for this literary material.

First printing

This is a work of fiction. Names, characters, businesses, places, events, and incidents are either the products of the author's imagination or used in a fictitious manner. Any resemblance to actual persons, living or dead, or actual events is purely coincidental.

ISBN: 978-1-68513-410-5
LIBRARY OF CONGRESS CONTROL NUMBER: 2023950316
PUBLISHED BY BLACK ROSE WRITING
www.blackrosewriting.com

Printed in the United States of America
Suggested Retail Price (SRP) $21.95

Stumbling Stones is printed in Sabon LT Std

*As a planet-friendly publisher, Black Rose Writing does its best to eliminate unnecessary waste to reduce paper usage and energy costs, while never compromising the reading experience. As a result, the final word count vs. page count may not meet common expectations.

Dedicated to the Heppenheimer women,
past, present, and future.

STUMBLING STONES

PROLOGUE

April 2018

Our early morning flight out of Tel Aviv took off an hour late and failed to make up any time on the way to Frankfurt. We only had forty-five minutes to catch our connecting flight back to Washington, D.C. Plenty of time, we said hopefully to each other as we quickly descended the stairs of the plane. We ignored both flight attendants, who told us that there was no way we could make our flight, given that the terminal was on the other side of the Frankfurt airport. We ran across the tarmac to the bus that would take us to the terminal, and then waited another fifteen minutes for the bus to leave. We jumped off the bus as soon as it stopped, raced through the doors of the terminal, and ran to the gate. I looked at my watch. We still had five minutes left. But as I looked up, I saw that the door to the plane had already closed. The airline employee gave us a sympathetic smile when we asked whether they were still boarding and then looked at her screen for the next available flight to Washington. A few taps later, she informed us that there was nothing available for another twelve hours. Twelve hours! We had been in Israel for two weeks on vacation and were eager to get home. But what else could we do? So, we told her we would take those seats, and then sat down to catch our breath and try to figure out what to do for the next twelve hours.

My husband Bruce is never one to wait at an airport and twelve hours is too long a time, even for me. But first, I needed some caffeine. I got up to buy myself a cup of tea and when I returned, Bruce immediately said to me, "Let's go to Frankfurt. We can get something to eat and walk around the city. It will be fun." I took a sip of my tea and said, "Sure. Let's go." And so we checked our carry-on bags at the airport, hopped on the train, and went to Frankfurt.

We had been to the city once before, also because of a missed flight. That time, we spent about four hours roaming the city. This time, we had more time to kill. It was a lovely spring day, and so we decided to try to explore more of the city than we had on our previous visit. We started in the center of the city, crossed and re-crossed the Main River, and walked around some of the residential neighborhoods.

Bruce's father Curtis was born in Mannheim, about an hour south of Frankfurt by train. He had lived there until he had fled to America in 1937 at the age of 17 to escape the Nazis. Bruce knew almost nothing about his father's life in Germany, since Curtis rarely spoke about that period. Bruce's mom Millie had more of a connection to her family – also Jewish refugees from Europe – and she had made it her mission to try to stay connected with some of Curtis' family, but Bruce only knew that the people he had visited were "cousins" of his father. As Bruce and I walked the streets of Frankfurt, Bruce said he believed that some of his family had also lived in Frankfurt, but he couldn't remember who. The only thing he knew was that they, too, had been forced to leave because of the Nazis.

As we were walking through Frankfurt, Bruce and I began to notice brass plates on the sidewalks. We read the plates and saw that they identified Jews who once lived at the addresses, but had been persecuted by the Nazis. I took out my phone and did a quick search and discovered that these were Stolpersteine, or "Stumbling Stones" in English, and that they had been placed around many cities in Europe to remember those who were either murdered or forced to leave their homes during the Holocaust. Given our recent visit to Yad Vashem, the Holocaust museum in Jerusalem, I was curious about these memorials.

The Stolpersteine website had a list of stones in Frankfurt, so I scrolled down the list as we walked through Frankfurt. I stopped when I came to the surname "Heppenheimer." This was my father-in-law's surname before he shortened it after he left Germany. Two women had this surname. I showed Bruce my phone.

"Do you think it's possible that these women were related to your family?"

"I have no idea. But we are just a few blocks from these stones. Let's walk over."

We soon turned onto Boemerstrasse. In front of the apartment building at Boemerstrasse 60 were three brass plates: "Lippmann ('Leo') Lewin, Selma Lewin born Heppenheimer, and Emma Heppenheimer." *Heppenheimer.* We assumed that Lippmann and Selma had been married and that Selma was Emma's daughter. But who were these people? Bruce was as curious as I – maybe Emma and Selma were distant cousins? I took out my phone and took a picture of the brass plates.

We had been walking nearly three hours and were tired and hungry, and so we stopped at a nearby restaurant and ordered lunch. We talked about what we wanted to see in the afternoon, but my mind kept coming back to Selma and Emma Heppenheimer. My curiosity was too strong, and Bruce knew better than to try to stop me. I pulled out my phone and began a quick search. I promised I would stop looking when the food arrived. According to the stones, Emma was born in 1861 and

Selma was born in 1900. Curtis' father's name was Max, and Max had siblings. I opened up my Ancestry.com account and typed in names. I pulled out a piece of paper from my purse and began to make a crude family tree.

As much as I could tell from this limited research, Max's father Joseph had two wives. With his first wife, Joseph had five children, including Bruce's grandfather. After his first wife died, Joseph married Emma and had two daughters – Alice and Selma. I read off the names of Max's siblings from the first marriage – Bruce vaguely knew who they were. But Bruce had never heard of Emma or Alice or Selma. After a quick calculation, we determined Max had been 6 years old when Joseph remarried and Emma became Max's stepmother. So, essentially, she was his mother, and was Curtis' grandmother. We both wondered out loud why my father-in-law had never mentioned this grandmother.

We knew that both Selma and Emma had perished in the Holocaust from the Stolpersteine. I continued to look on the Ancestry website, but could find nothing about what happened to Alice. I was not surprised, since a number of European countries had made access to records after 1900 a bit of a challenge. Even Selma's death record was not on the site. This would take more research, perhaps a lot more research. Since Bruce only knew about the children of Joseph through their children, who had emigrated to America, both of us wondered if it was possible that Bruce didn't know about Alice because she had survived the war but had no children. Maybe she had moved to California. Or maybe she had moved to Israel. Maybe we had unknowingly walked past her descendants during our trip to Israel. I remembered reading recently about brothers who had been reunited many years after the Holocaust; neither had known that the other had survived. Wouldn't it be wonderful to discover that Alice had also survived the Holocaust? But I had spent more time on my phone than the thirty minutes I had promised Bruce and our food was getting cold, and so I put my phone away. Still, throughout lunch and the rest of our brief visit to Frankfurt, we both kept coming back to the same question. What had happened to Alice?

CHAPTER 1

Nuremberg, May 1920

Alice was practically running to the tram stop, hoping that she would make the next tram. She was wearing her new Mary Jane pumps, and was worried about scuffing her shoes. Fortunately, she arrived at the tram stop just as the tram was about to leave. She climbed the two steps and found a seat. Alice looked down at her watch. 9:30 am. The train from Frankfurt was scheduled to arrive at 10 am. She should have no problem reaching the Nuremberg Central Station before the train arrived, assuming the tram kept to its schedule. Still, Alice could not stop worrying about being late. Her mother Emma was always late, which often made her father late. But Joseph Heppenheimer never tolerated his children being late. If Alice could make the tram go faster, she would.

It was all Tante Ida's fault. One of the conditions in her parents agreeing to allow Alice to leave Frankfurt to attend the Nuremberg Arts and Crafts School was that Alice agree to live with Emma's widowed second cousin, whose only child had left home to marry and who thus had a spare room to rent. On the day she moved in, the cousin insisted Alice call her Tante Ida. But this cousin never felt like an aunt to Alice. She was often stingy with meals and mindful of any additional expenses resulting from

Alice living in the apartment, such as Alice using too much coal for the stove to heat the apartment. When Alice was in the apartment, Tante Ida would often prattle on about nothing in particular. That was the case this morning, and Alice finally had to interrupt Tante Ida to remind her that Alice was going to be late to meet her parents. Alice could hear Tante Ida grumbling about the rudeness of her "niece" as Alice was leaving the apartment.

When the tram finally arrived at the train station, Alice quickly got off and raced through the doors of the station. She looked up at the large clock. She still had fifteen minutes before the train was scheduled to arrive. She stopped to catch her breath and found a bench to sit and wait. She looked around the large main hall, which had recently been rebuilt. She did not really like the station's Neo-Baroque façade, but loved the main hall's art nouveau features and the beautiful tile mosaics embedded in the walls. Every time she was in the main hall, she would design new tiles in her head. Now, she was trying to distract herself by designing a new tile. After all, she was getting married tomorrow and she wasn't sure her father would behave.

At exactly 10 am, the train pulled into the station. Alice got up from her bench and smoothed down the front of her dress. The dress was short – just above the knee – and she was wearing new silk stockings. She had chosen a dress with more muted colors, but she would not wear a long skirt, not even for her parents. She was also feeling good because she had kept her weight down and the dress was very slimming. As she walked toward the platform, she could see her sister Selma bound down the steps, followed more slowly by her mother and father. She was particularly struck by how her father was negotiating the train stairs, taking one stair at a time. It had been three months since she had last seen him, and he seemed to have aged since that family dinner. The family dinner that had almost ended her engagement, she thought to herself.

Selma was the first to see Alice and ran to hug her sister. Her mother followed and then her father, and Alice kissed both her parents. Her mother was the first to speak. "Alice, what have you done to your hair, your beautiful hair?" Alice had been worried that her mother would say something about the short dress or the Mary Jane shoes, accusing her of dressing like a "flapper." But, instead, her mother had focused on her hair. It really should not have been a surprise, Alice thought to herself, since she had had long hair for as long as she could remember. But Alice did not respond to her mother's comment. She wanted to keep the mood calm, so she changed the subject. "Hello, Mama, Papa. I hope you had a nice train ride. You are so lucky with the weather. It has been so cold and dreary, but today is a warm, sunny day."

But Selma did not take the hint – or chose to ignore it. "Oh, Alice, I love your hair. I have seen it in all the magazines. Mama, it is called a bob. All the women are doing it. Alice is so fashionable. I am thinking of doing it myself." She said the last comment with a bit of a smirk. Alice could hear her father grunt. Alice knew her father was still not happy about Alice going to the art school. Bobbed hair was likely a reminder of how far Alice had come from her life in Frankfurt. Selma knew that her comment would likely rile her father, but Selma didn't care. Actually, that wasn't true – she wanted to rile him. Selma had been trying to leave her job at Gebrüder Heppenheimer, the family's scrap metal company, and her father wouldn't let her – not until she married. And so any time Selma could annoy her father, she would.

Alice decided to side-step this battle. "Mama, Papa, let's get your bags and then we can go to the hotel. You will like this place. It is in a beautiful part of the city, just inside the old city walls. And you can take a rest before lunch. Ludwig and his family will meet us at the restaurant in the hotel for lunch." They walked out of the station, hailed a cab, and went to the hotel.

Alice had chosen the Hotel Plaut on Hallplatz because it was one of the few kosher hotels in the city, and kosher food was important both to her mother and, surprisingly, to her brother Max. Actually, her half-brother. Max was the youngest child from Joseph's first marriage to Mina, but always felt like a full brother to Alice, and Alice was very happy he was coming to see her marry. Max was arriving by train from Mannheim later in the day, but his wife Recha, who had recently given birth, was staying home with the newborn. Joseph's other four children from his first marriage – Bertha, Johanna, Jacob, and Benno – were not coming, but mostly because Alice had wanted to keep the wedding small. Although none of them had really pushed to attend.

After her father checked into the hotel, the bellhop picked up their bags and escorted her parents to the elevator. Alice had told her parents that she would let them get settled and would walk with Selma to the art school, which was only a few blocks from the hotel. Selma seemed happy to leave their parents, practically flying down the front stairs of the hotel. Alice had to run to catch up with her sister.

Once they were a block from the hotel, Selma turned to her sister and said, "Alice, you look wonderful. I love your hair, and that dress is lovely. And the dress matches your hat and your purse. And those shoes! I have seen advertisements in the magazines for Mary Janes, but Mama won't let me buy a pair. She says they are only for flappers. Ever since you wrote to her about seeing that movie "The Flapper," she has worried that I will turn into a flapper. Of course, with that new haircut of yours, Mama probably thinks you already are. I am assuming you made the dress yourself."

"I did. And the purse. Everything a well-dressed flapper needs." The two sisters giggled, and Alice continued, "Actually, I have been experimenting with different materials and different needle work for the purse. The dress is made with a silk fabric imported from China. A professor of mine told me about this importer, who brings in all kinds of exotic fabrics. It is pretty tricky to sew, but I think it turned out quite well. And you should look at the stitching."

Selma laughed. "You know I can't tell one stitch from another. But Alice, you are a magician with design. You know I love everything that you design. I actually can't think of a time when you were not designing something."

Alice also could not remember a time when she was not interested in fashion and design. As a young child, she loved to dress her many dolls. When she was old enough, her mother taught her how to use the treadle sewing machine, and Alice then designed dresses for her dolls. Alice designed dresses for herself as she got older, although she could not wear them outside the house. No daughter of Joseph Heppenheimer would be allowed to wear home-made dresses. While Alice's mother Emma did not share her daughter's passion for fashion, she always encouraged that passion and was happy to spend time with her daughter at Alice's favorite place, the Kaufhaus Wronker. The largest department store in Frankfurt, the Kaufhaus Wronker, had multiple floors of both ready-to-wear items and fashionable custom-made wear. The Kaufhaus Wronker even had an art salon and a gallery of decorative arts and graphics. After a morning exploring the latest fashions and viewing the art exhibits, Alice and her mother would have lunch at the Kaufhaus Wronker café. This was often the favorite part of the day for both mother and daughter, since Emma could enjoy a cup of coffee while happily listening to her daughter talk about her dream of opening her own fashion studio.

As they walked, Alice turned to her sister. "Selma, Papa seems to be walking a bit slower since the last time I saw him. Is everything okay with him?"

"Papa is fine. You would actually think that he would slow down since his retirement from Gebrüder Heppenheimer, but he still goes into the office most days and he is always pestering me when he is there. And when he is not going to the office, he is racing off to another spa 'to take the cure.' Perhaps he is tired and just needs to slow down."

But Alice thought that there was more to her father's slower gait than just tiredness. She had to admit that, even though he had retired in 1917, he didn't really behave like someone who had retired. Still, there was something about his walk that had changed. Maybe he was just getting older and Alice could see it only because she didn't see him every day.

"Selma, I thought it would be nice to sit down in the art school's library for about an hour. That would give Papa and Mama time to rest and to get ready for lunch. Erna said she would try to stop by to meet us there, if she has time. She has to speak with the office about an issue with her apprenticeship, which is starting next week."

Alice could see her sister force a smile. Alice knew Selma was jealous of her friendship with Erna, and had tried to reassure her sister about their own relationship multiple times. Still, Erna was her best friend at art school, and Alice knew it would calm her nerves if she could see her friend before the family lunch.

Alice met Erna when she first moved to Nuremberg in the fall of 1917 to begin art school. Alice had learned so much in the three years she had attended school. She learned about drawing and painting; about form and function; and about textiles and fashion. She loved those three years and had made great friends. Because of the Great War, more than half the students were women, and many had enjoyed the freedom to explore their talents for the first time in their young lives. That was certainly the case for Alice. She was sure that a number of these women would remain her friends forever. But she had no better friend than Erna.

Unlike Alice, Erna had started art school right after she graduated from high school at 16. Erna was younger than Alice's sister Selma and five years younger than Alice, but the two had a connection that she had never shared with her sister, or really with anyone else. Erna was from a small town Alice had never heard of and she wasn't Jewish. In fact, Alice was Erna's first Jewish friend. But that didn't matter – the two connected immediately and became instant friends.

Alice and Selma walked through the large wooden doors of the library and found two seats near the doors. They sat down and Alice took a small sketch book out of her purse and began to sketch. Sketching usually relaxed Alice, and she needed to be calm before the lunch, and then the dinner.

Selma started to laugh. "Is there ever a time when you don't have a sketch book with you? Even that little purse has a sketch book in it!"

Alice smiled. "I was actually thinking about a design on the way to the train station this morning and I wanted to sketch it before I forgot it. But I can put the book away."

"Don't bother. You will be too distracted unless you put it down on paper. You have always been this way. If Mama had not finally convinced Papa to let you attend art school, you would have made us all miserable."

Alice nodded at her sister and thought about the challenges she had faced to attend the Nuremberg school in the first place. It had taken five years to convince her parents – really her father – to allow her to leave Frankfurt and attend the arts and crafts school. Alice had graduated from the Philanthropin, a Jewish school in Frankfurt, in 1912 at 16 and immediately started working in her father's scrap metal business, as had her older sisters before her. Her sisters had married after a few years of work and her father expected the same for Alice. But Alice had other ideas. She wanted to be in the fashion industry and thought the best way to make that happen would be to attend an arts and crafts school.

Frankfurt had an arts and crafts school, but it only accepted men. One of the only schools in Germany to accept women at the time was the Nuremberg school. Admittedly, Alice had her concerns about attending school in Nuremberg. Nuremberg was a medieval town and tied to its old-fashioned ways. And while it had a Jewish community, it had a long anti-Semitic history. It was hard enough to be a Jew in Frankfurt. Her father was initially adamant that Alice would go nowhere near this Bavarian city.

But Alice was just as adamant that she be allowed to attend this school. She started her campaign to attend the art school as soon as she graduated from the Philanthropin. Her two older sisters, Bertha and Johanna, were her father's daughters from his first marriage and were much older that Alice. Alice was not particularly close to either sister, and both were married and with children, and so were focused on their own lives. She couldn't really expect much help from them. Her younger sister, Selma, was the other child from her father's second marriage, and Alice and Selma were close. Selma would want to help, but at the time, she was still a child.

As Alice continued to sketch in her book, she said, "I was actually surprised that, when I first raised the idea of moving to Nuremberg to attend school, Mama was not opposed to the idea."

"That also surprised me. But it may be that Mama knew what it was like not to have choices and wanted you to have the choice to pursue your art. Plus, I think she knew how much fashion meant to you." Alice shook her head in agreement, and thought about what her mother had done for her. Emma Baer had married Joseph Heppenheimer in her mid-30s, after helping to raise her younger siblings after her mother's death. Joseph had five children of his own, the youngest of whom was only four years old when his first wife died. Alice believed that her mother felt like she had traded raising one set of children for another when she married Joseph, but saw the emerging opportunities for young women like Alice. Emma could only be a wife and mother, but perhaps Alice could be more.

Alice looked up from her sketchbook just as her friend Erna was entering the library. Alice called out to her friend, who then waved to Alice. Alice stood up and gave Erna a hug. Selma also hugged Erna. The three then sat down.

"Selma, it is so good to see you. And Alice, I see you are sketching in your book. As usual. Everything okay with your parents?"

"Yes. They are in their hotel room, hopefully resting. As you know, my parents have not yet met Ludwig's mother, and knowing my father, things could go very wrong at lunch."

"Alice, I am sure your father will behave."

Alice was not so sure. "Selma, you remember how Papa was during my visit to Frankfurt three months ago. Just after Ludwig and I announced our engagement." Her parents had seemed excited when Alice called her parents using Tante Ida's telephone (with the promise that she would reimburse Tante Ida for the long-distance call). Alice and Ludwig took the train to Frankfurt on a Friday morning just after her last class. The plan was for both to stay in her parent's apartment, since the large apartment had four bedrooms, and only Selma was still living at home. They arrived in Frankfurt in the early afternoon. Selma was at the station to greet them and the three took the tram to the Roderberg Weg apartment.

Alice continued with the story. "It had been a while since I was in the apartment. Erna, remember I told you how surprised I was that nothing had changed in the kitchen – they still had the old coal stove and the ice box, even though the apartment had recently been wired for electricity. When we arrived at the apartment, my mother was in that antiquated kitchen, telling Sarah the cook what to do and not do. Erna, I believe I told you that my mother had to take care of her younger siblings after her mother had died, and because her father was a biblical scholar who could not afford any help, my mother had to learn to cook. My mother is probably a better cook than any of the cooks she has employed, but no wife of Joseph Heppenheimer would be cooking."

"Alice, I have been trying to convince Mama to modernize the kitchen, to install an electric stove and an electric refrigerator. All of my friends have electric refrigerators. It seems like we are the only family in the neighborhood still receiving an ice delivery. Papa agrees with me. Remember, he had to convince Mama to move to Roderberg Weg in the first place."

Alice smiled. "Erna, I have told you that my father is very careful with his money, and so the move to Roderberg Weg in 1914 was a big deal for our family. My father had been living in the East End of Frankfurt since 1880, but in more modest apartments, first with his first wife and then with our mother. But the Roderberg Weg apartment, on a large and very fashionable street, was a big change for all of us. The apartment building was relatively new, and while the apartment did not have electricity at the time, it had gas lights. Selma and I still shared a room, but the room was quite spacious, with very large windows overlooking the street. I loved that new apartment. And our mother loved it too, after she got over the fact that she was forced to move by our father. She especially loved being so close to the zoo."

Selma wanted to stop talking about the apartment and get back to the story. "Yes, yes, we love our big, modern apartment. But did you tell Erna what Papa said to Ludwig? And what Jacob said to Ludwig?"

"Okay, okay, back to our visit to Frankfurt. After we got settled, we met my parents in the parlor. My mother poured the coffee and served us cookies and asked us about our trip. I told them about the train ride, and my father immediately grilled Ludwig about why we had not travelled in first-class on the train, how Ludwig should never subject his future bride to anything other than first-class. 'Nothing but the best for my daughter,' he said. How ridiculous. Anytime he could avoid paying more for anything, he would, particularly when it came to his children. I couldn't tell if he was being overly protective or if he was signaling to Ludwig that he knew about Ludwig's business struggles. But I knew I needed to rescue Ludwig, who seemed to disappear before my eyes. I mentioned to my father that Ludwig was interested in the history of Jews in Nuremberg, and that was all I needed to say.

Selma, you know how much Papa loves to talk about Jewish history. So, my father began asking Ludwig questions and I left them in the parlor to talk about history."

It was clear to Alice that Selma was anxious to get to the worst part of the evening when Selma said, "I guess the visit would have been okay for the two of you if it had only been just the five of us for dinner. But the whole family came to dinner that night, and Jacob was brutal."

Alice knew Selma was having issues with their domineering older brother, and Alice often tried to avoid getting into the middle of battles between Selma and Jacob, but Selma was right. Jacob had been awful that night.

Erna reached out and lightly touched Alice's arm. "Alice, I remember you telling me about that dinner when you came back to Nuremberg. It sounded like an absolute nightmare. And poor Ludwig, who is normally a quiet man, being bombarded with all of those questions from your brothers."

Alice thought about everyone who had joined them for dinner that night. The children from Joseph's first marriage: Bertha and her husband Marcus and their daughters Bettina and Erna; Johanna and her husband Isadore and their daughter Martha; Jacob and his wife Johanna and their children Mellie and Ernst; and Benno and his fiancé Margot. Max and his new wife Recha were then living in Mannheim and could not join them. Alice understood, but was disappointed. Alice was a small child when her half-sisters Bertha and Johanna married, so she barely remembered living with them. Her brothers Jacob and Benno were significantly older and had lives of their own, and they rarely paid attention to their younger half-sister. But Max was just eight years old when Alice was born and loved being a doting older brother. She had only warm memories of growing up with Max, who lived at home until he went off to war in 1914, just before they moved to the Roderberg Weg apartment. She loved when he would come into her bedroom after a night out with friends or a date with a new girl and tell her about his night, careful not to wake up Selma.

Alice looked at both her sister and her friend. "Yes, that was an awful night. I knew Jacob was going to be a challenge, but I did not expect him to be that difficult." After Jacob and her cousin Adolph had taken over the family scrap metal business, Gebrüder Heppenheimer, after her father's retirement in 1917, Jacob had begun to assume the role of patriarch of the family, at least when her father allowed him to assume the role. Jacob, who had always been a bit of a know-it-all, was now assuming more responsibility, both in the company and in the lives of his siblings. But her father still remained a strong presence in all of their lives and exercised control, when he was up to it. For Alice, she sometimes felt like she had two fathers.

Selma, impatient to get to the real drama of the evening, continued the story. "We had just finished saying the blessings over the wine and the challah when Jacob started asking Ludwig one question after another about his failed attempts at business. And I remember Jacob saying to Ludwig, 'Well, don't worry about finding a successful business. You will come to work for Gebrüder Heppenheimer, just like our brothers-in-law Isadore and Marcus. That is what we do for family, right Papa?' And then our father agreed, and said, 'Ludwig, you can start as soon as you and Alice are married and move to Frankfurt.' I remember Ludwig saying nothing. How awful that must have been for him. I don't even remember Ludwig speaking again that night."

Selma had remembered that night exactly as it happened, Alice thought to herself. Ludwig said nothing to her the rest of the night, even after her family left. And he didn't really talk the next morning as they said their goodbyes and left for the train station. Fortunately, her father did not raise the subject of working for Gebrüder Heppenheimer at breakfast. She had hoped at the time that her parent attributed Ludwig's near silence to the number of family members he had met the night before and the fact that dinner did not end until almost midnight. Or that Ludwig was a quiet man. But Alice knew something was wrong, since he was quiet with her even when they were alone before breakfast. He didn't even kiss her good morning.

"Selma, I didn't tell you what happened after we left the apartment. Ludwig said nothing to me until the train left the station for Nuremberg. Then he turned to me and said, 'Alice, I want to marry you. I would not have asked you to marry me if I didn't want to marry you. But your family already seems to have decided that we are moving to Frankfurt and that I will work for them once we marry. As I said to you, I won't leave Nuremberg, and I can't work for your family's company.' He had never directly said why he wouldn't work for the company, but I have my suspicions. Papa's sons and nephew have ownership interests in the company. But each son-in-law is an employee in the company and neither has an ownership interest – that would only be available for blood relatives. I think Ludwig believes that he would have second-class status if he joined the company, which is probably true. Plus, for some unknown reason, Ludwig is tied to his family and never wants to leave them, even though his mother always treats him badly. And then he stopped talking, took a deep breath and said, 'Maybe it would be better if we didn't marry.'"

Selma grabbed her sister's hand and exclaimed, "No, he didn't say that!"

"Yes, he did. As you can imagine, I was shocked and upset. But knowing him and thinking back on that terrible evening, I couldn't really blame him for what he said. Jacob had been so hard on Ludwig. And no one had defended Ludwig, not even me. I could have said no, Ludwig doesn't want to leave Nuremberg, he doesn't want to work for Gebrüder Heppenheimer. But I said nothing. So not only did Ludwig feel ambushed, he must have also felt abandoned by me. I said to him, 'Ludwig, I understand why you feel this way. I am sorry that I didn't stand up for you. This is what happens when I am with my family; I get completely overwhelmed by them. I don't want to move back to Frankfurt. And I don't want you to work for my family's company. I want us to stay in Nuremberg once we are married, assuming you still want to marry me. And I want you to get a job doing something you want to do.' And then I took his hand and said, 'So should we still get married?' And fortunately, he said yes."

Selma squeezed her sister's hand and said, "Alice, how awful for you. I didn't know that Jacob almost ended your engagement. What a brute he is!" Alice looked up at her sister and saw tears in Selma's eyes. Alice agreed that Jacob had been unnecessarily hard on Ludwig, but Alice suspected that Selma's tears were more likely caused by Alice's statement about not moving back to Frankfurt. Through her years in art school, her family had pressured her to return home. No child of Joseph Heppenheimer had left Frankfurt until Alice. And even though Max had recently moved to Mannheim, he was there only because of the business. But Alice had no interest in returning to Frankfurt.

During that dinner, Jacob had said some other things that Alice chose not to share with Selma. No need to give her sister more ammunition in her battles with Jacob. At one point in the evening, Jacob had said how terrible it would be if Alice were the success in his family. Alice pretended not to listen, because she knew how devastated he would be if Ludwig knew that Alice had heard this awful comment. Alice knew about his insecurities in business, and she had to admit that that last statement also rattled her, since she also worried about whether Ludwig would be able to support both of them, and also children, once they had them. She worried Jacob would make Ludwig feel bad about himself every time the two were together. So, she made herself a promise that she would work to keep them apart, even at family functions. Alice was relieved that Jacob would not be attending her wedding.

Erna looked at her watch. "Looks like it is time for you two to walk back to the hotel. I hope everyone behaves themselves. Sorry I won't be able to take part in the festivities until dinner."

"If you are feeling badly about missing family craziness, why don't you join us for lunch?"

Selma immediately responded. "Alice, I am sure Erna has too many commitments already today." Alice had not been serious about the suggestion, but forgot about Selma's jealousy.

But Erna saved her friend. "I wish I could, but I've got to run before the school office closes. Last-minute issues with my apprenticeship. Sorry."

Alice winked at her friend. "Coward! But I will make sure I save some of the craziness for dinner!"

As they walked back to the hotel, Alice could sense that her sister was troubled by the time they had just spent with Erna, and so Alice decided to distract Selma by asking for her sister's help. "Selma, I have told you all about Ludwig's mother, about how she is not a very warm person and often criticizes Ludwig. And how she favors her younger son. I need your help with Ludwig's mother and brother at lunch."

"You know I am always happy to help. And don't worry – I will do my best to make sure everyone is having a good time." Selma winked at her sister, and Alice felt some relief. When Selma tried, she could be quite engaging and charming.

Alice and Selma were walking arm in arm as they entered the hotel. Ludwig had already arrived and was sitting in the lobby. He stood up and kissed Alice. When he stood, it reminded Alice of one of the reasons she liked being with Ludwig. Alice was tall – at 5 feet, 8 inches, she was taller than her three brothers and taller than the few men Alice had dated in the past. But Ludwig was taller than Alice. Ludwig then gave Selma a kiss on each cheek, and the three sat down to wait for their families. Alice was a little early, and she was sure that Ludwig had been sitting in the lobby for at least 30 minutes. Ludwig was never late, particularly when it involved his mother.

As Selma and Ludwig began to talk about the next day's wedding plans, Alice thought about when she and Ludwig first met. It was early December 1918, just after the Armistice was signed that ended the Great War. Alice was in the beginning of her second year at the art school. Ludwig's army unit had just returned to Nuremberg, and he was at a restaurant with some of his army buddies. Alice was in the same restaurant, having dinner with friends from school. It was a quiet night, and none of the other tables were occupied. The two tables started talking, and at some point, Alice realized she had been talking only to Ludwig. During their conversation, both shared that they were Jewish. When one of her friends announced it was time to leave, Ludwig asked if he could call on Alice. She gave him Tante Ida's telephone number.

For their first date, Alice wore the blue dress she had recently designed, having used one of the school's sewing machines to make the dress. She knew that the dress was flattering and brought out her blue eyes. When she opened Tante Ida's door to greet Ludwig, she was pleased with what she saw. She remembered he was tall, but she forgot he was actually an attractive man. And he was wearing a fashionable double-breasted suit, which she took to be a good sign.

During their date at a nearby restaurant, Ludwig told Alice that his father had owned a small factory in Nuremberg, but had died in 1910, and the factory had been sold after Ludwig went off to war. Now that the war was over, Ludwig intended to be a businessman. Ludwig told Alice that he was currently unemployed and living at home, but expected to find a job soon. Alice told Ludwig of her interest in working in fashion and her dream of opening her own studio. Unlike her father, Ludwig did not dismiss her goal, and even seemed to share her excitement. She had never met any man who thought a woman could pursue such a dream. Alice thought this had been a good first date and agreed to see him again. And they kept seeing each other, although Alice continued to make her studies a priority. And Ludwig understood.

Before she met Ludwig, Alice had dated little. In fact, Ludwig was the first man she had dated seriously. She had been focused on her studies since she had started art school. Plus, the war kept the men away, so there hadn't really been many opportunities to date. Alice had the sense that Ludwig had dated before, since he seemed to know what to do, but he didn't share his dating history and she didn't ask. They went to restaurants and cafes, they went to the theater, they went to the silent pictures. They took long walks along the cobblestoned streets of the old city. She felt comfortable with him.

Alice and Ludwig had been dating about a year when Ludwig asked her to marry him. She was in the middle of her last year of school, and she began to think about an apprenticeship after graduation. Ludwig understood that and said that he hoped that she would remain in Nuremberg after graduation and that the two would live in Nuremberg. He said he would be happy to wait until she graduated to marry. Alice also wanted to stay in Nuremberg, and Ludwig's proposal would keep her in Nuremberg. Plus, Alice was so thankful that Ludwig was interested in her fashion ideas, and supported her dream of opening a studio. Alice did not share Ludwig's love of politics, but was happy to listen to him speak about politics, which he did often, since he was happy to listen to Alice discuss fashion. She had never been in love before, but thought that what she was feeling was love, and so she said yes. Ludwig said that he loved her, and Alice said it back.

Alice was smiling to herself as she remembered that moment. And then she looked up and saw Selma and Ludwig staring at her. Alice asked, "Did you two just say something?" Selma and Ludwig both laughed.

"Ludwig and I have been asking you the same question for five minutes. I finally had to tap your knee. Several times. Ludwig, does Alice disappear on you, too?"

"As a matter of fact, she does. Often. But we can forget the question, which wasn't that important anyway, since my mother and brother have arrived."

It was precisely noon, and Ludwig's mother Lucille and brother Ernst strolled into the lobby as if they owned the hotel. Right on time, thought Alice. She knew her father would want to be on time – he was always on time for business – but worried that her mother would make them late. "Hello Frau Alder, Ernst. I hope you were able to follow our directions to the hotel."

"The directions were a little confusing, but Ernst knew how to get here." Just perfect. She found a way to criticize Alice and to praise her younger son, both in the same sentence. In the year since they first met, Alice had learned one important lesson – not to react to whatever Lucille Adler said. Frau Adler would never stop the criticisms and she would never stop favoring her younger son over Ludwig. Instead, Alice said, "I am glad you were able to find the hotel. My parents should be down soon. Frau Adler, this is my sister Selma."

"Selma, it is lovely to meet you. I understand you are just a year older than my Ernst. But please don't steal him away from his mother." Selma smiled, shook Lucille's hand, looked over at Ernst and was clearly trying to mask the face she was making when she saw the pudgy pimply-faced boy. Alice thought to herself, "No need to worry, Frau Adler."

"Where are your parents? I would have thought that they would be on time for our first meeting." Don't react, Alice. "Perhaps they were having a problem with their room, or maybe one of them has taken ill." Really, don't react. Fortunately, at that very moment, her parents came into the lobby.

Her father spoke first. "Good afternoon everyone. I assume you are Frau Adler? It is lovely to meet you. Alice has told us such wonderful things about you and how you have made her feel a part of your family. I am sorry we are a little late. This is my wife Emma Heppenheimer. And this must be Ernst. A pleasure meeting you as well." Looks like her father decided to turn on the charm. It was moments like this that made Alice understand why her father had been so successful in business. Alice had told him almost nothing about Frau Adler; she had told her mother that Frau Adler was a cold, controlling, and difficult woman, and assumed that she had shared that information with her father. And she never knew which father would show up. Clearly, the charming one did today. He always knew what to say to turn a room to his advantage, and he was using those skills today.

And it was working. "Herr Heppenheimer, Frau Heppenheimer, it is so lovely to meet you both. Alice is a darling, and we are certainly happy to have her join our family." Alice's father put out his arm for Frau Adler; and then walked her into the restaurant. Everyone else followed them.

•   •   •

Alice's father had done such a good job over lunch that the parents were getting along well during dinner. Selma successfully avoided speaking with Ernst, even though he tried several times, and even though Alice had specifically asked her to pay attention to him. Several of Ludwig's relatives were also at dinner, although Alice said little to them; she left that job to Ludwig. She mostly spoke with Max, who was seated to her left, and Erna, who was seated to her right. She had not seen Max since his own wedding last year, and she had a lot of catching up to do. While Erna was speaking with one of Ludwig's relatives, Alice asked Max about his new responsibilities in Mannheim.

While Max was still serving in the army, Jacob and her cousin Adolph had purchased an old smelter facility in Mannheim for Gebrüder Heppenheimer. They had also decided that, once it was refurbished and fully operational, Max would run the facility. They only told Max about this decision when he came home from the war; they told him he would need to move to Mannheim just after his wedding to Recha in 1919. Alice knew Max did not want to leave Frankfurt and hated the idea of operating a smelter facility. She knew that he really wanted to go to a university and study chemistry. But he had no choice. At least, that was what he was told at the time.

"Max, I know you hate the smelter facility. Why don't you tell Jacob that you want to study chemistry?"

"It's not so bad. I am getting better at it. And there is some chemistry involved. Plus, I have a wife and a baby now. I can't study at a university. It's too late. Maybe I could have when I was younger. Maybe if there had not been a war. But I can make it work at the smelter facility."

"I wish things had been different for you. I hate that Jacob just ordered you to move to Mannheim. He thinks he is the boss of everyone."

"Well, these days, he and Adolph kind of are. But let's talk about you. First, congratulations on graduating from the art school. I am really proud of you for pursuing your dream."

"Thanks, Max. Given that my wedding was going to be a week after graduation, I decided not to make a big deal of graduating. Ludwig and I went out to dinner with some of my art school friends to celebrate. I am just happy that all of you were able to come to my wedding." Although, in truth, Alice would have liked it if one member of her family had come to see her receive her diploma. But she understood that, in her family, marriage was more important than graduation.

"Alice, I also want to congratulate you on your apprenticeship. How exciting! You are so talented, and I am so proud of you. I know it won't be long before you have that studio, just like you have always wanted."

"Well, it will be awhile before I have the necessary experience to open my own place. But I am very excited about starting the apprenticeship at the factory next week. And Ludwig is very supportive, so that is a relief."

"And now the question you probably hoped I wouldn't ask. Have you told Papa and Mama about the apprenticeship and your plans to remain in Nuremberg?"

Alice smiled at her brother. "Yes, I actually told them today after lunch. As you can imagine, they were not entirely happy. In fact, Mama tried to change the subject. But then Papa asked me about the apprenticeship and seemed to be impressed with the business. And then we spoke about other things. They didn't mention the apprenticeship again. So, I hope that means they finally understand that I am not moving back to Frankfurt."

"Well, it's good to know that they understand where your future lies. At least, they understand that for now." With that last statement, Max winked at his sister and then they both laughed. For the rest of the evening, Max and Alice spoke about family members, and then Max listened to Alice and Erna gossip about schoolmates.

After dinner, Alice walked Erna back to Erna's boarding house. They went inside to the common room to share some tea. Sitting on one of the couches, both talked about the evening and agreed that the dinner had been a success. The parents seemed to get along, and no one made Ludwig feed bad. In fact, Ludwig was smiling through much of the evening. And the two friends talked about their future plans. Alice had told Erna early on about her dream of opening a studio, and Erna told Alice that she would love to help make that happen. Erna herself had no such dream; it was not who she was. But she would love to be Alice's right-hand person, the person who would be there to help make Alice's dream a reality. Alice and Erna spent another thirty minutes discussing fashion, and then Erna toasted Alice with her tea cup. Alice left her friend's place, feeling excited about the next day. She splurged on a taxi back to Tante Ida's apartment.

•   •   •

The wedding service at the Grand Synagogue of Nuremberg the next morning was short and attended only by the immediate family and a few of Alice's friends, including Erna. Erna had helped Alice design her wedding dress – it was white silk and above the knee. Erna and Alice together designed the beaded bodice, which had white and ivory beads, and both agreed that it had turned out beautifully. Even Emma was impressed with the dress, and told Alice so that morning. Ludwig wore a simple suit, but Alice had bought him a tie that matched her dress.

Alice did not like the façade of the synagogue, which reminded her of the Main Synagogue in Frankfurt. Both synagogues were styled like churches, and were overly ornate. Alice liked the clean lines of more modern buildings. Alice had purposefully chosen one of the smaller sanctuaries in the synagogue for her wedding ceremony, which was less showy than the main sanctuary, but had beautiful stained glass windows. She thought the room looked beautiful that morning, with the morning light streaming through the windows. Alice was happy during the ceremony, smiling at Ludwig and then at her parents. Ludwig was not smiling, but Alice assumed it was because he was nervous. After the wedding ceremony, Alice and Ludwig took pictures, and then joined the rest of the party for a reception in one of the reception rooms off the sanctuary. After the reception, Alice said goodbye to her parents and Selma. They were heading back to the hotel to pack, since their train was leaving at 2 pm. Alice was happy that the wedding had gone smoothly, and with no drama.

Alice and Ludwig went to Tante Ida's apartment to finish packing and to move her things to the new apartment at Burgschmietstrasse 8, just beyond the old walls of the city. They took a taxi, since they were also moving Alice's prized gramophone. A gift from her parents when she first moved to Nuremberg, Alice would have been devastated if anything had happened to her gramophone. There had been a number of nights when listening to one of her favorite jazz records on the gramophone was the only way she could make it through another night at Tante Ida's apartment. Alice and Ludwig rented the new apartment the previous month. It was small, and a little dark, with a single room that combined the living room, dining room, and kitchen, and a separate bedroom. But the apartment included a private bathroom, which was important to Alice, and the neighborhood was pretty. Plus, there was a housing shortage, so they could not be too picky. And, most important of all, they could afford it (at least, with the help of her parents, who insisted on helping them so that Alice could have the private bathroom). They couldn't afford a telephone or an apartment with electricity, but Alice assumed they would move to a better place once they were both working. Ludwig had come earlier to the new apartment to unload his things and to move in the furniture his mother had given them – cast-offs from Ludwig's family. Alice had grown up with beautiful furniture and servants, but she was not spoiled and was fine with the old furniture. She was, after all, an artist and didn't artists starve for their art?

Alice was met by an enticing aroma as she crossed the threshold into the new apartment. She could smell her favorite meal – roast duck stuffed with apples. Not only had Ludwig arranged the furniture, but he had also arranged for a wedding dinner for them and had even set the table. What a lovely way to start their marriage, she thought. He really was a thoughtful man, when he tried. Alice dropped her suitcases on the floor of their bedroom and returned to the main room. She looked at the table – Ludwig had even filled wine glasses with champagne.

"Ludwig, what I nice surprise. Everything smells wonderful. Where did you get the food?"

"Alice, I am so happy you like the surprise. My Tante Bertha had her cook make us a wedding dinner as a wedding present. I know I am not always the most demonstrative person, but I wanted to show you how happy I am that you married me. I wish I could have afforded to take you on a lovely honeymoon or rent a better apartment. But I promise that I will work as hard as I can to be a success. I really did think that the wholesale coffee business would work. But a cousin has told me about another business opportunity and we are meeting next week."

"Ludwig, let's not talk about any of that. Let's just enjoy the lovely dinner here."

"Alice, I love you. And have I told you how beautiful you looked in your wedding dress? And how beautiful you look right now?"

It was always hard for Alice to hear from anyone that she was beautiful. Ludwig rarely said it, and when he did, she didn't really believe it. But she felt beautiful at that moment and full of optimism about their future. "I love you too, Ludwig." They toasted to their new life together with the champagne and then sat down to enjoy their wedding feast.

•   •   •

During her last semester in art school, Alice had secured an apprenticeship in a handbag factory. In art school, Alice had focused on the use of different textiles in women's fashion. Women's handbags were of particular interest to Alice, especially since more and more women were now carrying handbags. The combination of more women in the work force and more active social lives resulted in women needing a place to store small items. And handcrafted purses had become especially fashionable, with purses made to match both dresses and gloves. In fact, many women had at least two handbags now, one for daytime use and one for the evening. Alice believed that this was an area of fashion where she could succeed. After all, handcrafted purses could be a big seller in a small studio like the one Alice hoped to open one day. The factory she would apprentice in was larger than she had wanted for her first apprenticeship. But Alice believed she could learn a lot about the handbag business, and the owner had expressed an interest in seeing her designs. Perhaps he would allow her to design a purse one day.

Alice began her apprenticeship five days after her wedding. She was motivated to succeed, and so beginning on her first day of work, Alice arrived every day before 8 am. She often arrived before her supervisor Herr Schneider, which she thought was important. There wasn't a task that was beneath her. Whatever she was asked to do, she did. Initially, the workers in the shop looked askance at the arts and crafts school graduate, anticipating a superior attitude. When none came, they relaxed a bit. And as she took on more tasks, she thought they were respecting her more. She didn't think she would ever be friends with these workers – who were mostly older than she – but she was happy that they appeared to respect her.

Which is why it came as a surprise when she saw a note on her chair one morning about a month after she had started her apprenticeship. It said, "Jew, go back to Poland." Her first thought was, "But I was born in Frankfurt." But then she understood. This was an anti-Semitic act. She had experienced nothing like this before. When she lived in Frankfurt, boys would sometimes yell anti-Jewish slurs as she walked from Saturday morning services with her mother. One time, she was actually hit with a coin. And her father had spoken of the anti-Semitism he experienced in business, which was often more subtle. But this was different. Maybe they thought she was Polish; since the war, Polish Jews had been moving into Germany, including Nuremberg. Ludwig had told her about recent efforts by the government to oust these Polish newcomers from the city, fearing they would take scarce jobs from local workers. But when she thought about it, no one could have thought she was from Poland. She had told her co-workers that she was born in Frankfurt. No, this was clear – someone here didn't like her because she was Jewish. But what would be the point in telling her supervisor? She had been raised to ignore anti-Semitic remarks. She was just going to have to ignore the note. So, she folded it, put it in her purse, and returned to her work.

Her father had warned her before she had left for art school that Nuremberg was an anti-Semitic city. Alice knew that this was true, but she also felt that this was one more way for her father to dissuade her from leaving Frankfurt. She had heard a few anti-Semitic remarks in art school – or at least what she thought were anti-Semitic remarks. In her first year in school, someone in her drawing class talked about how Jews never fought at the front – they sat behind desks to avoid combat. She knew this was wrong – at the time, her brother Max was fighting at the front. But she said nothing – she had learned from her parents to ignore such comments. But she had never experienced anything in school like what she had experienced in the factory that morning. And then she started thinking that maybe accepting an apprenticeship in a non-Jewish business had been a mistake. But, no, this was just one person. She would just do her work well, she told herself, and the notes would stop.

However, over the next several months, she received more notes on her chair. And with each note, the ugliness of the message increased. One note in October accused Jews of murdering Christ. Another note was simply a cartoon of a Jew with a large nose counting money, standing on the backs of workers. But she really liked her apprenticeship, so she continued to ignore the notes. And she didn't tell Ludwig. His cousin had introduced him to a wholesale butcher supply dealer, and he was learning the business. Hopefully, this would work out for him, and she didn't want to worry him.

By November, things had become very busy at the factory. Unemployment in the city was high and prices were rising, but Christmas was coming and purses made nice Christmas presents, even for those who struggled financially. Plus, this factory produced a more economical line of purses. Alice had been asked to retrieve some fabric, and was returning to her desk when she saw someone putting a note on her chair. She backed up and hid behind an open door. When she looked back at her desk from behind the door, she saw it was Rudolph.

Rudolph was a fabric cutter. She didn't know him well, but she always tried to say hello to him. He would give her a strange smile back, but she thought it was just his way. She had heard from others that he was a member of some extreme right–wing party. When they thought she wasn't listening, someone said that this party wanted to get rid of Jews in Germany because they were responsible for the high prices. This person also said that Rudolph hated the Weimar Republic, calling it the "Jews Republic." Alice thought that Rudolph might have been the one leaving the notes on her chair, but then she remembered all the help she had given him. Surely, he couldn't hate her if he actually knew her. After he left, she walked back to her chair and opened the note. It said, "Leave or die."

Alice was stunned. This note was different from the others. This note was a real threat to her. She understood she needed to do something. She knew she needed to tell Herr Schneider about the notes. But first, she sat down at her desk to try to calm herself. She thought it would be better for her to be calm when she went to speak with her boss.

Alice found Herr Schneider in his office later that morning and asked if he had time to speak with her. He smiled at her and told her to come into his office. Alice showed him the note. He then got up and closed the door. She told him about the other notes, and that she thought she could just ignore them. But this note was different. It scared her.

Herr Schneider took a deep breath. "Alice, you have done very good work here. We would be sorry to see you go, but if you feel you can't work here anymore, perhaps you need to find another apprenticeship. We will miss you, but I would be happy to give you excellent references. I can even help you find another apprenticeship."

"Herr Schneider, I don't want to leave this apprenticeship. I really enjoy working here and I have learned a lot already. I told you about the note because I thought you might be able to speak with Rudolph."

"Alice, as I said, I would be happy to find you another apprenticeship. You can finish out the rest of the week here. I will make a few calls and I will let you know what I find out." He then rose from his chair and opened his office door. Their meeting was over. Alice left his office and went back to her desk. It was like they were having two different conversations. She was complaining about a co-worker's bad behavior and he was hearing that Alice was not satisfied with her apprenticeship. She never thought her raising the issue would cause her dismissal. What was she going to do now? And how was she going to tell Ludwig?

Surprisingly, two hours later, Herr Schneider sent for her. Alice thought that he had decided to let her stay. But, instead, he told her he had made a few calls and had found her "the perfect place." It was a smaller factory, but it manufactured higher-end purses. And he spoke with them about the designs she had shown him and they were interested. "You can start on Monday. Here is the information about the company." He then handed Alice a piece of paper with the name, address and telephone number of the company. Alice had heard of Wertheimer Handbags. It had a reputation for good work. And, interestingly, it was owned by a Jewish family.

"Thank you, Herr Schneider. I really appreciate you finding me this position."

"My pleasure. I think you will be happier there. Good luck."

And then she left his office. The whole thing had been so strange. It was as if she had gone to Herr Schneider and complained that her apprenticeship was not fulfilling and he had found her a new apprenticeship. She suspected that, when he discussed her leaving with others, that is precisely what he will tell them. But what had really happened? Alice wondered, "Why was it better for him to get rid of me rather than speak with Rudolph? Was he afraid of Rudolph?" Maybe Alice needed to be afraid of Rudolph and this party he was a member of. But she couldn't remember its name.

When Alice came home that night, she told Ludwig what had happened, although not about the previous notes. Before she left work, she had called Wertheimer Handbags to make sure she actually had the position. She spoke to one of the owners, and he seemed excited for her to begin the apprenticeship. Herr Schneider had apparently told him she was from Frankfurt, and he and Alice compared notes on who they knew. After she hung up the telephone, Alice thought it might actually be a good thing to work for a Jewish company, especially after everything that had happened. But Ludwig was angry. Alice tried to calm him, explaining that this apprenticeship might be better for her, better for them. But then she let him rant.

"Was he a Nazi? Did you hear them say Nazi? They are the worst of the right-wing parties. There might have been a Nazi working in your factory. They are taking advantage of the financial challenges facing people to spread their lies and hate. And they really hate the Weimar Government. They are trying to overthrow it. Fortunately, from what I have read, it is a small group of extremists. But why would Schneider take their side? It he afraid of them? Or maybe he is one of them. And where does he send you? To a Jewish factory! Nuremberg has a liberal mayor, thankfully, but we need to watch out for these fanatics!" Ludwig continued to rant on, but Alice had stopped listening. It had been a hard day, and she was mostly exhausted. She really didn't need to hear such vitriol. Mostly, she needed a hug, but she was clearly not getting one. She told Ludwig she needed to start dinner, which finally stopped his rant. But she had to admit to herself that she was actually excited to start her new apprenticeship, to a place that made high-end purses. They might even let her design purses. And she was relieved that there would be no more anti-Semitic notes!

CHAPTER 2

Nuremberg, February 1923

Alice was annoyed. It was 6:30 pm, Erna and her husband Alfred were coming at 7 pm for dinner, and Ludwig was still not home. Ludwig told her the night before that there was a lot to do at the Central Association headquarters that day and he wanted to get there early. When he left that morning, Alice reminded him he needed to be home by 5:30 pm because they were having company. Ludwig assured her he would be home on time. And now he was late!

Alice supported Ludwig's work with the Central Association of German Citizens of Jewish Faith. The Central Association had been founded at the end of the nineteenth century to protect the rights German Jews had secured after they were emancipated in 1871. And the Central Association was doing important work now, at least that is what Ludwig reminded Alice almost every day. Alice had never been very interested in politics before she met Ludwig, but Alice tried to learn more about what was happening in Germany because this was Ludwig's favorite topic of conversation. And Alice knew it was important to become more knowledgeable, given all the recent changes in Germany. After Germany's loss of the Great War saw an end to the German Empire and the Kaiser, Germany had become a democratic republic. Ludwig believed that this change would be good for German Jews. And Alice was most excited about one important change – women could now vote. She hadn't really been bothered about the inability to vote before she started art school, but between the talk on campus and Ludwig's excitement about the new republic, Alice was excited to vote for the first time in January 1919. Following the elections, a new constitution was adopted in July. Alice went back to her art studies, but felt like she had been a part of the process that had secured democracy for Germany. And Ludwig continued to be engaged in politics, even joining the Central Association soon after their marriage.

Ludwig's recent decision to become more involved with the Central Association was mostly because he had lost his position at the butcher supply company at the end of 1922. Alice didn't always like the time Ludwig was devoting to the Association, but she had to admit that the distraction was important to Ludwig. Ludwig had been working at the butcher supply company since the beginning of 1921, and seemed to be happy with his job, but the inflation of 1921 turned into hyperinflation by the middle of 1922. The butcher supply company was forced to close because of the economic crisis. Things were not much better for Alice. Her apprenticeship in Wertheimer Handbags had resulted in a permanent position, but the company also was struggling because of hyperinflation, and Alice lost her job at the end of 1922. Alice had been picking up extra work from a few women's tailors, and she even did some dress designing for a few friends. She was also doing some piecemeal work for a few handbag factories. But she and Ludwig were also relying on money her mother was sending. Fortunately, her mother was not pressuring her to leave Nuremberg.

Alice stirred the stew on the cast-iron stove, the stove that also heated the apartment. Alice had been working to improve her cooking, but she just didn't have the knack for cooking. As talented as she was with fabrics, she simply had no talent in the kitchen. But she picked up a nice bread and an apple strudel for dessert, so dinner should be fine, she thought to herself.

Alice heard a knock at the door and took off her apron. "I can't believe that Ludwig is still not home!" she muttered aloud. She walked across the small living room to the door. Alice and Ludwig had been living in the same apartment since the start of their marriage in 1920, and they were really feeling the challenges of the small and dark space. The cast-iron stove often smelled, and the coal dust seemed to settle into every corner of the apartment. Even the faded flowered wallpaper seemed to have a constant film of coal dust no matter how hard Alice scrubbed. But now was certainly not the time to be looking for another apartment.

"Hello Erna, hello Alfred. Right on time!" Erna gave her friend a kiss on each cheek, and Alfred did the same. Alice could see that Alfred was looking around the room for Ludwig, but said nothing. Instead, Alfred handed Alice a bottle of wine, and Alice closed the door.

"Alfred, thank you so much for the wine. A Riesling! Ludwig's favorite! Give me your coats and we can sit and wait for Ludwig. Unfortunately, he is a little late."

As Erna and Alfred were handing Alice their coats, the front door opened and Ludwig came racing in.

"Hello Erna and Alfred. Sorry I am so late. I had hoped I would get home earlier, but we are so busy at the Central Association. So much important work to do! Let me just change quickly and we can eat." He gave Alice a quick kiss and went into their bedroom. Alice smiled at her guests and went over to the stove to stir the stew one last time. She was angry at her husband, but she needed to calm down, since the last thing she needed was to fight with Ludwig in front of Erna and Alfred. She just wished that he would sometimes make her a priority, especially when they were having company.

Ludwig changed quickly and sat down at their small table. Erna and Alfred joined him, and Alice brought the stew to the table, along with the bread and the wine.

"A Riesling. Thank you, Alfred. After the day I have had, it will be nice to have a glass or two of good wine."

"I have been traveling a lot for work lately, but I have read a little about the work of the Central Association. What has the Association been up to lately?"

"I understand making money is important, but, as a Jew, you should understand that there is nothing more important than the work the Central Association is doing for German Jews." Oh no, Alice thought to herself. The four of them were going to a cabaret after dinner, and she had wanted them to have a nice time at dinner before going out. But Ludwig now thought that Alfred was criticizing him about his lack of a job. He really is overly sensitive, Alice thought to herself. She was about to say something, but, fortunately, Alfred understood Ludwig had misunderstood his comment.

"Ludwig, I agree that the Association has always done very important work. I was really just asking about what the Association is doing now."

"I'm sorry – I guess I just get a little passionate about the work. We are doing so much. You undoubtedly know about all the claims made by the right-wing groups after the Great War about the Jewish people being responsible for Germany losing the war. That Germany was actually winning the war, but that the Jews forced Germany to sign the Armistice and then the Treaty of Versailles. That the Jews stabbed the Germans in the back. This inflammatory talk has led to violent actions, including the assassination of Walther Rathenau, the German Jewish Foreign Minister, last year. The Association has been distributing materials that refute those charges, and now the Association is using the courts to fight anti-Semitism. So far, we have been successful in assessing fines against a number of these thugs."

"Ludwig, that is great work. I am happy we have people like you who are fighting for the rest of us. But do you worry that these right-wing groups will think that the fines are just the cost of promoting their hate?"

"No, I don't. We cannot let them succeed with their hate. We must educate all Germans about all the great things that Jews have done for Germany. And how we were great patriots during the war. Do you remember when the Prussian Minister of War started that study in the middle of the war to prove that Jewish soldiers were deliberately evading front-line military service? The study actually showed the opposite – that we were overrepresented at the front, although the newspapers never reported the actual results of the study. You were at the front, I was at the front, we know first-hand what Jewish soldiers did for Germany."

"I remember when they announced the start of the study. It was in all the papers. All it did was fuel the anti-Semitism we sometimes faced when we were on leave. But I never felt anti-Semitism at the front, with my fellow soldiers. But the war is over. I have to believe that the Weimar government will work to make sure that the right-wing groups remain fringe groups. So Alice, Erna told me you and she recently saw an exhibit at the Nuremberg Kunsterhaus."

Alice could see Ludwig grimaced at the abrupt change in subject, but she was happy with the change. She knew that Alfred did not really like discussing his experiences during the war. And Alice was always hearing about the "important" work of the Association from Ludwig, and so was happy to talk about something she was actually interested in, although she did sometimes feel a little guilty that she was not more interested in Association's work. She knew that anti-Semitism had been a bit of a problem, but she thought it was time for Jews to focus on the future. Germany was now a republic and Nuremberg had a liberal mayor. Plus, she was just tired of hearing about all the problems

Jews were facing. Alice believed that her main problem was that her husband did not have a paying job.

"Yes, they had an exhibit that showcased student art from the Nuremberg Arts and Crafts School. They really have had some great exhibits recently. Because the Kunsterhaus was closed during the war, I was not aware of the extent of its collection. I do love most of the modern art, especially the works by the German expressionists, but of course I am partial to the craft-related exhibits. They even had a small exhibit showing new purse designs."

Erna added, "Alice began taking notes of the different designs for those purses. There was one particular purse we both loved, with the Art Deco beaded designs. That purse must have taken hours to make!"

"Yes, Erna, I did love that purse. And the purse with the cubism designs. When you and I finally open that studio of ours, we will be able to showcase purses with similar designs."

For the rest of the dinner, Alice, Erna, and Alfred discussed other exhibits they had seen at the Kunsterhaus, and then a silent picture Alfred and Erna had recently seen. Ludwig remained quiet, but Alice didn't mind. She thought they all had heard enough from Ludwig. After coffee and the strudel, Alice and Erna washed the dishes, and then the four left the apartment and hurried to the tram stop. The cabaret show would begin at 9 pm, and they wanted to get there a little early to get good seats. The tram arrived soon after they reached the stop, and they were able to get to the theater by 8:30 pm. Alice and Erna walked arm in arm through the doors, excited to be attending the show. Alice had to be careful about spending money, but she and Ludwig agreed it was worth going out once in a while. Plus, a friend of Ludwig had recommended the cabaret because one of the sketches in the revue was political. Ludwig and Alfred paid for the tickets and they found seats close to the stage.

The show began with a dance routine. Alice thought the costumes were a bit revealing, but she loved the colors, as well as the large feathers that were used in the routine. Next came a tenor who sang a number of songs by the popular cabaret songwriter Kurt Tucholsky. The songs were very funny and, at the same time, rather critical of the right-wing parties. And then there were two skits. The first one was a silly story about star-crossed lovers, but was still funny and everyone laughed. The second was a parody of some recent statements made by the right-wing parties against Jews. The skit even included the hapless leader of one of the parties. Alice was a little surprised at how pointed the satire was in the sketch, but Ludwig was clearly enjoying it. After the sketches, there were a few more dance and song routines, and then the show was over.

Outside the theater, Alice could tell that Ludwig wanted to talk about that second skit, and he even suggested that the four go out for some coffee. But Alice was tired of talking about politics, and she could see that Alfred and Erna were ready to go home.

"Erna and Alfred, what a wonderful evening. I am sorry the stew was a little burned. As much as I try, I can't seem to get the hang of cooking."

Erna gave her friend a hug. "Alice, dinner was fine, and that strudel from Friedmann's Bakery was delicious. And Ludwig, the cabaret was quite fun. It was a great suggestion. It is rather late, though, so Alfred and I will say goodnight."

Alice watched Erna and Alfred leave, and turned to Ludwig, who seemed to be disappointed that he wasn't able to discuss the skit. "Let's walk to the tram stop. I am exhausted and ready for some sleep."

On the tram, Ludwig turned to Alice and said, "Whenever we are out with Erna and Alfred, I rarely see the two of them talk to each other. Either you talk to Erna or you talk to Alfred. And you do talk to Alfred a lot. But do you think they ever talk to each other?"

Alice ignored the comment of her talking too much to Alfred. "I am sure they talk to each other. Maybe when we are together, they are happy to talk with us." Alice was too tired to talk about Erna and Alfred with Ludwig. She knew that Ludwig and Alfred never had much to say to one another, and that the four of them went out because Alice and Erna were best friends. Ludwig was quiet and mostly wanted to discuss politics when he was with people other than Alice. Alfred was gregarious, and was be able to converse on a range of topics, although he was less interested in politics. To Alice, it was hard to imagine anyone as interested in politics as Ludwig. Alfred worked for a watch company and traveled throughout Bavaria selling watches. Alice could understand why he was successful at his job, even during the hyperinflation period. Alfred could easily talk to people.

But Ludwig was not done with the conversation. "I just think it is strange that they seem to have nothing to say to one another. I have never really understood why those two married. They are from such different worlds. Of course, it is our fault that they are even together."

"Ludwig, they just fell in love." Alice would never use the word "fault," but it was true that they played matchmaker, although wholly unintentionally. Alice's mother had written to her that her good friend Auguste Falkenstein's son Alfred was moving to Nuremberg for a job and she wanted Alice and Ludwig to invite him for dinner, since he didn't know anyone in Nuremberg. Alice and Alfred were in the same grade in the Philanthropin, but he left to attend a yeshiva for high school, and she had not seen him since. She wrote to her mother to have Alfred contact her when he arrived in Nuremberg, and she would invite him to dinner. The Alfred she remembered was short and chubby and shy, but the person standing at the threshold to her apartment when he came to dinner was tall and good-looking and grinning broadly. She stared at him for a few seconds, and then recovered and invited him in. She had invited her friend Erna to join them, anticipating that the conversation might lag and having an additional person would help. But Alfred turned out to be a great conversationalist, and both Alice and Erna were enjoying themselves over dinner. Ludwig said little, but mostly because they were not discussing politics. When the dinner was over, Alfred asked Erna if he could walk her home and both left.

Several days later, Erna stopped by Alice's apartment and told her she had already been on a date with Alfred and they were planning on going out that weekend. Erna asked Alice if she thought it was okay to date Alfred, even though she was not Jewish. Alice told her friend that she thought it was okay, but was secretly hoping that the relationship would soon fizzle, mostly because she did not know how to tell her mother that she had inadvertently matched her friend's son with a non-Jewish woman. But the relationship only strengthened and Erna soon told her friend that Alfred had said that he was no longer religious and marrying Jewish was not a priority for him. So, Alice was not surprised when Alfred asked Erna to marry him. Erna and Alfred married in 1921.

Alice also knew that Ludwig was jealous of Alfred. When they first started to double-date, Alice often talked with Alfred about Frankfurt. From those conversations, Alice could tell that he missed Frankfurt, but there was also a part of Alice that missed Frankfurt, and she enjoyed those conversations. One night, the four went to a jazz club. Alfred knew Alice loved to listen to jazz on her gramophone and suggested that the four go out to a club to hear some jazz. After a few drinks, Alice suggested to Ludwig that they dance. Ludwig said no, but Alfred immediately stood up and pulled Alice onto the dance floor. It might have been the few drinks that she had had or the wonderful jazz, but Alice was soon dancing with abandon and laughing with Alfred. When the music finally stopped, she was still laughing when she looked over at her table. Ludwig was glaring at her and Erna was staring down at her drink. Alice stopped laughing and immediately returned to the table. They soon left the club, and the four had not gone dancing since. Alice didn't want to upset Ludwig or hurt Erna, and so she decided she would try to limit the time she spent alone with Alfred.

Ludwig waited a few more minutes and finally raised the topic he had hoped to discuss just after the show. "So, what did you think of the skit? I thought it was absolutely brilliant!" And then he started to talk about why he thought the skit was important. Alice only half listened, since she knew she really didn't need to contribute to his monologue. Instead, she was thinking about what Ludwig said about her friend's marriage. He was right – she rarely saw Erna and Alfred talk to each other when they were all together. But then she thought about her own marriage. How often did she and Ludwig talk, other than Alice listening to Ludwig's political rants?

•　　•　　•

The next morning, Alice had a quick breakfast and began working on a dress for a friend. Alice had purchased her treadle sewing machine second-hand just after her wedding. She had been able to earn good money at the end of 1922, with extra handbag and dressmaking work because of the Christmas holiday – even with hyperinflation, women still wanted to dress well and carry nice purses. And even after the holidays, the piecemeal work continued. She was actually quite busy, between the dressmaking work she was doing at home and the handbag work she was doing at the various factories.

It was a particularly cold morning, and she had asked Ludwig to put some extra coal into the coal stove. They were always mindful of how much coal they used to heat the apartment, but Alice was feeling a bit more optimistic about their finances, given all of her recent work, and thought they could afford a little more coal in the stove. She was singing to herself as she was working when she heard a knock at the door. She looked up and saw that

Ludwig was still eating his breakfast and not moving. She stopped the machine, got up from her chair, and walked to the door. When she opened the door, she could see the uniform of the telegram messenger. He asked whether Alice Adler lived in the apartment. She said that she was Alice Adler, and he handed her the telegram.

Alice worried whenever she saw the uniform of a telegram messenger, since it generally meant bad news. She and Ludwig could still not afford a telephone, so the only way family members could contact her quickly was by telegram. Alice quickly opened the telegram, and then read it aloud – "Alice, I have very sad news. Your beloved father has passed away. The funeral is tomorrow. Please come home."

Alice sat down in one of the chairs, the telegram still in her hand. Ludwig sat down next to her.

"I am so sorry about your father." He then touched her hand with his hand.

"Thank you, Ludwig. I knew from my mother that he had recently begun experiencing heart failure. But with all of those visits to the spas, I thought he would have another few years. I am not surprised by the news, but it is still sad. It is just hard to imagine my father gone."

"Alice, do you want me to go with you to Frankfurt?"

Alice wasn't thinking about the funeral at that moment, and was a little surprised by the question. Not go to the funeral? Her father would find the notion of a son-in-law not attending his funeral unthinkable. But her father was gone and they had very little money to spare, and she did not want to ask her mother for money. Plus, just by asking, it seemed Ludwig did not want to go to Frankfurt. She could hardly blame him. Jacob was never very nice to him whenever they were forced to be together. She would come up with some type of excuse for why Ludwig was not at the funeral. "Ludwig, I think it might be better, given our finances, for me to go alone." Ludwig nodded in relief and returned to his breakfast.

Alice packed quickly and boarded the noon train to Frankfurt. On the train, she thought about her father. They had never been very close, not in the way that she was close to her mother. Her father was in his forties when she was born, and already the father of grown children, and he was always working. Still, he was a strong presence in the family, and he would be missed. While she felt sad for the loss, she knew that his death would be hard for her mother and she mostly worried about her.

All of Joseph's children were at the funeral. Max, Recha and their son Kurt had come from Mannheim. The rest of Joseph's children and grandchildren lived in Frankfurt, so it was easy for them to attend. The funeral was also packed with friends and business associates. Joseph had operated one of the larger scrap metal companies in the city and was well respected by the business community. Joseph was also a generous contributor to a number of Jewish institutions, and those institutions were represented at the funeral. Alice noticed that her mother was holding up well and was gracious to every person who expressed their condolences for losing her husband. Alice thought to herself, "I think she will be okay."

Following the funeral, her mother opened her apartment for people to stop by to pay their respects. Alice was surprised by the amount of food on the family's dining room table. It would take them a month to eat all of that food. Ever the proper host, Emma wanted to make sure that no one left hungry.

Alice grabbed a plate and filled it with a variety of meats and salads and sat in one of the side chairs. Her brother Benno came over and sat down next to her.

"Benno, I can't believe how big Hans is. And how active he is. He looks like he is about to start walking."

"He is only ten months old, and Margot had hoped he would wait a little on walking. But can we ever really control our children? But changing subjects, I wanted to talk with you about a vacation idea for the summer." Alice thought it was a little strange to bring this up at their father's funeral. Moreover, she and Ludwig had no money and so could not go on any vacation. But she said, "Sure. I would love to hear about your vacation idea."

He told her he and Margot were planning on spending a few weeks in the resort town of Norderney in the North Sea with their baby. Norderney was well known among German Jews. Often referred to as the "Jewish Bath," the town openly courted Jews from across the continent. Benno said that he had spoken with Jacob about joining him and Margot, and Jacob said that he needed to work but that his wife Johanna and children would join them. "He has already decided that he needs to work through the summer. It is only February! But we are all going and Max and Recha also said that they are interested in going. You and Ludwig should come, and Selma could come too."

"Benno, we have no money to go to Norderney. This hyperinflation has been really hard on us. It was hard to even pay for the one train ticket here. Mama has been a big help to us, but until things get better, we will need to stay home."

"Don't worry about the money. The company is doing okay. At this point, we are sitting on a lot of inventory. While business in the Ruhr Basin have been quiet because of the current French occupation, Jacob is optimistic that the German mark will be revalued soon. The company will pay for everyone's vacation. So you and Ludwig should come with us. We will all have a great time." Alice had been wondering how the company was doing. Ludwig had been complaining about the French occupation of the Ruhr Basin after Germany stopped paying reparations under the Treaty of Versailles, the treaty that had ended the Great War. Ludwig told Alice that, because of the occupation, German industry was at a near standstill. It was good to know that Gebrüder Heppenheimer was at least solvent and could actually afford to spend money on vacations. There was no way that Jacob would have permitted this if it were not the case.

Alice told Benno that she would talk to Ludwig when she returned to Nuremberg. And then she thought to herself, "a vacation." And to a resort that is mostly Jewish. No worrying about money, no worrying about working, no worrying about any anti-Semitism. And she had never been to Norderney, which was supposed to be beautiful.

She took the train home the next day and told Ludwig about Benno's offer. She was expecting him to say no, to complain about how her family never appreciated their financial circumstances. Instead, Ludwig immediately agreed to the trip. Alice knew it was hard for Ludwig to be out of work, and would likely be hard for him to spend three weeks with Benno, who was part of a successful company that was paying for their vacation. By agreeing to go, Alice thought to herself, Ludwig must really need this vacation. Maybe, like her, he needed to escape the reality of hyperinflation and spend a couple of weeks living in luxury. And so she wrote to Benno with the good news.

The family spent the next few weeks planning the vacation. They had decided to stay in a small hotel called the Pension Haus Grimm, which was less expensive than some of the larger and fancier hotels. They would leave at the beginning of July and stay for three weeks. There was a small wrinkle in their plans when Max wrote to Alice in June to tell her that Recha was pregnant and the doctor advised them to remain at home. Alice thought it was more likely that Jacob told Max that he needed to remain in Mannheim to oversee the smelter facility. Her mother had told her that Max was having some trouble with the facility. Max's excuse sounded plausible enough and she would not embarrass him by asking about the "real reason" for his cancellation. She merely wrote back to him, "Mazel tov, Max, but we will miss you." But she was also grateful that Jacob had not re-considered his decision not to come on the trip.

When she agreed to the vacation, Alice didn't appreciate that the trip to Norderney would be so complicated and take so long. She and Ludwig packed enough clothing for three weeks at the beach and boarded the express train to Hamburg. Even though it was an express train, it still took nearly 24 hours before they arrived in Hamburg. Once in Hamburg, they met up with the rest of the family, and then boarded the ferry to Helgoland, a small island in the North Sea. After about three hours on the ferry, they arrived at Helgoland, and then boarded another boat to Norderney. Because there were no cars on the island, the taxis were horse-drawn carriages, and the carriage seemed to take forever to get them to their hotel. After the long and exhausting trip, everyone went to their rooms and slept for several hours. They agreed to meet later for dinner, at which point their vacation would really begin.

Alice was surprised at how quickly the three weeks went. The weather was hot during the day, but the sea breezes at night cooled everything off. Their hotel was close to the sea, and they spent at least some part of every day at the beach, unless it rained. In the evening, they strolled the streets of the town or went to the Kurtheater, which had recently installed a projector for silent films, but also presented plays and lectures.

Alice was most surprised by how relaxed Ludwig and Benno were. Benno knew Ludwig was not working, and yet he said nothing about Gebrüder Heppenheimer or the fact that the family had once offered Ludwig a job. Alice sensed Benno was happy to be away from the business. She never spoke with Benno about his working at Gebrüder Heppenheimer or his having to work with Jacob and Adolph, their cousin. Even though Benno owned an equal share of the business, they were Benno's bosses and acted like Benno's bosses. Perhaps being away from both of them was just what Benno needed.

It was also nice for Alice to spend time with Selma. Since moving to Nuremberg, Alice had spent less and less time with her sister. Alice and Selma shared a bedroom growing up in Frankfurt and had always been close, but close in a different way from Erna. Alice and Selma probably would not have been friends if they had not been related. Perhaps it was the fact that their half-siblings were older or that their parents were older, but Alice and Selma always felt that they shared a special bond. And that bond was renewed in the three weeks they spent in Norderney. While Ludwig read the morning papers, Alice and Selma took long walks or relaxed on the front porch. Benno and Margot were often playing with Hans, but Johanna and her children Mellie and Ernst would sometimes join Alice and Selma on their morning walks.

Selma was clearly happy to be away from Frankfurt. Their father's death had been hard on their mother, and Selma had been spending many evenings with Emma. Selma was okay about supporting her mother in the beginning, but she was having a hard time being that selfless. Alice understood it was not in her sister's nature. Selma preferred to be taken care of. But their mother seemed to be doing better. She declined the invitation to join them for the vacation – she did not feel comfortable vacationing so soon after losing her husband. But she encouraged her children to go and enjoy themselves, and Alice believed she wanted them to do just that.

On one of their walks alone, Selma spoke about some recent dates she had had. She told Alice that she was not in a hurry to marry. She said that, while she didn't like working at the company, it did get her out of the house, and she was happy about that. She was not interested in attending a university, but she had been taking classes at the Jewish Lehrhaus. She was meeting new people at those classes, including some interesting men.

"Papa might not have approved of me attending some of these classes, but he always supported learning, particularly Jewish learning. And Mama likes that I am out meeting new people. She hasn't been putting any pressure on me, but I know she would like me to find someone and marry. I know she wants more grandchildren." Alice knew that last comment was directed at her. Her mother never asked, but she knew her mother wondered why she and Ludwig had had no children.

"I guess that will just put more pressure on you to marry and have children." Alice had hoped that glib comment would stop the discussion, but Selma looked more directly at her sister and ask, "So when can I expect to be an aunt again?"

"With Ludwig not working, it makes no sense to have children at this point." But she didn't share that she wasn't sure she wanted children with Ludwig. Ludwig's inability to hold a job had been a strain on their relationship. And he seemed to be getting angrier and angrier at the right-wing extremist groups in Nuremberg he always railed against. Alice agreed that some of the groups' actions were troubling, but he didn't need to spend all his time reading about them and ranting to Alice. Perhaps it was all the time he was spending at the Central Association. But Selma didn't ask for more details, and Alice didn't volunteer. Selma soon changed the subject, discussing some drama involving friends in Frankfurt. Alice was happy to just listen.

Alice was surprised to find that she was also enjoying spending time with Ludwig. She assumed it had to do with being away from the stresses of their life in Nuremberg. She was reminded of the early days of their relationship, when everything was new and a little exciting. She was also enjoying spending time with the rest of her family. Norderney seemed to be neutral ground for everyone.

In the second week of their vacation, Alice was sitting on the front porch of the hotel, thinking about different designs. She suddenly noticed Selma sitting beside her. "Alice, do you know that I have been sitting next to you for five minutes? It really is amazing your level of concentration! What were you thinking about?"

"I was thinking about a few purse and dress designs. And you really haven't been sitting next to me for five minutes!"

"No, you're right. It was really more like ten minutes. Just like when we were children. I used to joke with Papa that you left your body and went to outer space."

"I can assure you that I have been here the whole time. I guess I was just lost in thought. But if I were travelling in outer space, I must have really built up an appetite, since I am starving. Let's go have breakfast." The sisters went inside to join the rest of the family.

During the breakfast, the family decided to arrange for some pictures at the beach. Beach photographers walked along the beach looking for customers, so finding a photographer would be easy. "And it would be nice to have a postcard made of the photographs to send to Max and to Mama," Alice said. She continued to feel guilty that Max had been forced to remain in Mannheim and hoped that he would like a postcard from them.

After breakfast, the family packed up their clothing and food and walked the short distance to the beach. Each changed in one of the changing rooms located along the promenade. Alice put her beach pajamas over her one-piece bathing suit. Beach pajamas were the one item Alice purchased for both her and Ludwig before they left for vacation. Alice wore the pajamas every day, and felt very stylish in the silk pajamas, with the flared pants. She also had a matching Japanese sun umbrella and a close-fitting cloche hat, which she thought completed the outfit. Alice came out of the changing room and saw both Ludwig and Selma in their beach pajamas; Selma purchased a pair as soon as she found out that her sister had purchased them. Ludwig was wearing his for the first time. Alice looked over at her brother and sisters-in-law – Benno was wearing a one-piece bathing suit and her sisters-in-law were wearing simple black cover-ups over their suits. Johanna was shaking her head and smiling.

"Alice, I always feel so dowdy next to you. And now you have Ludwig and Selma joining the fashion show!"

Alice knew that Johanna's comments were made in good-fun and were meant, on some level, to poke fun at herself. So, Alice laughed along with her sister-in-law and then said, "Johanna, I would be happy to help you pick out some silk pajamas."

"If I did that, I would need to leave them here. Could you imagine what Jacob would say if he saw me wearing silk pajamas at home?" Alice winked at her sister-in-law and then the two laughed.

Benno had arranged for six beach chairs near the water, and they put down their baskets of food. Baby Hans was asleep in the baby carriage, so Benno waved over a beach photographer, and everyone walked to the water to have the picture taken. The photographer then suggested that they take a picture in the water, so they walked back to the chairs to take off their cover-ups, and the women put on bathing caps. The photographer thought it would be fun for the women all to lay facing down in the water, with Benno, Ludwig and Ernst sitting on three of the women. Alice did not want to get wet yet, and so Ludwig volunteered to lie in the water, with Alice sitting on Ludwig's back. Ernst sat on his sister Mellie and Benno sat on Margot's back. The photographer said "smile everyone" and took several pictures. The photographer told them he would return with the pictures the following day and went to find other customers.

Selma said to everyone, "It is so nice when we accomplish something! And Hans will get a special treat from me later for being such a good boy and staying asleep. But I am exhausted from all of that smiling and now it is time to rest in our chairs. After all, we are on vacation!" Everyone laughed and returned to the chairs to enjoy the sunny day.

The one thing Alice became aware of on her vacation was the fact that fewer and fewer of the North Sea resorts were allowing Jewish vacationers. Alice knew that there were hotels in Nuremberg (and even in Frankfurt) that did not allow Jews to stay, but they were small in number. But whole resorts on the

North Sea islands? Guests at the hotel spoke about how "Jewish" Norderney had become, especially since places they had vacationed at in the past no longer allowed Jews to stay. Alice was a little surprised at this. While she generally avoided discussing politics with Ludwig, she did ask him what he thought. He said something that would stay with her for years. "This is the canary in the cave, Alice. I think this is only the beginning. It will be harder and harder to be a Jew in Germany." After he said this to Alice, Alice decided not to think any more about politics and instead to enjoy the rest of her vacation.

The glow from the three weeks on the North Sea lasted for weeks after their return to Nuremberg. Ludwig came back to Nuremberg relaxed and ready to try to find work. Hyperinflation was as bad as ever, and Alice was still struggling to find different jobs to help them pay rent. But Ludwig seemed optimistic, and that optimism rubbed off on Alice. The financial crisis couldn't last forever – things would get better soon. Alice was thinking that very thought as she was walking home from a sewing job when she noticed a flier tacked to a wall announcing a rally for September 1st and 2nd. She was struck by the bright colors of the flier, but didn't really pay much attention to it.

When she arrived home, Ludwig was sitting in a chair reading the paper. When he looked up at her, he seemed agitated. "The right-wing extremists are planning a rally for next month in Nuremberg."

Alice remembered the flier she had just seen. "I saw a flier on the way home tacked to a wall. It was advertising the rally. What is the rally for?"

"Do you remember that person who left those notes on your chair at your apprenticeship? Remember how I said that he might have been a member of this new party, the Nazi party? The party has grown since and has been aligning itself with other right-wing parties. Apparently, they are organizing a German Day Rally here in Nuremberg. They are expecting thousands of people to attend.

They will be marching in the streets. It won't be safe for us to be out, or for any Jew to be out. We will need to stay inside until they leave."

Alice had never seen Ludwig this upset. She wondered if his obsession with the right-wing parties in Nuremberg was getting to him. Maybe this would not be as bad as he suggested. She knew that right-wing groups had been making more trouble in the city. There had even been some vandalism the previous year at the Jewish cemetery. But the city's liberal mayor, Hermann Luppe, would make sure that the city's Jews were protected, she thought. It was difficult to believe that anything serious could happen, but just to be safe, she agreed with Ludwig to stay home those two days.

There was a crazy energy in the city the day before the rally, and Alice could see men in different uniforms roaming the streets. But one uniform stood out – a uniform with brown shirts. Ludwig explained that these were the Storm Troopers, or "SA," and that they served as security for Adolf Hitler, the head of the Nazi Party. As Alice and Ludwig continued to walk, Alice recognized someone, and then grabbed Ludwig's arm and dragged him down a side street.

"Alice, what's wrong with you. You practically pulled my arm out."

"Do you remember that person we were just talking about who wrote all of those horrible anti-Semitic notes? The one who got me fired from my first apprenticeship?"

"Yes, I even remember his name. Rudolph."

"I just saw him. In a brown shirt. I am sure he didn't see me, but I didn't want to take a chance. He really scared me."

"And for good reason. Wearing that brown shirt means he is a member of the SA. And a Nazi. You see, Alice, I was right about him."

Alice and Ludwig remained at home on the days of the rally, and finally left the apartment on the morning after the rally was over. There was still trash in the street, but nothing was broken. Ludwig bought the morning newspaper and they walked back to the apartment. After he read the lead article, Ludwig told Alice that 100,000 people had attended the rally.

Ludwig continued, "According to the article, Hitler spoke at the rally. The article says that he was a dynamic speaker who riled up the crowd. Hitler said the Jews, Marxists, and the French were to blame for hyperinflation, said the Treaty of Versailles would be the ruin of Germany, and advocated for the overthrow of the Weimar Government. Then, for two hours, he reviewed formations of these nationalist forces." It sounded very militaristic to Alice, who found it all a bit frightening.

Rosh Hashanah was the following week and Alice and Ludwig attended services at the Grand Synagogue, where they had married. Because of an increase in anti-Semitic activities and the recent rally, there were security guards in front of the synagogue. Ludwig and Alice rarely attended religious services, but always went for the High Holiday services. Neither remembered ever seeing security guards at the synagogue. Were things changing for Nuremberg's Jewish community? Or was this a small blip, with things returning to normal after the current economic crisis was over? Alice was hoping for the latter.

CHAPTER 3

Nuremberg, October 1926

It was an unusually cold day for October, but Alice hardly noticed. After she left City Hall, Alice walked on the cobblestone streets past the Main Market, and crossed the Pegnitz River. Normally she would have taken the tram home, but she decided to walk. It was only a thirty-minute walk home. Plus, the walk would do her good. It had taken her six years to see her dream a reality, and she wanted to enjoy this moment before she had to face Ludwig. She was so excited she was almost skipping home.

An arts and crafts studio! And a women's handbag factory! She had just received business licenses for both. A little late for her thirtieth birthday, but not a bad birthday present. Her apartment on Wodanstrasse was a little small for her new ventures, but she would make it work. It certainly was larger than their last apartment, and much less gloomy. Plus, she and Ludwig were hoping to move to a larger apartment next year. Her art school friends would be able to sell their work at her studio, even in her current apartment.

Alice had worried that she would never see her dream become a reality, but over the past two years, things had fallen into place. First, prices finally began to fall in the middle of 1924 after the reparations payments forced on Germany after the Great War were reset to more sustainable levels and after a new currency for Germany was adopted. Women began to buy fancy purses again. Alice was able to get some work at Wertheimer Handbags, the factory she had apprenticed in, by the end of 1924, and that work soon turned into a full-time position when they hired her as a purse designer. Ludwig was also working, selling spices wholesale. The trade was not very lucrative, but it was consistent, and he had been working steadily for two years.

Even during the hyperinflation years, when Alice could only secure piecemeal work, she still worked to perfect her craft. She was able to audit classes at the art school and attended as many lectures on fashion as she could. Any time there was a fashion show, Alice found a way to attend. And Erna had been perfecting her craft, as well, learning more about the textiles and other materials used in the manufacturing of purses. Unlike Alice, Erna had been able to secure an apprenticeship in a handbag factory right after graduation that turned into a full-time position, and kept that position through the hyperinflation period. But each friend continued to support the dream of an arts and crafts studio, and now that dream would become a reality. The friends agreed Erna would keep her job for now, and help Alice before and after work. Alice was able to negotiate a flexible position with Wertheimer Handbags, being paid for each handbag she designed.

While Alice was excited and optimistic about her future, she wished things were better with Ludwig. The two years Ludwig had been out of work had been very hard on both of them, and their relationship. Ludwig had spent most of his time sitting at home and reading the various newspapers, or at the Central Association office. His worries about the right-wing organizations had become an obsession and he was constantly tracking where they were meeting in town and what rallies they were holding. When the publisher of the Nuremberg-based *Der Stürmer*, Julius Streicher, was suspended from his teaching position because of his participation with Hitler and other Nazis in a failed attempt to topple the Weimar government at the end of 1923, Ludwig rejoiced. But Hitler, who was sentenced to five years in prison for leading this "Beer Hall Putsch," only served eight months in what was essentially house arrest, and was now more popular than ever, promoting the so-called autobiography he wrote in prison, "Mein Kampf," a political manifesto that envisioned an Aryan nation free of Jews. Ludwig told Alice that Hitler had transformed the Nazi Party from one bent on revolution to one focused on winning elections. Streicher followed this approach, soon rising to power in the Nuremberg government, with *Der Stürmer* becoming an important paper of the right-wing parties. Ludwig was furious, complaining to Alice that the Nazi Party might actually gain political power in Germany. Alice believed that the best thing that happened for Ludwig was that he was finally able to secure a job – after hyperinflation ended – and he was out of the house and not so fixated on the Nazi Party. But working had not seemed to fix his relationship with Alice, and they had grown more distant. They rarely talked when Ludwig was home, and when they did, he was generally surly. Alice told him about opening the studio, only because it would be in their apartment. He had been so supportive earlier in their marriage, but he simply said, "Fine" when she told him. Alice was not sure what she had expected from their marriage, but things were certainly not right. Still, Alice was finally opening her studio, and that was her focus now.

Alice adjusted the route to her apartment in order to pass by Erna's building. It was more than just an adjustment since she would have to re-cross the river, but she really wanted to share the news with her friend. She knew that Alfred was travelling for business, and so only Erna would be home. And she knew that Erna would have just come home from work. Alfred had been just as excited about Alice's new ventures as Erna, and she was happy to talk to both when both were together. But Alice was still mindful that Erna seemed a little uncomfortable if Alice was speaking with Alfred alone, and so she still avoided situations where it was just Alice and Alfred.

Alice opened the front door at Laufer Torgraben 6, walked down the hall and knocked. Erna must have known it would be Alice, since Alice could hear her running to the door. As soon as she opened the door, the two friends hugged. Alice then showed Erna the two licenses and both women shrieked. Erna rarely showed strong emotion, so Alice knew her friend was really excited. To avoid the stares of nosy neighbors, Erna grabbed Alice and they both went inside.

"I can't believe you finally did it!"

"I can't believe <u>we</u> finally did it!" Alice wanted her friend to feel that she was part of the new ventures.

"Alice, it is wonderful for you to say that, but this really is your studio. But I am happy to be a part of it." Alice understood her friend's reluctance to be too visible to the world, and so didn't challenge her friend. But in her mind, Alice felt like the friends were partners. And Alice knew Erna would do whatever she could to make these businesses succeed.

"So Alice, explain to me again what it means to have the licenses? Can we get started right away?"

"We can start the arts and crafts studio immediately. The second license provides that the handbag factory will start after January 1st of next year, so we have a little time to begin. You and I will need to decide what we will need to purchase and who will display their works in the studio. We will then need to determine what we need to do to open the factory, and we will need to do that soon. But for now, we just need to focus on getting the studio open, before the holiday season. We can reach out to everyone we know asking about their interest in displaying their art. Certainly, you and I have enough items to start the studio. And we will need to do all of this before our opening reception."

"I still can't believe you are finally opening the studio. This really is so exciting!"

Alice was about to remind her friend about "we" and then thought better of it. It just wasn't in Erna to accept that they were partners, but the reality was that they were not really partners. Alice was putting up all the money, and so was really taking all the risk. If the studio failed, only Alice would be liable for any debts. As the daughter of the owner of a large and successful scrap metal business, Alice understood the concepts of risk and liability. Erna, whose father had been a civil servant, was not really mindful of such issues as they were preparing to open the studio, and was not worried about risk or liability. But Erna agreed to only take a percentage of what the studio sold rather than a salary, so, in a way, she was taking a risk; just not as large a risk as Alice.

"Alice, why don't you stay for coffee. I have some cookies from our favorite bakery."

"Oh, Erna, you know how hard it is to resist an offer for Friedmann's cookies, but I am really trying to lose a little weight. And I told Ludwig that I would be home in time to make dinner, so I really should be going. But let's plan on meeting early tomorrow morning at my apartment before you need to get to work and start making plans for the studio. And you can bring those cookies."

"Wonderful. See you tomorrow, my friend. And I won't forget the cookies." The two friends smiled and then hugged again. Alice left the apartment, truly excited about opening the studio – and opening it with Erna. She bundled up her jacket and walked to her apartment. She wasn't sure how Ludwig would respond to actually seeing the licenses, but she would deal with that when she got home. She had dealt with his moods before.

•   •   •

Alice arrived home around 6 pm and climbed the stairs to their first-floor apartment. There were two apartments on this level, and both were relatively small. Alice's apartment was a one-bedroom apartment, with the all-important private bathroom. But unlike her last apartment, this apartment had a much larger main room. And unlike the previous apartment, the living room's wallpaper was new and had a more modern Art Deco pattern. The kitchen was in the corner of the room and could easily be hidden behind screens, which would allow for a large space for the studio. Alice took out her key and unlocked the door. Ludwig was in his chair, reading the newspaper. Alice thought he was probably reading the *Central Association Zeitung*, which was issued weekly and reported on the hundreds of cases the Association was bringing in the courts. He must have just come home from work, she thought, since he still had his suit jacket on. Ludwig raised his head, waved, and returned to his paper. He knew Alice had gone to City Hall to obtain her licenses, but he did not ask her how it went. Alice decided it was better not to volunteer information. She walked past him and went to the stove to prepare dinner, a simple chicken stew. She added coal to the stove and began to heat the pan. She was a bit annoyed with Ludwig for asking her nothing about the licenses, but it really did not dim her excitement about the day. She was really starting her studio and the handbag factory!

Half-way through her dinner preparation, Ludwig walked over to her. Alice was not aware that she had been singing to herself, and perhaps that was why he had gotten up from his chair. She stopped singing and asked him if there was something that he needed.

"No, I'm fine. When is dinner going to be ready? I was thinking about taking a walk."

"Dinner will be ready by 7:30 pm. Is that okay for you?"

"Yes, that's fine. I will be back shortly."

Alice heard him put on his shoes and leave the apartment. Still, nothing about her day, one of the biggest days in her life, Alice thought. She grunted out loud, louder than she had intended, but he had already left and didn't hear her. She finished preparing dinner and then went into the bedroom to take a rest.

Alice had fallen asleep and awoke when she heard Ludwig close the apartment door. "What time is it?" she wondered aloud. It was getting dark outside, so she guessed she had slept about 30 minutes. Clearly, she needed the nap. She got up from the bed, brushed her hair, and left the bedroom. She was rather startled when she saw Ludwig holding a beautiful bouquet of flowers. She could not remember a time Ludwig had bought her flowers. Even early in their marriage, Ludwig was just not demonstrative in that way. Alice had always loved flowers, but never expected Ludwig to buy her flowers. Alice often wondered why Ludwig had not figured out that she loved flowers, given the flowers she included in her dress and purse designs.

"Oh, Ludwig, they are beautiful!" She gave him a kiss on the cheek.

"Well, I thought it would be nice to get you some flowers to celebrate your new studio." Ludwig handed Alice the flowers. Alice walked over to one of the cabinets next to the stove. She knew there was a vase in the back of the cabinet. She thought to herself, "I don't think I have ever used this vase. I can't even remember who gave this to us as a wedding present." When Alice turned around, she saw that Ludwig had returned to his chair and his paper. She had hoped that Ludwig would have asked her about the process for getting the licenses. But Alice understood how hard it was for Ludwig to make even this small gesture, and so said nothing more. Alice knew Ludwig had complicated feelings when it came to her opening a studio, and then a factory, especially given the last few years. So she was happy that he at least acknowledged the studio. Perhaps this represented a first step toward a better relationship for them.

Alice placed the flowers in the center of the dining table. This would be one of the last dinners they would eat at this table, since Ludwig had agreed to allow Alice to use the dining table for her studio until they were able to move into the larger apartment. They would use a smaller table closer to the stove for their meals. Alice set the table and she and Ludwig sat down to eat. Ludwig remained quiet through dinner, and Alice knew not to push him to talk. The flowers were the most that Ludwig could do to celebrate Alice's big news.

Alice understood that Ludwig wanted to be successful at some type of business, but over the course of their marriage, Ludwig struggled with one business failure after another. His father had a small but successful factory, but that business was sold after he died and Ludwig went to war. His mother always favored her younger son Ernst, who was now studying medicine. His mother often asked Ludwig why he was such a failure at business when his father was such a success. She didn't add "and like your brother is such a success," but Alice heard it, and she was sure Ludwig did, as well.

It likely didn't help that Alice's efforts were finally paying off. Since she graduated from art school, Alice had been designing and making her own clothes, and she had been designing clothes for friends. She had designed her own handbags, as well as hats, scarves, and shawls. She was experimenting with various fabrics, and her friends from art school spent more and more time in her apartment, discussing designs and studying the latest fashions.

Alice's various side jobs had helped to pay the rent and provide food for them. During the two years that Ludwig was out of work, it was the only money the two had, other than the money provided by Alice's mother. They didn't talk about money, since it would only have reinforced Ludwig's image of himself as a failure. He had been working the past two years selling spices wholesale, but he barely made enough for them to cover their rent. Certainly, there was no extra money to do something like start two businesses.

When Alice finally decided it was time to start her businesses, she did not ask Ludwig for the money, since he had none. And she did not ask his permission, since they had already spoken about this dream of hers multiple times. But she needed to tell Ludwig that she would be asking her brothers for help in starting the businesses. Hearing that was hard for Ludwig – Alice knew that – but to his credit he did not dismiss the idea of asking her brothers for money, asking instead how much they were giving her and whether they were expecting her to pay them back. She told him they were giving her RM 500 and they were considering it a gift. He said that this was very generous of them and that he was happy that she was finally going to realize her dream. He didn't say that he was sorry that he could not help her make this dream happen, but she knew he felt it. It would have simply been too much for him to say.

•   •   •

Erna was at Alice's apartment at 7 am sharp the next morning. Erna immediately put down her things and began walking around the room that would be the studio. "I love this space. The windows bring in the natural light and we can enhance that light with lamps. And if we make the shades, we can also sell the lamps." Erna was truly in her element – she was using her color and spacial talents to find the best attributes of the room to help to sell their art. And she was thinking about all the items the two could sell. Alice was so happy to have her friend to help her with this business venture. "We can move the dining room table against the wall, and put other smaller tables along the wall. We can also place mannequins in different parts of the room to highlight the best of your dress and shawl designs. Oh Alice, this is really going to be great!"

"Erna, I love your enthusiasm! And you are absolutely right about the dining room table. And the mannequins. Let's have some coffee – and a few of those fancy cookies – and think about what the room should look like before you need to leave for work.

We also need to decide who we will invite to show their work, besides our own."

The friends sat down to their coffee, excited about their new venture. Alice felt that there was nothing to stop them from succeeding. Alice did wish that Ludwig was a little easier on her, or at least felt more confident about his business prospects. The economy was better and women were buying her designs. And she was making a name for herself, at least within her small fashion community.

"Erna, we can open the studio in two months, don't you think? Just in time for the holidays. We can advertise in my synagogue newsletter for free. And we can tack up posters throughout the art school campus. And for the opening reception, we can invite our friends, and encourage our friends to invite their friends. We can serve cookies and coffee. People will come, don't you think?"

"They will absolutely come, Alice. Let's start planning."

•　•　•

Erna had been at Alice's apartment for most of the day, preparing for the studio's opening that evening. Alice was a nervous wreck, and while Erna was doing her best to calm down her friend, it wasn't working.

"Erna, do you think we have enough scarves on the table?"

"Yes, we have plenty of scarves. And more in the bedroom."

"I just don't think we have enough items on the table. And where is the food? It was supposed to be delivered by 2 pm, and it is nearly 3:30. And the reception is supposed to start at 5! But it won't matter, since no one will come anyway!"

"Alice, the food will be here soon. And we will have lots of guests this evening. What else will people be doing on a Sunday evening? But you need to relax. I have never seen you this nervous about anything. You need to leave the apartment and take a walk."

"But I can't leave now. The food still hasn't arrived!"

Erna handed Alice a jacket and hat and pointed to the door. Alice took a deep breath and took the jacket. Erna was right – a brisk walk outside would do her good. As she was leaving her building, she saw the cart from Friedmann's Bakery. Okay, well at least there will be food, she thought.

Alice began walking toward the Grosser Dutzendteich, the largest of the ponds near her apartment. The ponds had been created by an emperor centuries earlier by damming several streams, but the large pond was more like a lake. When she needed a place to think or relax, she always walked to this pond. She started to think about the reception, about who might show up and what pieces might be sold. She was so lost in her thoughts that she almost bumped into an elderly woman carrying groceries home. Alice was about two blocks from the pond when she noticed some young men who were walking behind her. She thought little about them initially, but they got closer and then she felt something hit the back of her jacket. It soon became clear that they were throwing pebbles at her.

"What do you think would happen if we threw this Jewess into the pond," one asked. "Would she float or would she sink?"

"Maybe she would just melt!" another said. They all laughed.

"Let's try it," said a third one.

Alice turned onto another street and began to run. The men threw the rest of their pebbles at her, but did not follow her. They just laughed. They only wanted to scare her, and they had done a good job.

Alice was out of breath by the time she reached her apartment. She climbed the stairs, but stopped at the door. This was not the first time that someone in Nuremberg had approached her on the street because she was Jewish, although nothing bad had ever happened to her previously. These boys today only wanted to scare her. Ludwig had warned her about the increase in violence against Jews. He was particularly concerned about the recent decision of the Bavarian government to lift the ban on the Nazi Party imposed following Hitler's trial in 1924. Ludwig also told her about recent riots in Berlin, particularly in neighborhoods where Polish Jews were living, and he was worried about possible riots in Nuremberg. But nothing bad had happened to her today, and they had actually done her a favor, she told herself. She was no longer anxious about this evening's reception. She took a deep breath and entered her apartment.

Alice looked to her left and saw that Erna had already set out the cookies and cakes on the small table. And next to that table was another table for hot and cold drinks. Then Alice looked around the room. The large table along the wall contained the various purses Alice and Erna had been making over the last few years, several tapestries and scarves that Alice and Erna had designed, and other crafts from art school friends. Another table held ceramic, wooden, and brass pieces made by artisans she had met since art school, as well as jewelry designed by another friend from art school. On the three mannequins were what Alice thought were the best of her dress designs. Looking at the calf-revealing lengths and the lower necklines of the dresses, Alice thought that her mother would probably call them "flapper dresses" in a dismissive tone. But Alice loved the straight lines and bold colors of the dresses, and thought that each would look great with a long strand of pearls. And on the walls were Art Deco lithograph prints from another art school friend. Everything looked wonderful, thought Alice. Tonight would be a success!

• • •

The last of the guests left the apartment around 9 pm. All the food had been eaten and everyone seemed to have had a good time. Erna helped Alice move the dirty plates into the kitchen. Ludwig was sitting in the living room chair reading the newspaper, although Alfred had volunteered to help the women. He was not about to wash or dry a dish, but said he would be happy to collect the garbage and take it outside to the trash can. Alice was happy for the help. Alfred was gathering the waste when he said, "Alice, I think this reception was a big success. Sometimes I couldn't move around the living room because of all the people. Erna told me that the two of you sold a few pieces tonight. So, you can now say that you have already made money!"

"Thanks, Alfred, and thanks for all your help. I am pretty pleased at how everything went this evening."

"I was actually listening in on some of the conversations. Some of your art school friends are jealous that you have been able to make this happen. I have the sense that several of them will want to display their pieces here, now that they saw things were selling. Who knows? Pretty soon you may have to turn away your artist friends." With that comment, he smiled at Alice and took the garbage downstairs to the outside can. Alice was not aware that she was also smiling, but then looked up and saw Ludwig staring at her. She looked away and continue to pick up the plates to be washed. She assumed Ludwig would return to his paper and sulk.

Not unexpectedly, Alice found Erna at the sink, washing dishes. Erna looked up at Alice and said, "I meant to tell you that both Catherine and Gerta asked if we would show their work, and I told them I needed to speak to you."

"Wow, their work is beautiful, particularly Gerta's beaded purses. Getting more work to show would be great. Let's sit down tomorrow morning and make a list of who is interested and who we should reach out to. We should also make a list of who we should invite to future shows. I really think this is going to work."

"Me too."

The two friends were working in companionable silence when Alfred came back into the apartment. Alice could hear him speaking with Ludwig, and then the two came over to Alice and Erna. Alfred had a newspaper in his hand. "I found this on the hall floor in front of your door. Someone must have left it during the reception." Alice looked at the paper – "*Der Stürmer*." The cover of the paper was particularly heinous – there was an image of three ugly Jewish men sucking the blood of a dead Polish girl. The implication behind the image was clear – Jews engage in ritual murders of children. They had heard such allegations for years.

Of course, Ludwig was the first to speak. "*Der Stürmer*, the worst piece of filth. The publisher, Julius Streicher, is such an embarrassment to mankind. Look at these lies he is spreading. And he is only getting more popular. The Central Association has been bringing lawsuits against this horrible man for years. We have been able to assess fines against him, but his position as a Bavarian government official has given him parliamentary immunity, so no jail time. Whoever put this paper at our door is clearly making a statement. I wonder if it was one of our neighbors. Who else would know we are Jewish? Or maybe it was one of your art school friends. And now we have it, right on our doorstep! I need to show this to the leadership at the Central Association. We need to stop these Nazi attacks!"

Leave it to Ludwig to focus on the political aspects of this anti-Semitic act and not think about how it might be affecting Alice. And also to suggest that one of the people at Alice's reception left this garbage at their doorstep. But Alfred seemed to be aware of the impact this paper was having on Alice and Erna. "Erna, Alice, how terrible for the two of you that someone would leave that at the door, especially given how hard the two of had worked to make this evening a success. My guess is that it was someone in the building or in the neighborhood. I don't think anyone attending the reception would be trying to send a message to you about your business. Still, the two of you should monitor the people who come to the studio. I am sorry this person has tainted what really was a wonderful opening for the studio."

Alice decided to ignore this awful incident, whatever the point of it was, as she had the earlier encounter near the pond. "Alfred, I agree. Erna, we had a great success this evening and let's just enjoy that. Let's put this trash where it belongs – in the trash can." At that moment, she looked up and saw Ludwig glaring at Alfred. Really, Ludwig, she thought, is that really necessary?

CHAPTER 4

Nuremberg, June 1930

Alice stood before the door to Breite Gasse 2. She had had an early morning meeting with a potential supplier and was ready for some coffee. But she stopped outside the building to enjoy a few last moments of quiet. At that moment, the door to her right opened and Herr Liegel, the owner of the hairdresser shop, came out to throw some trash into the trash can.

"Good morning, Herr Liegel. Lovely morning."

"Good morning, Frau Adler. Another busy day for your factory? I have already seen a few of your young ladies arrive for work."

"Yes, Herr Liegel. We have been pretty busy. I guess women love to buy handbags."

"Particularly your handbags, Frau Adler. My wife has already purchased three! She seems intent on bankrupting me."

Alice smiled at the hairdresser and waved goodbye. She then entered the building and walked up a flight of stairs to the first floor. She could hear the chatter of her employees as she opened the door to her factory. Her factory! It had been open since January, but she still got a thrill every time she said it to herself. She greeted her employees. "Good morning, Ladies." The three ladies called back, "Good morning, Alice." And then Helga came up to Alice to let her know about a problem with an order. Her day was already beginning, thought Alice. But she was happy. At least, mostly happy.

When she first opened her factory on Breite Gasse, Alice thought about the stories her father Joseph had told about when Gebrüder Heppenheimer was successful enough to open a separate office. It was 1879 and at the time, both Henry and Joseph and their families were living together in a small apartment. The brothers had started the business in 1877, but worked out of the apartment for two years. Even after they opened the separate office, they remained in the same apartment for another year, until the business was successful enough for them to afford two apartments. Nine little children living in a single apartment! But the focus was on the long-term success of the business and not the short-term discomfort of the family. Alice had also waited until she could afford to open a factory outside of her apartment, although she didn't have any children.

A year after Alice opened her arts and crafts studio in 1926, she and Ludwig had moved to a larger two-bedroom apartment on Hallerstrasse, with both a living room and a dining room, as well as a separate kitchen. Still, it wasn't until 1928 that she could finally manufacture handbags in the apartment. When she began the factory, the arts and crafts studio occupied half of the living room and all of the dining room, and the factory occupied the rest of the living room and one of the bedrooms. She soon hired one woman, and then a second woman, to help her make the beaded, fabric, and embroidered bags. The bags were being purchased by women throughout the city. In 1929, Alice obtained a city license to sell textile goods, so that she could sell her handbags directly to women's shops. With the opening of the factory in her apartment, Alice was finally able to stop doing the piecemeal work for Wertheimer Handbags.

When Alice was ready to open the handbag factory in 1928, she decided to ask her brothers for a loan. She needed to buy some additional sewing machines and other equipment, as well as supplies for the handbags. She also needed to pay her employees, and it would take some time to see a profit. Because she had no collateral, no bank would lend her the money. Her brothers had given her a small amount of money to start the arts and crafts studio, but this time she was going to need more money and she wanted it to be a loan – she wanted to pay them back. It was never easy to go to her brothers – especially Jacob – for anything. But if she wanted to start the factory, she needed the loan.

Alice was planning a visit to Frankfurt in June 1928 to meet Selma's fiancé Leo Lewin, and decided to combine that visit with a meeting with Jacob and Benno to ask for the loan. For the first two days of her visit, Alice helped Selma plan the last few details for the wedding, which was to happen in the beginning of 1929. Selma told Alice that she had decided to make the wedding small, with just family and a few friends. Selma told her that the brothers had suggested that the wedding just be with the immediate family, and what her brothers said was generally followed. But Alice sensed that something else was going on.

Selma had always dreamed of a large and fancy wedding. She loved to dress up and she loved to eat well. Alice had always been a little surprised that Selma had not found someone earlier. After all, she hated working at the company and was only working until she married. Alice knew Selma had dated other men, but Selma never confided in her why none of those other prospects had worked out. Alice had never met Leo, but he seemed like a nice enough man, from the way her mother and her sister had described him. And he seemed to love Selma. Plus, he did not seem intimidated by her brothers, which Selma probably liked. Leo was in the wholesale coffee business, working on commission for a Dutch coffee exporter. But he was hoping to start his own wholesale coffee company, and Selma was excited about his prospects. Emma had written to Alice that her brothers were worried about Leo's ability to make enough money to support Selma, but that may just have been her brothers.

Still, why was Selma not getting her big fancy wedding? If her father were still alive, Selma would have had that wedding. And why was Selma being so agreeable about a small wedding? Alice decided not to push.

Alice had sent her brothers her loan request and supporting materials in a letter a few weeks before she went to Frankfurt. Alice sat down with Jacob and Benno the third day she was in Frankfurt at her mother's apartment to discuss the proposal. She remembered the important meetings her father conducted in the apartment's parlor and decided she would meet with her brothers in the parlor. Alice understood Jacob made the decisions about money, and so focused her attention on him after they sat down in the parlor.

After she was finished with her presentation for the loan, Jacob had a question. "Where is Ludwig?"

"Ludwig had business and couldn't get away." Jacob knew about Ludwig's business challenges and Alice was pretty sure Jacob knew about her marriage problems. So, he would not make this easy.

"It just seems pretty strange that his wife is meeting her sister's fiancé for the first time and Ludwig is too busy to join her. If it were me, I would have made it a priority to come." Alice remembered the trip she and Ludwig had taken with Benno and his wife Margot and Jacob's wife Johanna and their two children – but not Jacob – to Norderney. This was one of a long list of vacations where Jacob was absent. Business was everything to Jacob, and when it was a contest between business and family, business always won out. But this was not about family or Ludwig. It was about making Alice feel badly because Alice had left Frankfurt for art school and had not returned. It may be that Jacob also blamed Alice for his own daughter Mellie's decision to attend a university when she graduated from high school. She was currently at the Sorbonne in Paris, and not working for Gebrüder Heppenheimer.

"Jacob, he just couldn't get away. Could we concentrate instead on my request for a loan? And it really would be just that. A loan. I will pay you back as soon as I make a profit, which should be next year."

"Alice, you know we are always happy to help you, and we have helped you in the past." Alice hated when he reminded her of the help he had given her. "You are asking us for 3,000 Reichsmarks and normally that would not be a problem for us, but much of our money is tied up in several investments right now. We have reviewed all of your financial information – very impressive, by the way – and have decided that we can lend you the money. We can lend you half now, but you will need to wait two years for the rest. Based on the projections you have shared with us, that should not be a problem. And we have every confidence that your business will succeed."

Benno said nothing during the meeting and Alice couldn't tell if he agreed with his brother about giving her only half of what she had requested. She also couldn't tell how much the economy was affecting Gebrüder Heppenheimer, although she suspected that there were financial issues with the business, at least based on what Max had said with respect to the Mannheim scrap metal facility. RM 3,000 was what was needed to get the business fully operational, but she could make it work with RM 1,500, provided her brothers came through with the other half. She believed that her factory would need to be in a space separate from her apartment in order to be truly successful. But that would need to wait if they were only giving her half of what she had asked for. She would just need to adjust her business plan. "Jacob, Benno, this is really generous of you and I really appreciate the faith you have in me. RM 1,500 would help me get the factory off the ground, and the second installment should come at the right time for me. Thank you." She didn't say that, without that second installment, she could not make the business work.

"Wonderful. Now let's have dinner with what's-his-name." Unfortunately, Jacob was not shy about expressing his sentiments about Leo. But Alice was hoping that he was wrong and that Leo would be just the man that Selma needed. But then Alice understood why the wedding was so understated. It wasn't just that the brothers (or at least Jacob) had concerns about Leo. They were also worried about money. Her mother had mentioned that there were continuing problems with the Mannheim smelter facility. But Alice now understood that the company was likely having money problems beyond the smelter facility. And Selma, working at the company, must have understood that the company was having money issues. While Alice had problems with Jacob, at that moment, she was grateful that her brothers were giving her the money she needed.

The RM 1,500 allowed Alice to purchase two sewing machine, as well as fabrics, beads, and other supplies, and the factory opened in her apartment in early October 1928. She had enough resources to advertise and to pay her employees, and she and Erna were working hard to increase business. Customers liked their handbags, and they were sending friends to the factory. Alice was relieved that the business was growing and it was wonderful to have her friend Erna working side by side with her in the apartment. The factory was finally making enough money by the beginning of 1929 that Erna quit her job and came to work full time with Alice.

While her business was doing well, it was clear to Alice that her marriage was failing. Ludwig continued to sell spices wholesale – at least he was finally able to keep a job – but he was not a natural salesperson and he never made the money that others in his company did. His mother knew the owner, and Alice suspected that was why Ludwig was hired in the first place and why he had not been fired. But Ludwig knew he was not good at his job, and as Alice's fortunes increased, Ludwig's resentment at her success also increased. When he was home, Ludwig mostly stayed in the second bedroom. Soon after the factory opened, Ludwig and Alice began to sleep in separate rooms, although she did not share this with anyone, including Erna. When she closed the factory for the day, Alice took out a cot and slept in the bedroom with the sewing machines.

By the fall of 1929, Alice decided she was ready take the next step. She knew that, if she was going to succeed, she needed to open a factory separate from her apartment. And she needed her friend to help her with the move. So, Alice asked Erna to meet her for breakfast on an early October morning to discuss Alice's plan. Alice was excited to share with her friend this exciting step. But Erna had something she needed to tell Alice, as well.

Erna had been her friend since the beginning of art school, and they had talked about opening an arts and crafts studio together since the early days of their friendship. It was Erna who had encouraged Alice to open the studio and the handbag factory. It was Erna who had calmed Alice down when she worried about the business or finances. And it was Erna who Alice confided in about her problems with Ludwig after the studio and the factory opened.

Erna never discussed her marriage with Alfred, and Alice never pushed, although it was Alice's sense that the two were not well suited for each other. Alfred was naturally gregarious, and Erna was very quiet. When the four had double-dated years earlier and Alfred and Ludwig were not talking about politics, it was often Alice and Alfred who did most of the talking, and often to each other. When Alice was with Alfred and Erna, Alice found herself mostly talking to Alfred. Alice loved Erna, but she wondered what Alfred and Erna talked about when they were alone. Adding to the problem was the fact that Alfred was frequently away on business, traveling around southern Germany selling watches. Alice often had the sense that Erna was actually happier when

Alfred was away; she could work with Alice or she could be alone in the apartment and didn't need to talk to anyone. Still, it came as a bit of a surprise when Erna came to the apartment that October morning and, before Alice had a chance to discuss the new factory, announced to Alice that she was divorcing Alfred and moving back home. She didn't want to talk about the divorce, or the reasons for the divorce. She also didn't want to talk about remaining with the business.

Because it was Alice who was the sole investor in the businesses and the licenses were in Alice's name, the business was technically hers. But Alice would have been happy to discuss a financial arrangement with Erna to reflect her contribution to the business. Erna immediately cut her off when Alice began to talk finances. But more puzzling, she didn't seem to want to talk about anything. She just hugged her friend and left the apartment. Alice was stunned, but let her friend leave. Alice understood when Erna needed to be alone, although Alice had never been completely shut out by her friend. She gave Erna a week, and when Alice had still not heard from her friend, Alice went to her apartment. Alice assumed a week would be enough time for Erna to reconsider the move away from Nuremberg; perhaps Erna could move into Alice's apartment until she could afford a place of her own. Alfred answered the door and informed Alice that Erna had already left.

"What do you mean she left? She didn't even say goodbye!"

"It was very quick. She packed her things and left five days ago." Five days ago, Alice thought to herself. So, she had left Alice's apartment, packed her things and left two days after they had spoken. And without even saying goodbye.

"Alfred, what happened? Why did she leave without saying goodbye to me? Everything with the business has been going so well, and Erna seemed happy. But she came to me a week ago, said the two of you were divorcing, and that she was going back to her town. I didn't even know the two of you were having problems. She wouldn't tell me what had happened and I didn't push. You know Erna. But maybe I should have pushed."

"Alice, it is a bit complicated and I really don't think it is my place to talk about this. If Erna didn't want to talk with you about it, I should respect her decision."

"What do you mean you should respect her decision! You are also getting a divorce! What happened? And why did she leave?"

Alfred looked at Alice, but the look was not of someone in pain, someone distraught at having to face a failed marriage and a spouse who had left. It was something else, almost like relief. And it was making her uncomfortable, so she decided it would be best to leave. She asked Alfred for Erna's address and he gave it to her. And then he said, "Alice, whatever happened between Erna and me, you should know that Erna loved you and it hurt her more than anything to leave you and to leave without saying goodbye. She loved working with you and hated leaving you alone with the business. All that I can say is that she really couldn't talk to you about why she was leaving Nuremberg – trust me that it was just too hard." Alice could see that there was no point in continuing. Alfred was not going to tell her anything more, and so she left.

Over the next few weeks, Alice sent Erna several letters, but Erna never responded. Erna had been Alice's best friend and support, and Alice was hurt and bewildered by her friend's rejection and disappearance. On a selfish note, she also felt Erna's absence, since it was only Erna in whom she had confided about her own failing marriage. She hadn't really discussed her problems with Selma, although she was pretty sure that Selma – and her mother – knew that there were problems in the marriage. But for now, with her friend and support gone, she really needed to keep focused on her business in order to make it a success. And she went ahead with her decision to open the factory outside the apartment.

Sometimes Alice wondered if her drive to succeed had something to do with the problems in her marriage. Ludwig had wanted to succeed as a businessman, but perhaps he just didn't have it in him. At some point, Ludwig had pushed Alice to have children, but how could she bring children into a marriage where the husband could not support the family? She was now thirty-four years old, the same age her mother was when she had Alice. It was not too late to have children, but for Alice – if she was being honest with herself – her business was her baby. Alice found a space in the center of the old city and moved her sewing machines and other equipment to the space in December. By January 1, 1930, the purse factory was up and running on Breite Gasse.

After the factory opened, Alice continued the arts and crafts studio in her apartment, but generally limited art showings to one evening a week. Her main focus was now on the factory. She developed relationships with several stores, and they were carrying some of her purses, particularly the cheaper ones. She spent much of her time going from store to store, and when she wasn't selling, she was designing or helping her ladies finish the purses. For the moment, they were making clutch bags, to be worn under the arm, and reticules, which were pouches with a drawstring or a frame. Alice was particularly proud of the framed reticules, which were lined in silk and had a row of fringes hanging from the bottom.

Alice was working long hours at the factory. It was not unusual for her to arrive before 7 am and leave after 8 pm. Her only day off was Sunday, since all businesses were required to be closed on Sunday. She sometimes took work home with her in the evenings. Of course, she needed to manage the business side, which she usually did on Sunday in her apartment. And because Alice and Ludwig were essentially leading separate lives, her long hours had little effect on their relationship. After the factory was moved to Breite Gasse, Alice permanently moved into the second bedroom. And given how busy Alice was, she hired a cook to feed both her and Ludwig, which allowed them to eat separately. Alice knew that her marriage was in trouble, but she was simply too busy to think about what to do about it.

Other than the time she spent selling her handbags around town or going to the factory on Breite Gasse or showing art at her studio, Alice mostly stayed in her bedroom, listing to music on her gramophone. The music often calmed her after a full day at the factory. She was no longer going to the cinema or exhibits at the museum. She sometimes met friends, but that was mostly for an early breakfast or a lunch date. But it wasn't just that she was very busy. She had finally admitted to herself that it had become dangerous for a Jew – particularly a Jewish woman – to be outside alone. And she certainly avoided being outside by herself at night. She often took a taxi home after work, rather than risk walking home in the dark.

It felt like everything had really changed since the 1929 Nazi rally. The Nazis had held rallies in 1923 and 1927, but the 1929 rally in August was different. Like the earlier rallies, thousands of Nazis had shown up and marched in the streets, but this time, local Communists and Social Democrat supporters also showed up, and there were clashes throughout the city. Two people were killed in the clashes and the city council banned future Nazi rallies. But while the Nazis might have been forced to leave the city, their anti-Semitism remained. And Streicher, the publisher of *Der Stürmer*, continued to stir up trouble in his paper, blaming the growing economic problems on the Jews.

Alice had never really wanted to pay attention to politics – that had been Ludwig's obsession – but she now felt like she had no choice. This was particularly the case as her business was growing and she needed more customers. The Jewish community in Nuremberg was smaller than Frankfurt, but was large enough to offer some support to Jewish artisans. But Alice's designs had gained interest beyond her community, and she hoped that the rising anti-Semitism would not hurt her business. Alice understood that her business would fail if she was limited to selling her purses to just the Jewish community in Nuremberg.

• • •

The following morning, Alice arrived at the factory at 7:30 am. She was reviewing invoices when Helga opened the door to the factory. Helga was often the first of her workers to arrive in the morning. Alice waved her over to review a problem with an order, and then Alice walked over to the small kitchen to pour herself a cup of needed coffee. As she took the first sip of her coffee, Alice thought about how well the factory was doing, but then thought about what Max had said to her about the risk in opening the factory during troubled economic times. Alice remembered the screaming newspaper headlines at the end of October 1929, referring to the crash of the German stock exchange as "Black Friday" and calling the subsequent crash of the New York exchange "Black Tuesday." Max told Alice that the stock market crash was already having an effect on Gebrüder Heppenheimer's business and warned her that the whole of the German economy would soon be affected because Germany's economy was built upon foreign capital, particularly American capital. "No one would buy fancy handbags and dresses if they were struggling to put food on the table," he had told her. Alice had seen that first hand during the hyperinflation period. But she was finally succeeding in her dream, and nothing was going to stop her. Alice was going to open her factory, no matter what. And so far, she was doing well.

Alice also believed that Max's worries had more to do with his own troubles managing the Mannheim smelter facility than the German economy. When Max was first told by his older brothers that they had purchased a smelter facility in Mannheim and that he would need to take his new bride Recha to Mannheim to run the facility, it was Alice who listened to her brother complain about having to move away from his family and friends in Frankfurt. She knew he was really complaining about having to work for the family business and not being allowed to attend a university to study chemistry. And she listened to him complain about his brothers sending an employee from Frankfurt in 1924 to help Max run the facility. Alice knew Max should never have been made to run the facility – Max was not a businessman and was much more suited to an academic life. So, it was not a surprise when Max wrote Alice a long letter in the beginning of 1930 to tell her that the business was failing and that he was worried that Gebrüder Heppenheimer would close the facility. He blamed the stock market crash, but Alice knew it was more than that.

Alice was taking another sip of coffee when she heard the telephone ring. It was not unusual to get early morning calls, and Alice answered the telephone, expecting to hear from one of her suppliers about an order that was late. She had placed an order for silk and had still not received the order. She had called her supplier the previous week, warning him she would cancel the order if she had not received it that morning. She was worried that he was calling to ask for additional time, and she was planning to say no.

Instead, it was her brother Jacob. A long-distance call was rare, and still rarer from her brother. In fact, any call from Jacob was rare. Jacob apologized for the early call, but said he had something important to tell her. Not one for small talk, Jacob got right to the reason for the call. "The Gebrüder Heppenheimer board met yesterday and made some important decisions about the company. First, we voted to close the Mannheim smelter facility. Your brother drove that facility into the ground, and now he will be responsible for liquidating it." Oh no, thought Alice. Poor Max. Everyone will blame Max. She knew some of it was his fault, but the economic situation did not help. Jacob continued. "The board also decided to close the main office and consolidate operations in the old office." Gebrüder Heppenheimer owned two office buildings, but had moved the headquarters to the newer and more modern building in the early 1920s. Moving back to the older building said something. "We are re-evaluating all of our investments and need to be very careful about our finances, given the present economy. Unfortunately, we won't be able to lend you the additional RM 1,500. I know that is a disappointment to you, and I am very sorry, but my hands are tied. But we won't make you repay the RM 1,500 we already lent you. I am sorry about this, but I am sure you understand the situation. Anyway, as you can imagine, I have a million things to do. But I look forward to catching up with you at another time. Take care." And then he hung up.

Alice was stunned. Jacob spoke during the entire call and didn't even give Alice a chance to say goodbye before he hung up. Maybe he was feeling badly about completely blind-siding her. But she didn't care if he was feeling bad. She was angry, really angry. She was in the middle of orders, she owed suppliers money, she needed to pay her employees. In fact, she had made the move to Breite Gasse and had made some recent purchases in anticipation of the cash infusion, which she was supposed to receive at the end of the month. It was June and she knew she had only enough cash in the bank for another month or two, at the most. She was relying on that money from her brothers. She couldn't go to a bank for the money and there were no other family members to turn to.

After she hung up the telephone, she found the nearest chair and sat down. Her employees were looking at her and likely wondering why their boss had turned so pale. She knew she could not share this news with them yet. She really missed Erna at that moment – Erna would have been the rock that she needed to lean on. She told Helga that she needed to run some errands and left the factory. She needed to take a walk, to figure out what she should do next.

She walked for more than an hour, reviewing all of her options. Her purses were selling well, but her expenses still exceeded her income, and that would remain the case for at least the next few months. Each time she thought of a different option, she came to the same conclusion – without the RM 1,500, she could not keep the factory open. In that one call, Jacob had essentially doomed her business. After ten years of trying to make a go of living and working in Nuremberg, she knew it was over. She would have to let her employees go. And she would also need to tell Ludwig. She really dreaded having that conversation.

When she felt able to return to the factory, she climbed the steps and opened the door. Her employees looked at her and knew that something was wrong.

"Helga, Gerta, Ingrid, please put down your work. We need to talk."

Her employees were clearly devastated when she told them she would need to close the factory, but they were also wonderful. They understood why Alice needed to close the factory and told her they had loved working for her. Alice told them she would pay them until the end of the month, but that they should feel free to leave sooner if they found other employment. She told them she would close the factory early that day and that they should go home. After they left, Alice sat in one of the chairs and sobbed.

Ludwig came home from work at 6 pm and was surprised to see Alice sitting in a chair and clearly waiting to talk to him. Alice was rarely home before Ludwig and seldom wanted to speak with Ludwig when she was home. Alice asked Ludwig to sit with her, and then got right to the point.

"I received a call from Jacob this morning. Gebrüder Heppenheimer is having some serious financial problems because of the economy and they have decided that they cannot lend me the RM 1,500 they had promised me. Without that money, I can't keep the factory open. I am going to have to shut it down by the end of the month."

Ludwig was clearly stunned. "I am so sorry Alice. I know how much this meant to you." As much as Ludwig and Alice were essentially leading separate lives, Alice could tell that he was trying to be sympathetic and Alice appreciated the effort. Alice could have used a hug at that moment, but that would have been too awkward for both of them.

And then Alice faced her husband directly and said, "Ludwig, I can't stay in Nuremberg anymore. I need to close my business, and without my income, we can't afford to live in this apartment. I need to move back to Frankfurt." She purposely did not say "we need to move."

Ludwig seemed not to have heard what Alice was saying, or chose to ignore her last statement when he said, "Alice, you know I can't leave Nuremberg." But then he added, "I don't understand why we need to leave. Why can't you just get a job in a handbag factory. You know everyone in the business. Maybe you can even go back to the Jewish handbag factory. They loved your work."

Alice knew Ludwig would never leave Nuremberg. So why had she said that she needed to move to Frankfurt? She had actually surprised herself when she said it. Surely, she could find a job with a handbag factory. Lots of places would hire her in a minute, assuming they had no issue with hiring a Jew. But that was it! Her being Jewish in a city like Nuremberg. She understood why she had said that she needed to move to Frankfurt – she was tired of living in Nuremberg, or at least what Nuremberg had become. She was tired of trying to fit into a city that did not want Jews.

When she had moved to Nuremberg in 1917, Alice was excited to leave Frankfurt and test her limits in the fashion world. She had learned a lot and was excelling in her industry. But over the past few years, anti-Semitism had become a real problem for all Jews in Nuremberg. She also missed Erna. Running the business was just not as much fun since her friend had left. And she missed her mother and sister. It was hard being in a city with no family.

But more than anything else, she recognized her marriage to Ludwig was a failure. She realized early in her marriage to Ludwig that their marriage was not what she had hoped it would be. Earlier, she had believed that divorce was not really an option for her. But she also knew that, through the 1920s, more women were getting divorced in Germany – even Jewish women – and the stigma attached to divorce had lessened a little. Ludwig would never move to Frankfurt, so if she told him she needed to move, she could also raise the prospect of divorce.

And so she took a deep breath and said, "Ludwig, I need to leave, but I understand why you need to stay. But if you stay, we cannot remain married. It wouldn't be fair to either of us, to be married but living in different cities. I think we need to divorce."

Ludwig stared at Alice for a second and then left the room. He closed the door to his bedroom and remained there for the rest of the evening. The next morning, Ludwig knocked on Alice's bedroom door. When she opened the door, he asked her if they could take a walk. They both dressed, left the apartment, and walked towards the Great Pond. They stopped when they reached the water.

"Alice, let me speak and please don't interrupt me until I'm finished. I know I am a disappointment to you. I am often a disappointment to myself. I wish I had it in me to be the success your brothers are. I just can't seem to make it happen. But you are so talented and it was a pleasure watching your business grow. I really am so proud of you, and I am sorry you need to shut down your business. I know you need to do that, and you tell me you need to go back to Frankfurt. I can't go with you. If I tried, I believe it would kill me. I will be really sad to see you go. I don't want to get a divorce, but if that is what you want, I won't try to stop you. Just let me know how I can help you with that. It is the least I can do. And now I want you to leave me here. I think I need to stay here for a bit. And then I need to get to my office."

Alice left him at the pond and walked back to their apartment. She had to go to the factory and begin the work of shutting down her business, making the many calls to her suppliers and customers. And she needed to call her mother to let her know she would be moving back to Frankfurt. Her mother, of course, would be sympathetic, but also relieved. And happy that her daughter was finally coming back home.

CHAPTER 5

Frankfurt, November 1930

After the train left the Nuremberg station, Alice experienced two competing emotions. First, she was relieved that she was returning to Frankfurt, away from Nuremburg and all of her recent struggles. At the same time, she was experiencing dread at what she might face now that she would be returning to Frankfurt. Alice had felt nothing but excitement when she left Frankfurt in 1917, on her way to the Nuremberg art school. That was thirteen years ago. So much had happened to Alice – in fact, so much had happened to the family – since that day she stepped on the Nuremburg-bound train. She had thought Nuremburg would be her home. And it was her home. Or at least, it had felt like home for much of those years. And now she was returning to Frankfurt. She told herself that she would still follow her dreams, only now in Frankfurt.

She reminded herself about how unsafe she had felt recently in Nuremberg. She knew that the city always had an undercurrent of anti-Semitism, although it hadn't really affected her in the beginning – or at least, that is what she told herself. But only a Jew whose head was buried in the sand could not have noticed the change in the city in the last few years. And Ludwig made sure that Alice noticed. On the other hand, Frankfurt had elected a liberal Jewish mayor during the mid-1920s, and Mayor Ludwig Landmann was doing great things for the city. In response to the housing shortages in the 1920s, Landmann brought in a team of famous architects and urban planners that helped to build 12,000 new and modern apartments. During the 1920s, Frankfurt had also become a leading light in the avant-garde movement, in music, theater, literature, and, of course, fashion. Her brothers spoke well of their enlightened mayor, and Alice herself was excited about the great things happening in Frankfurt. She would just have to make Frankfurt feel like home again.

The train arrived in Frankfurt on time, and as Alice stepped onto the platform, she remembered how much she liked this part of Frankfurt. The station was just a few blocks from the family's headquarters until recently. When she worked for Gebrüder Heppenheimer after she graduated from the Philanthropin, she had worked in the old headquarters, before the company had purchased the large building in the early 1920s and moved the headquarters to the newer and more modern offices. They were now back in the older building, but Alice had visited the nearby newer building nearly every time she had been back to Frankfurt for a visit. Plus, Frankfurt's main theater, the Schauspielhaus, was near the train station, and her family went to the theater when she was a teenager, which often included a meal at one of the nearby restaurants. Memories of those visits came flooding back as she walked along the platform. And then she saw her mother and sister Selma waving excitedly and all she could feel at that moment was the love of these two women. She ran to them and fell into their arms. She was home.

•   •   •

As they drove to the apartment, Alice looked over at her sister. She had not seen Selma recently – Alice's business had kept her too busy – but her sister looked the same. She was 31 years old, but her skin was still flawless. She wore lipstick, but no other makeup; really, she needed no makeup. She had bobbed her hair in the mid-1920s, but, like Alice, Selma was now wearing her auburn hair slightly longer and parted on the side, with the waves fashionable for the period. She wasn't a classic beauty, but her face lit up when she smiled. Which she often did. Although there was something now about her smile that seemed a little off, a little forced, at least to Alice. Or maybe it was just Alice, who definitely felt a little off. She thought that she just needed to get herself settled.

"It was nice of Jacob to let us use the company car to take me to the apartment from the station. It is certainly making it easier to move all of my bags to the apartment." Alice was feeling generous at the moment, even towards her eldest brother.

"He is out of town on business. Besides, he's not driving the car. They pay Hans a salary, so it's not like it's costing him extra." Selma was obviously feeling less generous towards Jacob. "It would have been nice of him to send the car all the way to Nuremberg. I tried, but I got tired of listening to all the reasons the company could not afford to send Hans. Really, you would think they are about to go bankrupt."

Alice loved her sister, but knew that Selma always found a reason to complain about Jacob. Alice wrote to Max often about the problems at Gebrüder Heppenheimer. She understood why Jacob was complaining about the cost of sending the car to pick her up in Nuremberg. But she also knew that Jacob would have found any excuse not to be inconvenienced, even in better financial times.

"So, tell me about this new apartment I am moving into?" Alice could see her mother bristle at the question, but Selma was quick to respond, clearly excited about the new place.

"Oh, Alice, you are going to love this place. We have been trying for years to get Mama to move out of that mausoleum. So many rooms, and the neighborhood had really changed, with all of those Polish Jews moving in after the war. This new place is great. Smaller, obviously, but with three bedrooms, we all have our own space. Everything is new and modern. And the neighborhood is wonderful – lots of artists!"

"I am assuming Leo likes the place?"

"Oh, you know my husband. As long as there is dinner on the table at 7 pm, he doesn't care where he lives." But Alice knew that Leo also played a role in the move. Since their marriage two years earlier, Selma and Leo had lived with Emma on Roderberg Weg in the East End neighborhood. When Joseph first moved to the East End around the turn of the century, the neighborhood was very Jewish and very fashionable. It was still very Jewish, but many poorer immigrants had replaced the German Jewish families, who were moving to wealthier sections of the city. Leo and Selma were interested in a more modern neighborhood with more modern features, but Selma would not leave her mother behind. But it may have been Alice's recent decision to move back to Frankfurt – but not wanting to move back to the apartment on Roderberg Weg – that finally convinced Emma to move. Alice had explained to her mother that, although she loved living in the apartment as a teenager, she wanted to start fresh in Frankfurt in a new place. Leo, Selma and Emma had moved into the apartment in September, anticipating that Alice would move in with them when Alice returned to Frankfurt.

The car crossed the Main River and turned onto Schaumainkai – the street that paralleled the river. The car stopped at Schaumainkai 5a. Alice was getting excited. Hans helped Alice with her bags and they climbed the stairs to the first floor. They opened the door to a spacious living room with windows that looked out onto the Main River. Alice took a deep breath and smiled. She would have preferred living on her own, but now was not the time. She could be happy here, she thought.

"Alice, I assume that smile means you like the view. Mama, show Alice her bedroom and then both of you can join me in the kitchen. I have something special to show you."

Alice walked down the hall with her mother to the back bedroom, put down her bags, and walked with her mother back through the living room and into the separate narrow kitchen. Alice's first thought was how nice it will be to have a separate kitchen. She looked over at her sister, who then pushed a button. A single light bulb hanging from the ceiling lit up the entire room. Alice looked around and saw that the kitchen had both an electric stove and an electric refrigerator.

Selma was clearly enjoying the spectacle. "Alice, I kept this as a surprise. What do you think of our electric kitchen? They recently re-wired the room and added new cabinets. It is called a "Frankfurt Kitchen," because the design was invented here. Stove to the left, cabinets to the right. The kitchen didn't have an electric refrigerator, but we had one installed. No more cast-iron stove, no more ice box. No more schlepping up coal and blocks of ice. Everything is clean and modern and convenient. Don't you just love it?"

Alice had to admit to herself that she was very impressed with the design and function of this kitchen. And electricity! The rest of the apartment had not yet been wired for electricity – they would still need to use gas lamps – but how nice to have this modern kitchen. "I absolutely love it, Selma!" Alice turned to her mother. "Mama, what do you think?"

"Your sister likes it and Leo likes it. It's not for me to like. I actually cannot figure out how to turn on the stove. I liked my old stove. That I knew how to use."

Selma scoffed. "Mama, you simply turn the knob. It is that easy. Honestly, Alice, Mama could have lived with that dirty old coal stove forever. Plus, now that I am cooking, I absolutely love this stove."

Selma was cooking? That was news to Alice. Where was their long-time cook, Sarah, Alice wondered? Alice knew something was wrong, but she decided to raise the question of Sarah later. Instead, she asked, "Selma, what can I help you with? You know I am not much of a cook, but tell me what to do. I can chop vegetables, if nothing else."

"You don't need to do anything. Dinner is going to be very simple tonight, and it is nearly done. Just sit down and I will make us all some coffee."

"I am very good at sitting down. It is really among my best skills. Why don't you sit with me for a bit. I am sure I can teach you the finer points of sitting." Alice was hoping to have some time to talk to her sister alone, although that would need to come later. There was so much to discuss.

"I will sit down in a minute. Let me just get this casserole into the oven. You will be impressed with my cooking skills, especially since we had to let Sarah go." That last statement gave Alice the opening she needed, although she decided to wait until they were all seated. Alice looked over at Selma, who added the remaining vegetables to a pot, put the lid on the pot, and placed it in the oven. She then began to make the coffee and placed three coffee cups on the table, along with a plate of cookies.

Selma poured the coffee and all sat down. Alice then turned to her sister and asked, "Selma, why is Sarah gone?"

"Once we married and I stopped working at the company, Leo thought I should learn to cook. He told me he thought it was not good for me to be idle. He asked Sarah to teach me how to cook. When we finally moved here, Leo decided it was time to let Sarah go."

Alice was stunned by this. Leo telling Selma to learn to cook and then firing Sarah. "Mama, why? You loved Sarah."

Her mother said nothing. Alice saw the first glimmer of a crack in Selma's façade. "Mama wasn't particularly happy about letting Sarah go, and she told Leo so. But Leo has been trying to open his wholesale coffee business and is a little worried about money. Sarah is now working for a friend of Mama's. And I am actually finding cooking fun. I even made these cookies."

This is the first time Alice was hearing anything about a problem with money. Selma said nothing about this in the letters she wrote to Alice. But she thought now was not the right time to discuss this, when she was tired and Leo would be home soon. There was plenty of time to catch up and to do it in a way that would not upset her sister or her mother. And, of course, her sister and her mother would want to discuss all the things that made Alice want to leave Nuremberg and return to Frankfurt. Some things Selma and her mother knew, but not everything. But there was plenty of time for that. Plus, Alice dreaded having to discuss her failed marriage. For the moment, Alice just wanted to sit and have coffee and cookies with her sister and mother. As she took a bite of the cookie, Alice had to admit to herself that the cookie was as good as the cookies from Friedmann's Bakery in Nuremburg.

• • •

Emma had saved Alice's old bedroom furniture and had arranged for the furniture to be moved to the new apartment. The furniture was not to Alice's more modern taste, but she would make due for the time being. She was putting her clothing away in the dresser when there was a knock at the door. Alice knew it was her mother, since she had heard Leo and Selma leave the apartment after dinner.

"Come in, Mama."

"I just wanted to make sure that you were getting yourself settled and had everything you needed. Are you okay?" Her mother then sat down in one of the chairs. Alice knew that her mother had come to talk.

"I am fine. I am a bit tired from the train ride and am looking forward to a long sleep. The rest of my things are supposed to arrive later in the week. Thank you so much for letting me store all the things from my factory in the storage facility."

"I am happy it is getting some use. Although at some point I will need to figure out what to do with all the furniture from the old apartment, which just sits gathering dust in the storage unit. I was hoping that one of your siblings would take some of it, but no one is interested. I guess their tastes have gotten too fancy for the furniture." Her mother loved her stepchildren, but she never missed an opportunity to give them just a little dig when she could about money. Her mother recently mentioned to Alice that Jacob was a bit too free with his spending, and thought that his purchase of the fancy villa not too far from their current apartment was reckless, but Alice knew that her mother also believed that the refusal to take any of the old furniture was a snub directed at her mother. As hard as Emma tried, the older children – except Max – could never get past the fact that Emma was a stepmother.

Alice continued to put away her clothes and could feel her mother watching her. Alice knew that her mother wanted to say something and she knew what it was, but Alice was a little tired and was hoping to have this conversation tomorrow. But, no such luck.

"Alice, you know I am really happy that you have moved back to Frankfurt. I always worried about your safety in Nuremberg. Such a horrible city for Jews! But I don't understand why Ludwig did not move with you. Whatever problems you were having could be worked out here. Frankfurt is still a great place for a Jew to make a living. I know he had some problems in Nuremberg, but he could do fine here."

Alice really did not want to discuss her marital problems when she was so tired. But her mother needed to hear something from Alice. All Alice had told her was that she and Ludwig were separating. She had not yet told her mother that she had decided to divorce Ludwig. She hadn't even told Selma, since she assumed Selma would immediately tell their mother. She decided to be honest with her mother, who had always valued honesty. She stopped unpacking and sat down on the bed.

"Mama, you know that Ludwig and I have had problems for years. But I didn't share with you how unhappy I was with Ludwig. We had stopped sleeping in the same bedroom and we were barely talking. But I probably would have stayed with him if I could have made the handbag business work. But once I was forced to close the factory, I realized how unhappy I was living in Nuremberg and living with Ludwig. Plus, I missed my family. Ludwig would never leave Nuremberg, but if I were being honest, I don't think I wanted Ludwig to move with me back to Frankfurt. I really wanted a complete break from everything. I told Ludwig that I wanted a divorce and he agreed to help me get the divorce. He could have fought me on this but he won't. He is not a bad man. We were just not right for each other. I really hope you understand, Mama."

Alice could tell that her mother was surprised by the announcement. Alice knew that no one in her family had ever divorced. But she also knew her mother. Her mother would be much more concerned about how Alice was doing than about what other people thought. That was why she had worked to convince her husband Joseph to allow Alice to attend the Nuremberg art school. Still, her mother was quiet for a while and Alice couldn't tell what her mother was thinking. Finally, her mother spoke.

"Well Ludwig really never understood that staying in Nuremberg was a bad choice. I am sure his mother was a real poison to your marriage. Why he needed to be near that mother of his was a mystery to me. But that is his problem. I am happy that you are back and now you need to work your magic here to be the success that I know you can be." So, her mother blamed the divorce on Ludwig's mother. That's fine, thought Alice. Alice had always thought the woman was a rather dreadful person anyway. So if this makes the divorce easier for her mother, that was fine with Alice. As long as her mother did not oppose the divorce. Because Alice needed this complete break from Nuremberg.

"Mama, I think I am going to leave the rest of the unpacking until tomorrow. All of a sudden, I can't keep my eyes open." Her mother gave her a warm hug and a kiss on the check and said goodnight. Alice changed into her night clothes and got into her childhood bed. It was a little small, but it would do for now. Before she knew it, Alice was fast asleep.

CHAPTER 6

Frankfurt, April 1933

Alice looked down from her seat in the women's balcony and saw her brother Max on the bimah, the raised platform at the front of the sanctuary. Max was standing beside his son Kurt, who was now taller than his father. Max was the shortest of her brothers, and Alice thought that the weight he had put on recently made Max look even shorter. Alice looked around the open space of the sanctuary. The Klaus Synagogue had been recently renovated, and the bimah and Ark for the Torahs were made of a beautiful gray marble. The room had Moorish overtones, which was not to Alice's taste, but she appreciated the amount of work that went into the renovation. Max told her that the synagogue had more than doubled its seating capacity to accommodate a growth in the number of Orthodox Jews, mostly from Eastern Europe, now living in Mannheim.

Kurt was doing a masterful job reading from the Torah. Not a single mistake, at least as far as Alice could tell. Alice had received enough of a Jewish education to be able to read Hebrew and chant the prayers. But she did not know the trope for the Torah reading, and could not tell if her nephew was hitting every note of that chant. But so far, the cantor had not had to correct him once. Kurt's voice was still changing, and unfortunately there had been a few squeaks during his reading, but Alice thought Kurt conveyed a certain confidence as he read from the Torah.

When Kurt had finished, Max said a special blessing to his son. The Torah was then lifted for the congregation to see, and placed off to the side. Kurt had one more portion of the service to complete – the Haftorah – which is a short reading from the Prophets. As Kurt was reading, Alice looked over at Max, who was still on the bimah and smiling with pride. After Kurt finished, the Torah was returned to the Ark, and then the congregation broke out in a celebratory song. After years of Hebrew school and a year of intensive study with the cantor, Kurt was a bar mitzvah. Max hugged his son with pride. Alice looked over to Recha, who was sitting near her in the balcony (where all the women were required to sit), and saw tears in her eyes.

After the celebratory singing stopped, Rabbi Isak Unna went to the podium to deliver his sermon. Every other part of the service was in Hebrew – something Alice was not used to – but the sermon itself was in German. Max had told Alice about his rabbi's great oratory skills, and Alice was looking forward to the sermon. The Rabbi waited until the congregation was completely silent before he began.

"I first want to give a hearty mazel tov to Kurt on the wonderful job he did this morning. No mistakes, my young man. I am very impressed. I guess we all have Cantor Kohn to thank. And welcome to the rest of the Heppenheimer family, who I understand came to us from Frankfurt. I hope you enjoy your time in our lovely city. As I am sure everyone is aware, next Wednesday begins the Passover holiday. I know that all of you have been ridding your homes of leavened products and will bring your bread to me for the ritual burning. When the sun sets on Wednesday, you will gather your families together and begin the retelling of the story we have been telling for many generations, about how the Jewish people were able to free themselves from bondage with the help of Hashem. The Jewish people had no rights when they lived in the land of Egypt. They could not work where they wanted, they could not live where they wanted, and they could not marry who they wanted. They were treated as second-class citizens, as slaves. Some of you may remember a time in Germany when Jews also had limited rights, or heard stories about those times from your parents or grandparents. It was not until 1871 that Jews were emancipated. And with emancipation came the rights that German Jews had been hoping for for generations. We took advantage of the opportunities given to us and built successful businesses and became lawyers and doctors, all the while helping Germany grow and prosper. Many Jewish families lost sons fighting for Germany in the Great War. We live our lives in Germany as if we have always had the rights we have right now. We sometimes forget that it has only been sixty years since our emancipation.

"Last Saturday, on my way home from our beloved synagogue, I came upon a man wearing a brown shirt and a swastika on his left arm. This storm trooper yelled a Jewish slur at me, and nearly pushed me down. A woman who I know came up to me and was crying, telling me her husband had been assaulted by these storm troopers. I walked this woman home and spoke with her husband. He was badly shaken. I left the couple and walked home, passing signs encouraging Germans to boycott Jewish stores. During this past week, I have been speaking almost non-stop with rabbis in other cities, including the great Rabbi Leo Baeck. We discussed the plague of anti-Semitics acts following the appointment of the new Chancellor in January. We are working on plans to respond to those increases in actions against Jews. My congregation knows that, as much as I can, I avoid any discussion of politics, especially during the weekly sermon. Unfortunately, when politics threatens the very foundation of civil life, I must speak out. Anti-Semitism in any form is wrong. When our ancestors left Egypt, we declared we would not be slaves again. We are German Jews with all the rights of German citizens. We must be vigilant to stop this anti-Semitism before it leads to the end of German Jewry. And we must not be afraid. We must wear our Jewish identity with pride. And because we are in a synagogue, we must offer our prayers that the anti-Semitic persecution ceases." And then the rabbi offered a Hebrew prayer for the protection of German Jews, and everyone said "Amen."

The rabbi then continued with the service. The sermon was short, but powerful, Alice thought. And also surprising. The rabbi did not specifically mention Adolf Hitler, the new Chancellor, or the Nazis, but his meaning was clear to all who were listening – Hitler and the Nazis are an existential threat to the Jewish people. Alice looked around at the other women in the balcony. They all looked rather stunned. Alice thought that the rabbi's sermon should make for an interesting discussion among the family after the service.

The rabbi was leading the congregation in the last part of the service, all in Hebrew. Alice only attended services during Rosh Hashanah and Yom Kippur, but the services in Frankfurt were at the Reform Main Synagogue and were partly in German, and so more understandable. Alice stopped listening to the service and instead thought about the fact that this was the first time the family had come together since the financial crisis faced by Gebrüder Heppenheimer the previous year. Given everything that had gone on with the business and the recent anti-Semitic acts, Alice had expected some of her siblings to send their regrets. But she was pleased that all had come to Mannheim to celebrate Kurt's bar mitzvah.

Alice looked down and could see both Jacob and Benno sitting in the first row. They were talking to one another, not paying attention to the service. Likely talking business, Alice thought. She was still annoyed with Jacob over the failure of her factory in Nuremburg. He had gone back on his promise and that essentially doomed her business and forced her to move back to Frankfurt, although she had to admit that it turned out to be a blessing, given everything that had happened since that call in Germany. And it had allowed her to divorce Ludwig. But, unknown to her at the time, the issues Jacob shared with Alice that morning were just the tip of a much larger iceberg.

Alice remembered Max being summoned to Frankfurt by his brothers and his cousin to report on the status of his liquidation efforts of the Mannheim scrap metal facility. That was in 1931, a year after she had moved back to Frankfurt. When their father Joseph first moved to Frankfurt in the mid-1870s from a small town in southern Germany, he and his brother Henry established Gebrüder Heppenheimer. When Henry emigrated to America in the 1890s, he left behind his two oldest sons to help run the company. The oldest died in 1900, but the second son Adolph had remained with the company. After Joseph retired in 1917, Adolph became the Chairman of the Board, with Joseph's oldest son Jacob as Vice-Chair. Benno also had a seat on the board, but Max was left off the Board. Like his cousin and brothers, Max had an equal share the company's ownership, but he had no vote on any of the company's decisions. And to add to this humiliation, when the Board had called Max to provide them with a status of the liquidation, it was obvious that the Board blamed the failure of the facility on him.

After that meeting with his brothers and cousin in Frankfurt, Max stopped by to visit his sisters and his stepmother. After enjoying a delicious lunch cooked by Selma, Max and Alice decided to take a walk. It was a warm day and Alice could tell that Max needed to talk to her. Alice suggested they walk along the Main River.

It didn't take long for Max to share with Alice what had transpired during that earlier meeting. "The Board made me go through every transaction over the last three years, even though we are in liquidation. They made me explain what had happened with the facility and how I could have done things differently. They didn't say it – they never do directly – but everything they were asking suggested to me they thought that it was all my fault. It never occurred to any of them to think that this might have had something to do with the damn depression!"

Alice had never seen her brother so upset. Alice looked directly at Max and noticed for the first time that her brother had aged. His hair had grayed significantly since the last time she had seen him and he had put on weight. He was always fair-skinned, but his face now looked pasty. She could see that all the stresses in his life were getting to him. Jacob had served in the Great War, but had avoided the trenches, and Benno was discharged from the war early because of heat stroke. But Max had served four years in the trenches and had even received the Iron Cross for actions above and beyond the call of duty. He had been a quiet and studious boy before the war, but after the war, he became more reserved and it was harder for him to express his feelings. He also seemed to have a harder time dealing with stress. Perhaps that was why the Mannheim job was so hard for him. Alice understood that Max sharing so openly and colorfully meant that things must be really hard for him. She wondered if he was sharing any of this with his wife Recha. The best thing Alice could do for Max was to listen and not to judge.

"Adolph and Jacob and Benno just sat there listening to my report and said nothing. But I knew what they were thinking. And then the questions started and never stopped. And the lawyer and the banker – these Board members aren't even family and yet they just sat there judging me. I hated it. I couldn't wait to be done and leave."

"Max, I am so sorry you had to go through this. They have never been easy on you."

"It's so easy to blame me for everything, but after I was done and went into the side room to collect some of my things, I heard them discuss two things that were really worrisome, and nothing that I had anything to do with. The door was ajar, but they didn't seem to care if I heard. Maybe they wanted me to hear it. First, it looks like the Frankfurt smelter facility is also having financial trouble. They were discussing the fact that they were looking for a buyer and having trouble finding one. So maybe the Mannheim facility was not all my fault! Also, Adolph and Jacob had purchased a lot of lead and copper, hoping that the prices would go up. Instead, the prices dropped on both metals. The rest of the Board were not happy and someone mentioned 'breach of fiduciary duty.' Then Jacob claimed it was Adolph's idea to purchase the metals, and Jacob had initially objected to the purchase. Adolph then yelled something at Jacob, and I decided to leave. At that point, I really had had enough of all of them. There are certainly times when I am happy that I am not on the Board. Still, things don't seem to be going well for the company, and they certainly can't blame this on me!"

That conversation happened two years ago, and things only got worse for Gebrüder Heppenheimer. The lead and copper speculations turned out to be huge losses for the company. Adolph was forced to rent out his four-story villa and rent a smaller (although still large) apartment in the West End. Jacob was forced to sell his large villa and also rented an apartment in the West End. The Frankfurt smelter facility (which was located just outside of Frankfurt) was closed, and Benno, who had been living in a house attached to the facility, moved with his family to an apartment in the West End. Facing bankruptcy, Gebrüder Heppenheimer entered into a financial settlement with its creditors in 1932, just after the Mannheim smelter facility was closed for good. Alice had hoped that the financial settlement would be the end of the company's troubles, but now worried about what Hitler's appointment as Chancellor would mean for all of them.

Alice stopped thinking about Gebrüder Heppenheimer's troubles when the congregation stood for the blessings over the wine and the challah, the final prayers of the service. Alice helped her mother down the stairs of the balcony, followed by Selma, her older sisters Bertha and Johanna, Jacob's wife Johanna and

Benno's wife Margot. The women walked outside, and Alice's brothers soon joined them. Alice could see her nephew Kurt, smiling and surrounded by his brother Alfred, friends, and cousins. Alice was thinking how wonderful it was to be together as a family. The family then walked together to Max's apartment, which was just a few blocks from the synagogue.

It had been a while since Emma's last visit to Max's apartment, and Max and Recha took her on a tour while the rest of the family settled in the living room. Alice joined the tour. Alice could tell that Max was pleased that his stepmother had nice things to say about the new additions to the place. Certainly, Recha liked to hear how impressed her mother-in-law was with how well Recha had furnished the apartment. Emma was aware of Max's struggles with the company, and everything she said to her stepson was positive and supportive. Alice knew that her mother was sorry that she could not do more to help Max.

As the four returned to the living room, Alice could hear the family discussing the rabbi's sermon. Alice was expecting the discussion, although she had hoped the family would wait until they sat down for lunch. Jacob's son Ernst was speaking, with all the passion of a 19-year-old.

"The depression caused many Germans to blame the Weimar Republic, which they were told was controlled by the Jews, and the Nazi Party took advantage of this lie. And while they only captured about a third of the seats in the Reichstag in the 1932 elections, Hitler still got himself appointed Chancellor in January. And look at what the Nazis have done since. They blamed the Reichstag fire in February on the Communists and then issued a decree that suspended all of our hard fought-for rights. Hitler then called for new elections in March, which gave the Nazis even more seats in the Reichstag. They then passed the Enabling Act, which now gives Hitler the power to enact any law he wants without the consent of the Reichstag, and he was only able to accomplish that by arresting all the Communist Party members in the Reichstag.

He can now essentially do whatever he wants. Rabbi Unna is right. The Nazis want to take away all of our rights."

Jacob's daughter Mellie added, "I agree. Frankfurt's liberal Jewish Mayor Landmann has been replaced by that horrible Nazi Party official Friedrich Krebs, and he immediately ordered the removal of all Jewish employees and officials of the city. Some of my friends have lost their government jobs. And remember that I left the University of Frankfurt in 1931 to help Gebrüder Heppenheimer? Well, I was planning on re-enrolling to study chemistry, but now I hear that Krebs won't allow Jews to enroll in the University. And Tante Alice, he has even ordered the closure of the Städel Museum's modern art gallery. Do you remember you took me to an exhibit there last year?"

Alice nodded to her niece. "I remember that well, Mellie. We had a wonderful day. I was particularly sad when I heard about the closure."

Ernst picked up where his sister left off. "And now the one-day boycott last Saturday. Because the American Jews hurt the Nazis' feelings!"

Jacob responded only to his son's statements. "As everyone can tell, Ernst has been paying a lot of attention to politics lately. He has even become involved with the Central Association. I know the Central Association is worried about the Nazi Party, and to be perfectly honest, I am a little worried myself. But Paul von Hindenburg is still the President of Germany, and has been President since 1925. He is a friend to the German Jewish community and has assured the community that he would never tolerate the loss of our rights. Ernst, I am assuming you know that President Hindenburg even sent a letter last year to the Central Association expressing his disapproval of all the anti-Jewish attacks."

Ernst was not prepared to back down. "Hindenburg is an old man who is just a figurehead. Hitler has out-maneuvered him and is now the real person in charge. Hindenburg can do nothing to help German Jews. The one-day boycott proved it. The American Jews, under the leadership of Rabbi Stephen Wise, held a huge rally last month in New York to protest the boycott of Jewish stores earlier in the month by the Nazi storm troopers. They then issued a statement denouncing the Nazi actions. In response, the Nazis called for this boycott and said that they would resume the boycotts if the American Jews didn't stop what the Nazis claimed were false accusations. All the Americans did was tell the truth! We German Jews need to think about leaving Germany before things get worse." Alice was surprised at Ernst's passion. He had recently graduated from the Philanthropin and was apprenticing at a textile facility. He was never very studious and seemed more interested in having fun with friends than caring about politics. But Alice thought it had been hard for Ernst to ignore what was happening in Germany, especially as a young Jew. She had not heard that Ernst had become involved with the Central Association – she had not really paid attention to their work since she had returned to Frankfurt.

But Jacob dismissed his son's concerns. "You young people never really experienced anti-Semitism until recently. But Jews faced anti-Semitism in Germany in the past and thrived. As the rabbi said today, it was only recently that Jews in Germany could live where they want and could marry whom they want and could have the jobs they want. That was not the case for my grandparents, and yet they still succeeded. Papa told me that his father Jacob, of blessed memory, told him about how Jews were vital to the farmers around his village, because only the Jews would lend money to the farmers and that without Jews, there would have been no agriculture in southern Germany. And Papa always said that, without the Jewish metals traders, Germany would never have grown into the powerful nation it has become. And Jews did all this while facing anti-Semitism. Instead of fighting the Nazis, we must remind them of our significant contributions to making Germany a great country. And didn't the

Central Association encourage the American Jews not to hold the rally, to avoid antagonizing the Nazis? We have survived for thousands of years by not antagonizing those in power."

However, Ernst was not finished. "I don't agree with everything the Central Association says or does. I think the Association's Vice President Ernest Wallach was wrong in urging Rabbi Wise and the other American leaders to postpone the rally. The only way to prevent more Nazis actions against German Jews is to shine a light on them, all around the world. Over the last few years, the Central Association had been successful in challenging Nazi attempts to encourage Germans to boycott Jewish stores. They were even able to stop the publication of a list of Jewish merchants, doctors and lawyers. But they were not able to stop last week's boycott, and I worry that this is just the beginning. And the rabbi today spoke about the time before Jews were emancipated in Germany because he is worried that we might lose all of our rights."

Alice looked over at her niece Mellie, who was clearly not happy at being ignored by her father, and decided it was her turn to speak. "I disagree with Ernst about the American Jew's decision to hold the rally. As I am sure the rest of you know, I have been active in the Zionist Federation of Germany since I attended the University of Frankfurt. The Federation strongly believes that the solution for Germany's Jews is a homeland in Palestine, and has begun negotiating with the Nazi government to make that happen. The Americans need to stay out of our business and not undermine these negotiations."

It was clear to Alice that Jacob was ready to end the conversation. He did not like to be challenged by anyone, especially by his children. "I think I have heard enough from the both of you. Ernst, Herr Wallach is a very respected banker and Jewish leader and if he thought the rally should have been postponed, maybe Rabbi Wise and the other Americans should have listened. And Mellie, in terms of leaving Germany, I have read that even our great Rabbi Leo Baeck believes that only a small minority of German Jews could successfully leave Germany and that it would be better to work with the Nazi government. As Rabbi Unna reminded all of us, we must wear our Jewish identify with pride. But we must be smart, too. And we must not overreact. There is no need to leave our homeland. Ever. But this is enough talk about the rabbi's sermon." Jacob turned to his younger brother. "Max, mazel tov on the wonderful job Kurt did today. Reading the entire Torah portion! Very impressive. Ernst barely made it through his single Torah section."

Alice thought that her brother's last statement was less a congratulatory note to Max and more a way of putting his son in his place. But Alice understood that any thought of leaving Germany also had a financial component to it, one that was not really a concern for either Ernst or Mellie, since neither owned a business. She understood this because she was hoping to open her dressmaking studio within the next few months and was about to invest all of her money in that venture. Gebrüder Heppenheimer had taken a hit with the metals speculation and the closure of the smelter facilities. But they were still trading and they continued to own the two large office buildings in Frankfurt, which brought in rent from multiple tenants. There was tension among the four owners of the company – Adolph, Jacob, Benno, and Max – but they were committed to making the business a great success again, or at least that was what Max told Alice recently. Plus, all four knew that if they ever thought about leaving Germany, the Flight Tax and other measures would cause then to lose about fifty percent of the value of their assets. After the German bank crash of 1931, Germany introduced the Flight Tax to stem capital flight. And after the Nazis came to power, they reduced the threshold for application of the tax to limit the ability of Jews to take their money out of Germany. After working so hard to develop Gebrüder Heppenheimer, and after the recent losses to their business, the Heppenheimers were not about to give up any more of their assets. Plus, they were Germans. They would never leave their country.

Alice could see that Recha was worried that the family would continue to talk politics and ruin her son's special day. The one-day boycott from the previous week had already cast a pall over the day, so Alice decided to step in. Ever the peacemaker in her family, Alice said, "Recha, as we were taking a tour your apartment earlier, I could not help noticing all the delicious dishes in the dining room. I am assuming you have no intention of letting all of that good food go to waste."

Her sister-in-law smiled with relief. "Alice, you are absolutely right. And I am absolutely starving. Let's gather all the cousins and the bar mitzvah boy and have lunch." Max immediately walked over to his stepmother and put out his arm to escort her to the table. The rest of the family followed.

Before Alice returned to Frankfurt, Max asked if she would take a walk with him. Taking a walk with Max often meant that he had something serious he wanted to discuss with her, away from their siblings. They left the apartment on Richard Wagner Strasse and walked toward the Mannheim Water Tower in the Friedrichplatz. The weather was typical for April, and both needed warm hats and gloves. When they reached the plaza, Max told Alice that he felt that something was going on with the business, but he couldn't put his finger on it. His brothers seemed to be having meetings that didn't include him or Adolph. He asked Alice if she could find out anything for him.

"Max, you know I would be happy to try to find out anything I can. I hadn't noticed anything different about Jacob or Benno, but neither really shares much with me. And I don't really socialize with either, except for family events. I haven't even told them I am about to open my dressmaking studio. After everything that happened in Nuremberg, I thought it was best not to share the news of this new venture with them. But if I hear about anything, I will let you know."

"Maybe I am just being paranoid, but it also feels like they are giving me less to do in terms of scrap trading. They tell me it's the depression, but I know they are both pretty busy. And I know that scrap metal traders in Mannheim are pretty busy, including our cousin Leopold. They are still paying me a salary and between that and my share of the rents, we are doing fine financially. I am just a little worried."

"Max, let me see what I can find out and I will let you know."

CHAPTER 7

Frankfurt, August 1933

Alice was humming to herself as she walked back to the apartment. She was returning from the Kreishandwerkerschaft, the District Craftmen's Association. After several apprenticeships in Frankfurt following her return, as well as a demonstration of her competency, she had been approved for membership in the Dressmaker's Guild as a master tailor. She would now be able to open a dressmaker's studio. She could put the failed efforts in Nuremberg behind her and start anew. She smiled as she looked again at her new guild card.

After moving to Frankfurt, Alice thought about opening another handbag factory, but decided that a handbag factory, particularly one focused on high-end fashion, was probably the wrong approach during the depression. Even though Alice's factory had been doing well in Nuremberg, at least before Jacob failed to provide her with the promised cash infusion, Alice could already see early signs of a slowdown in sales. But every woman needed a dress, and even during the depression, women still needed fine dresses, particularly if those dresses were reasonably priced. She had designed dresses in Nuremberg, especially during the years before she opened her factory, and she believed that those skills would translate into a successful dress studio in

Frankfurt. And with her skills at beaded work from her years of designing and making handbags, she thought she could make beautiful and unique dresses. The heart of the German fashion industry was in Berlin, where most of the industry was run by Jews. Still, Frankfurt had dress designers and there was enough business for Alice, or at least she hoped. She would try to be a big fish (or at least a medium fish) in this smaller pond.

Alice was especially excited about the new trends in women's fashion. She had kept up with all the changes in design through the 1920s, but didn't support some of the more masculine boxy designs. But women's fashion was slowly becoming more feminine, with longer and fuller skirts and more closely fitting bodices. Alice was thankful designs were not returning to the fashions her mother still favored, but Alice preferred more feminine designs, and was happy that the fashion trends were now more consistent with her vision for women's fashion.

Alice learned her lesson about relying on her brothers for any financial help. Over the past three years, she had been earning money from her apprenticeships and her private dress design customers. She was contributing some to her share of the rent, but had been saving the rest of her money. She had also been able to take two of the sewing machines she had in Nuremberg with her to Frankfurt. She would need a third machine to really make this business a success.

She was grateful to her mother and sister for arranging for her place in their apartment, and for moving to the Sashsenhausen neighborhood. Selma had been right about the neighborhood, and Alice had taken full advantage of the many galleries near the apartment. And of course, there was the Städel art museum. The Nuremberg Kunsterhaus had great art, but that museum was not in the same league as the Städel. Georg Swarzenski, the museum's director, had been given financial support by Frankfurt Mayor Landmann to grow the collection's modern works, beginning in 1906, so that the museum had important new works by Paul

Cezanne, Claude Monet, Vincent van Gogh, and Pablo Picasso. Swarzenski also organized free concerts in the museum's rooms, and Alice tried to attend as many of these concerts as she could. Alice often attended the concerts with friends from her school days, but could sometimes convince her mother and sister to join her. Unfortunately, since the Nazis came to power, her favorite exhibits had closed, the art locked up in a storage facility. And there would be no more concerts.

But it was time for her to live on her own. She had wanted to have her own apartment when she first moved back to Frankfurt, but she could not afford it. She now had the resources (and the guild card) to start her own dressmaking business, and needed her own place to make that happen. Moreover, she was ready to leave her sister's apartment. It was hard to live with the constant fighting. There had been some disagreements between Selma and Leo when Alice first moved back to Frankfurt, but those disagreements had escalated into major battles over the past year. Selma was complaining constantly that there was not enough money for her to buy clothes. Leo told her she was spending beyond their means. And Leo had a temper he sometimes had trouble controlling. One night, following a particularly heated argument, Leo threw a lamp at Selma in front of Alice. Luckily, the lamp missed both sisters. The fighting worried Alice, but she was reluctant to raise the idea of divorce with Selma. One daughter's divorce was hard enough for her mother. But two divorces...

Alice entered the apartment and told Selma she needed to speak with her. Selma was expecting the conversation – Alice had been talking about moving out and opening her own dressmaking studio for more than a year. But Alice knew Selma had been dreading this conversation. Alice knew Selma really loved having her sister living with them. And Alice knew Selma worried about how things would be with Leo once Alice moved out.

"Selma, look, I just received my guild card. Isn't it beautiful? You know what this means?"

"I know, I know. I am so happy for you. But this could be good for us, too. You've been talking about moving across the Main River to be closer to customers, and I think this might be a good time for us to move, as well. And this way, we won't be too far apart. Plus, Leo's new business seems to be doing well, so it is about time we moved to a nicer place." Leo had finally opened his wholesale coffee business in July, and was travelling around the country, looking for new accounts. Alice had no way of knowing whether he was making any money yet, but Selma seemed to have decided that he was. Alice worried that this might not necessarily be the case, since money was mostly what they fought about – either Selma spending too much money or Leo not giving Selma enough money.

"I was think about moving to the inner city. You don't want to move there, Selma."

"No, but if we move to the West End, that would be an easy walk to the inner city. Plus, everyone we know has been moving to the West End. I am tired of being the only Jewish family for blocks and blocks. I even think that Leo and I would be happier there, which would mean less fighting."

"Selma, I would love to have you and Mama live nearby. Anticipating that I would be receiving my guild card today, I have actually found a place on Bleichstrasse, which I can start renting next month. It has a small bedroom, but a large living room. Space enough for several seamstresses and a changing area. Most exciting is that the entire apartment has been wired for electricity. I will finally be able to get an electric sewing machine, which should speed up my dressmaking. Of course, I will still use the two sewing machines I have in storage. And I will also install a telephone, so that I can speak with customers and suppliers."

"Wow, you have already found an apartment! You really are ready to go. Well, it looks like I will have to start looking for a new place myself. And I will need to speak with Mama and Leo about the move."

• • •

Some would think that, given the dwindling fortunes of Gebrüder Heppenheimer, and the Nazi takeover of the German government, opening a new business might not make much sense. But since the failure of the Nuremberg factory, Alice had been on a mission to open her own place and to be a success at it. And nothing was going to stop her, not even a government that had anti-Semitism as one of its core principles. And while her brother Jacob was not her favorite person, he was a good and knowledgeable businessman and if he believed that President Hindenburg would be able to protect the German Jews, she thought she could trust his judgement.

Alice decided to move into her new apartment the first week in September. Alice used some of the furniture her mother had put into storage after she first moved with Selma and Leo across the Main River. Regardless of how much money she had, Emma was always frugal and was not about to get rid of perfectly good furniture. Plus, she assumed that at some point someone would want some of the furniture. Well, maybe not Jacob, who only filled his place with the best. But her mother offered some of the furniture to Alice and she immediately accepted. Alice needed to use what money she had saved for the business. Perfectly good furniture from her mother's old place was just fine for Alice, even if the furniture was a bit old-fashioned. I will buy more modern furniture once I start making money, Alice promised herself.

Alice had arranged for movers to take one of the bedroom sets, some living room chairs, a couch, and a kitchen table from the storage facility. She purchased some tables for the three sewing machines, including the electric machine, and for measuring and cutting fabric. She also purchased a full-length mirror and a screen for a separate changing area. She would purchase other items as she started making money.

Her mother and sister offered to help set up the new place and Alice asked them to come after the movers left. She thought she would ask them to help put away dishes and clean up a little. She really couldn't afford a maid.

There was a knock at the door around 4 pm. Alice opened the door for her mother and sister, and just at that moment, a mouse ran into Alice's apartment from the hall. Alice screamed, "Eek!" She then jumped up on one of the chairs.

Selma laughed and their mother chased the mouse into a corner of the living room. "Alice, get me a glass jar." Alice was still up on the chair, so Selma went into the kitchen and came back with a jar. Emma took some newspaper and used it to push the mouse into the jar. Then Selma took the jar outside and came back inside laughing.

"Alice, you can come off the chair now. The mouse has gone back to his family."

"Very funny. You know how much I hate mice!"

Selma smiled at her sister. "I know you do, but it always makes me laugh whenever I see you climb on a chair to get away from a mouse. You are so fearless when it comes to the rest of your life. You argue with suppliers and bargain with customers, and you were able to walk away from your marriage to Ludwig. But when it comes to a tiny mouse…"

"Yes, I know, it makes no sense, but I can't help it. And of course, there is Mama, taking charge and rescuing me from that filthy rodent!" Alice knew her fear of mice was ridiculous, but at least she could laugh at herself. And clearly Selma had no trouble laughing at her.

After the drama with the mouse, Selma and her mother helped Alice with the apartment. Selma herself was not much of a cleaner, but Emma took some rags and soapy water and went to work on the apartment. Even after all of these years of help at home, Emma never forgot how to clean. And to her credit, Emma never thought she was above cleaning. Alice wanted to believe that she had inherited this trait from her mother, that she was never too good for any hard work. She sometimes struggled with this, but she liked to think that her better angels won out, at least most of the time.

When they were done, Emma and her daughters took a taxi home and enjoyed one last dinner together in the apartment on Schaumainkai. Tomorrow, Alice would be living on her own, for the first time in her life. And she couldn't wait. Alice thought to herself that the only thing that she would really miss about living with her sister was Selma's cooking. Alice had to admit to herself that Selma had become a very good cook. Selma had even begun experimenting with French cooking, although their mother complained that the food was "too fancy." Selma often teased Alice that, if there was a way for Alice to burn water, she would. But Alice readily acknowledged that Selma's joke was not far from the truth.

•   •   •

There was nothing specific she could put her finger on, but Alice also had the sense that something was going on with Jacob and Benno. Even at their infrequent family dinners, they were often separate from the rest and seemed to change the subject any time anyone would come near. After Kurt's bar mitzvah, Alice was focused on getting her guild card and then finding the new apartment. Alice was aware of the various anti-Semitic actions taking place around her. In May, university students burned thousands of books deemed "decadent," and she could not walk down a main street without seeing the horrific caricatures of Jews on lamp posts and building walls. But Alice chose to ignore these actions. She was focused on her big move to the new apartment, and was now working to set up her studio and hire help. She would officially open the second week in November and she planned to place her first ad in the *Frankfurter Israelitisches Gemeindeblatt*, the official paper of the Frankfurt Jewish community, in December. She was really excited, but really focused, and completely missed whatever signs of family disaster she might have seen had she been less distracted with her new venture.

The knock on her door came in the middle of October. It was highly unusual for anyone to come at 7 pm, especially someone who had not first called. She was nearly finished cooking her stew, but turned off the stove and walked to the door. She opened the door and there stood Max, white as a sheet and shivering. He had no coat on.

"Max, what are you doing in Frankfurt? What's wrong? Please, please, come inside."

Max remained at the threshold, and Alice had to grab his arm to pull him inside. She guided him to a chair in the living room and told him to sit down. She went into the kitchen to put the kettle on for some tea and returned to the living room. Max was staring into space and said nothing. Alice sat down in a chair across from Max and waited until he was ready to speak.

Max finally took a deep breath and said a single word. "Traitors." Alice heard the kettle whistle and went to the kitchen to make them both tea. She hoped he would be ready to say more when she returned with the tea.

She decided she would try to start the conversation and was hoping for more than a single word response. "Who are the traitors?"

"Jacob and Benno. All these months they have been lying to me and to Adolph. Well, I don't really care that they have been lying to Adolph, but they have been lying to me, their own brother. They told me that business is slow and that is why they didn't have a lot of scrap metal trading for me to do. Meanwhile, they were working to set up their own business. They are keeping our name "Gebrüder Heppenheimer," but adding "limited liability company" after the name. They are going to work out of our offices in the old building and they are going to take all of our customers. Just Jacob and Benno. They told me not to worry, that the old company will still exist and will own all of the buildings so that we will still be receiving our share of the rents. I know Jacob is tired of Adolph making decisions about the company, that he blamed Adolph for the metals speculation disaster. But did they really have to get rid of me and Isadore?" Isadore was their older sister Johanna's husband, who had been trading for the company for years. "They said that they felt like they could only survive as a company if the company were leaner. I guess they decided I was dead weight." With that last statement, Max seemed to sink further into the chair, almost like he wanted to disappear.

Alice now understood all the whispering and secretive conversations. Knowing her brothers, this was clearly Jacob's decision. For as long as she could remember, Adolph and Jacob had worked side-by-side in the business. While Joseph was in charge, Joseph made all the decisions. But when her father retired, he made Adolph Chairman of the Board. This was only fair, since Adolph had worked in the company longer. And it was named Gebrüder Heppenheimer – for the brothers Henry (the older brother and Adolph's father) and Joseph. Jacob understood the equity, but Alice thought he couldn't help but resent the decision his own father made. Plus, Jacob thought Adolph had taken too many risks as Chairman. The company had purchased 500,000 Marks worth of war bonds during the Great War, and while they were able to use the war bonds as collateral after the war, the war bonds lost all of their value during the hyperinflation period. Adolph also drove the company to make investments in other companies just after the war, and those investments also failed during the hyperinflation period. Adolph was the main driver in the decision to purchase the Mannheim smelter facility, although the failure of the investment was attributed to Max. And Jacob blamed Adolph for the decision to speculate in lead and copper. In an effort to get out of debt, that decision actually drove them further into debt and to near bankruptcy. Alice thought that the decision to open a new company was likely Jacob's desire to be free of Adolph. Was Max just collateral damage, or did Jacob also want to be free of having to take care of his younger brother? Alice knew that there had been troubling times for the business over the years, but, like Max, she could only think of one word to describe the actions of her brothers, but it was a different word – selfish.

CHAPTER 8

Frankfurt, September 1935

Alice put the strudel in the oven to warm up their dessert and sat down to glance at the paper. She already knew the big news, since the headlines were hard to avoid for any German Jew – the Nazis had just enacted laws that denied all Jews citizenship, voting rights, the right to marry a non-Jew, or to keep Government positions. We officially don't exist, thought Alice as she skimmed the lead article. The Nuremberg Laws had been enacted during the latest Nazi Rally in the town where Alice first started her career. The birthplace of the Nazi rallies. Good thing she had left that horrible city when she did!

"How are Jews expected to live in Germany? Are they really just trying to drive us out?"

"I believe they are, Alice. I don't know how much more time we have before we will need to think about leaving."

Alice shook her head. "That can't be. My dress shop is doing well. In fact, I have never been busier. Do you think we can find a way around these laws?"

"Maybe this year. And next year. But I don't know after that. It's not fair, I know. And after all the Jews have done for this country. By the way, how is Ruth doing in the studio? She seems very happy."

"I don't know what I would do without Ruth. She is a natural at fashion. Her work is beautiful and she has an eye for design and color. Plus, she does everything I ask. I don't know how I can ever thank you for sending her to me."

"Well, without her, we would not have connected again." He smiled and wiped his month with his napkin. "And thank you for the dinner. It was great, schatzi. "

"You are a very charming liar. I am sorry I burned the potatoes. But the salad was good, right?"

"The salad was perfect."

Alice smiled. Who would have thought that Alfred would came back into her life? And would stay. Alice thought about the call Alfred had made to her at the beginning of the year. She had not seen Alfred for over five years, since Alfred's wife Erna – her former best friend – left Nuremberg and Alice. When Alfred called, Alice was swamped with work, working on a challenging design for a particularly challenging client. It was just her and Greta working in the studio. Alice knew she needed to take on some additional help, but she simply didn't have the time to look. After exchanging pleasantries, Alfred asked Alice to lunch, and Alice agreed, curious why Alfred wanted to speak with her after all these years.

They met at a café down the street. Alfred looked about the same, although he had put on a little weight and his hair had grayed a little. He was still an attractive man, but what was most striking were his eyes. They were blue and seemed to see right through you. He was also taller than Alice, which she always appreciated after growing up taller than her three brothers.

Alfred started the conversation. "It was really nice of you to meet me for lunch. I heard you opened your own dress shop here. You were always ambitious like that."

"How would you have heard about my little dress shop? Aren't you still living in Nuremberg?"

"I heard from my mother, who still speaks with your mother. My mother is not doing well and I have been visiting her when I can. My sister has actually bought several of your dresses – Henny Bermann – and she also told me about your shop. I reminded her we were friends when you lived Nuremberg. She then asked me to ask you for a favor. I hope I am not imposing. My niece Ruth recently graduated from the Philanthropin and is interested in apprenticing as a dressmaker. She took dressmaking courses in high school and is really quite talented. Would you be interested in meeting with her? Even if you can't take her on, maybe you know of someone else who might be interested in an apprentice. As you can imagine, it is hard for a Jewish girl to find an apprenticeship these days."

"As it turns out, I could use someone right now. Ask your niece to stop by tomorrow and I would be happy to speak with her."

"Alice, I can't tell you how much I appreciate this. I am very close to my niece and she is a wonderful and hard-working girl. I think you two will really get along." They spent the next fifteen minutes talking about Alfred's business – he was still selling watches – and her family and his family. He said nothing about Erna and Alice was too nervous to bring up the subject. Then Alfred did something surprising – he asked Alice to join him for a concert.

"My mother has tickets for a chamber music concert at the West End Synagogue and she can't make it. It is this Saturday evening. Are you free to join me? You know how much I hate letting anything go to waste." With that last statement, Alfred smiled at Alice. He did have a way about him that always put Alice at ease. But Alice was confused – was he asking her out on a date or was this just a way for two old friends to reconnect? Alice thought he was probably just repaying her for agreeing to speak with his niece. Plus, he did say that he didn't want the tickets to go to waste, or maybe that was just a joke. And then she said to herself that she should stop worrying about why he was asking her to join him. She told herself to just say yes to Alfred's invitation. After all, what harm could there be for two old friends to go to a concert together? "I would love to join you," Alice told Alfred.

That Saturday, Alfred picked up Alice at her apartment and the two walked to the synagogue. Alice wore a gray dress she had made recently, one which was comfortable, but also flattering, just in case this was really a date. The weather was unusually warm and Alice was enjoying the walk. Alice had been a little nervous when he came to her door, but Alfred immediately put her at ease. She forgot how easy it was to talk with him. Alice told him about her meeting with Ruth and how much she really liked this sixteen-year-old.

"She is unusually poised and mature for her age. And she already has good skills from the classes she took in school. I offered her the apprenticeship on the spot and she accepted. She starts on Monday."

"That is great news. But I hope you are not giving Ruth the apprenticeship because of me."

"Trust me, Alfred. I would never sacrifice my business for friendship." And she smiled at Alfred. "I offered her the apprenticeship because I think she would be perfect for my business." And then Alfred smiled at Alice. Alice thought she felt a spark between the two, but immediately dismissed it.

After the concert, Alfred suggested that the two find a place for a late supper. Alice had not eaten before the concert and was hungry, so she readily agreed. They found a small café near the synagogue and they quickly ordered. Alice assumed Alfred was also hungry.

Alice was placing her napkin on her lap when she noticed Alfred fidgeting with his napkin. He seemed nervous. Twice, he started to say something and then stopped. Alice decided to let him figure out how to get the words out.

"Alice, thank you for joining me tonight. I wasn't sure you would come out with me, given everything that had happened in Nuremberg." Alice thought this was a strange statement. The only thing she remembered involving Alfred was that he wouldn't tell her why Erna had left Nuremberg. But he clearly had more to say and so she said nothing.

"First, I wanted to make sure you knew about Ludwig."

"Yes, his mother wrote to me he had died. She was pretty vague, but I had the sense that it had something to do with his lungs. Maybe pneumonia. I was sad when I received the letter. He was relatively young, and I had hoped that he would find happiness with someone else. Although I thought at the time that it was odd that he would die just months after the Nazis came to power. He had warned all of us about the dangers of the Nazi Party, and we never took him seriously. As it turns out, he was right all along."

"Yes, he was. And I agree it was sad. I liked Ludwig." Alfred stopped speaking and took a deep breath. "Alice, there is something else I wanted to speak with you about. I didn't think I would ever get the chance, but when my sister asked me to speak with you about my niece, I thought I would tell you what I wanted to tell you that day you came to my apartment in Nuremberg to find Erna. I know that Erna never spoke with you about our divorce – she told me you asked, but she said nothing. I take the blame for our failed marriage – I was probably too young to marry and all that travel was probably not good for us. Plus, Erna was sometimes hard to talk to, at least hard for me. When she found out about my indiscretions, and I admit I had some indiscretions, she was pretty upset. I think she was prepared to forgive me, but then I made the mistake of saying one thing too many. I told her I liked you. I don't know why I said it. Maybe I was worried that she would forgive me and stay with me. At the moment I told her, I had decided I didn't want to stay married to Erna, and I knew that telling her about my feelings for you would be too much for her to bear. But I only expected her to leave me. I never expected her to stop speaking to you. In hindsight, it is not surprising that she did, but I was just being selfish, and for that I am truly sorry. But what I said to her was the truth. I didn't try to pursue it, since you were married, and didn't try to contact you after you left Nuremberg. I did hear that you and Ludwig divorced, but I decided it was best for me to move on with my life. I don't know why I am telling you this now. Maybe it has to do with everything going on right now in Germany. All I know is, at this moment right now, I would like to see you again, if you are okay with that. I need to go back on the road for about two weeks, but then I will be back in Frankfurt to see my mother."

Alice was stunned. So that was why Erna didn't want to see her. Surely, Erna could not have thought that Alice had feelings towards Alfred. No, Alice was sure that Erna did not think that. But perhaps Erna was worried that something might have started between Alice and Alfred. After all, Erna knew how unhappy Alice was with Ludwig. Maybe Erna had assumed that something would have started between the two, and so she removed herself from the equation. Or maybe it would have been too hard for Erna to see the end of their friendship if Alice and Alfred started to see each other. All of this was making Alice dizzy. But, at the same time, she was intrigued by Alfred's request. She had always felt comfortable with Alfred, and sometimes sensed something more, which she immediately quashed. And what would be the harm in seeing him again, to see if there is something more?

"Alfred, this is a lot to think about, especially everything about Erna. Let's take it one step at a time. Let's have dinner again the next time you are in town."

So Alice had dinner with Alfred when he returned to Frankfurt. And she had more dinners with Alfred. She soon found herself falling for him, and falling for him fast.

•　•　•

After the strudel and coffee, Alfred helped Alice clear the table. She would let the burned pot soak overnight in the sink, but she washed the rest of the dishes. Alice then joined Alfred in the living room. There was a small space in the corner, away from the sewing machines, where they could sit and read. Alice returned to the article about the Nuremberg Laws. She read a few lines and then put the paper down. She could not read anymore.

Alice closed her eyes and thought about the year, about how things had been going so well for her, at the dressmaking studio and with Alfred. She had hired a second seamstress and so there were four of them, sewing and cutting and fitting the various customers. Alfred continued to travel and was technically still living in Nuremberg, but when he was not on the road, he was spending most of his time in Frankfurt and with Alice. More family members were worried about the situation for Jews in Germany and what should be done. Some of the younger ones had already left Germany. Jacob's son Ernst had left last year for America. The final straw for Ernst came during a trip to the mountains with some friends, when the proprietor of a hotel they had stayed at in the past told them she no longer allowed Jews to stay in her hotel. Jacob's daughter Mellie, the Zionist, had married last year and she and her new husband left for a honeymoon in Palestine and never came back. But, so far, none of Alice's siblings were seriously considering leaving. And things were going too well for Alice to consider leaving.

Alice could not help but be aware of the government's efforts to make life more difficult for Jews in Germany. German Jews had naively hoped that President Hindenburg would be able to rein in the more extreme elements of the Nazi Party, but that hope finally died with the President in August 1934. Following Hindenburg's death, Hitler combined the offices of President and Chancellor, becoming Fuhrer. Perhaps the scariest time was just before Hindenburg's death, when Hitler ordered the SS and the Gestapo to purge Hitler's political enemies, with perhaps hundreds killed throughout Germany. Alice remembered the chilling radio address Hitler gave to justify the killings in July 1934, claiming that those killed had been guilty of treason against Germany. "Jacob, I guess you were wrong about Hindenburg's ability to protect the Jews from Hitler," Alice had thought as she listened to the address.

Still, notwithstanding all the actions taken thus far by the Nazis against Frankfurt's Jews, 1935 had been a surprisingly good year for Alice and Alice was feeling optimistic about her future. Until that July day. That awful, awful day. The day was almost a harbinger of things to come. For Alice, passage of the Nuremberg Laws almost seemed like an inevitability following that horrible day.

That July day started like most days for Alice. She woke at 6:30 am, had her morning coffee and reviewed the appointments for the day. She checked the stock to determine what she needed to order. She had a wedding party coming in at noon and needed to make sure she had enough tulle to show the bride. She was focused on her supplies and was a bit startled when the telephone rang. It was 8 am, and she wasn't expecting a call that early. Perhaps one of her seamstresses was calling in sick. Not what she needed, she thought, given how busy she was. She answered the telephone. It was her mother. She almost never used the telephone. She hated using the telephone, Alice thought. Why was she calling? "Alice, I have some very sad news." She was crying and needed to stop talking for a second. And then she said, "Max has died. Please come right over."

Alice put down the telephone and stared off into space. Max is dead? Max is dead? This can't be real. When did she last talk to Max? Last month? The month before? She needed to focus. Her mother needed her to come right over. She needed to call Gretel to take charge. She didn't quite trust Gretel with the wedding party, but she had no choice. She trusted Ruth more, but Ruth was only 16 years old. She called Gretel and told her there was a death in the family. Gretel didn't need to know more. She then grabbed her purse and left the apartment. She was at her mother's place in ten minutes. Her mother answered the door and fell into her arms. And then she told Alice that Max had committed suicide.

Alice knew that the last few months had been bad for Max, but she didn't realize how bad they must have been. Max began his own scrap trading business in the beginning of 1934, after

Jacob and Benno started their company. Gebrüder Heppenheimer's scrap metal clients had been around the Frankfurt area, as well as north in the Ruhr Valley, so Max had no relationships with businesses in Mannheim. In normal times, it would have been a challenge to start a business. But the German economy was still in a depression. Worse, anti-Semitism was on the rise and businesses were reluctant to do any business with a Jew, particularly a Jew starting a new business. Month after month, Max knocked on door after door and received the same response – thanks, but no thanks. He was feeling pretty demoralized when he came home one afternoon in April of this year to find Kurt at home. One of the top students in his Gymnasium, Kurt had wanted to be a ship's doctor. But the Nazis had other plans for Jewish students. All Jewish students in the Gymnasium had been told to go home and not come back, including Kurt.

After Kurt had been thrown out of school, it seemed Max had lost all focus, at least that is what Recha later told Alice. He left the apartment in the morning, but Recha believed that he simply walked the streets or drank coffee in one of the cafes. When Kurt came home a month after he left school to tell his parents that he had found an apprenticeship in a paper factory, it was as if the remaining lights had turned off for Max. That morning in July, Max climbed the stairs of his apartment building to the roof and jumped to his death.

When Alice walked into her mother's apartment, she looked around and saw Leo and Selma. Leo was expressionless, but Selma was crying. Selma came over to her sister and gave her a hug and told her Benno and Margot were on their way over. "What about Jacob?" Alice asked. But why bother asking? She already knew the answer. "Jacob said that he couldn't get away from the office. But he said he would be at the funeral tomorrow."

Oh, the funeral. She hadn't really focused on that. If this had been any other member of the family, they may have waited beyond the 24-hour period prescribed for burial. But Max was an Orthodox Jew and he would have wanted to be buried within 24 hours of his death. She was sure Recha would insist, and it was her right. She had been through enough. Alice would arrange for a car for herself, her mother and her sister. As for her brothers, they could find their own transportation to Mannheim.

After she returned home from the funeral the following evening, Alice realized she didn't remember much of the funeral, or really much of the day. She remembered driving with her mother and sister from Frankfurt. Leo stayed home, and it was just as well – she couldn't imagine driving with the two of them fighting. Both Benno and Jacob came to the cemetery, but she couldn't remember how they got there. There were just two clear memories of the day. The first was the look on Kurt's face when he saw his two uncles. She had never seen such hatred in a single look. At that moment, she wanted to hug her nephew and tell him she agreed with him, that his uncles were responsible for his father's death.

The second clear memory happened just after the funeral was concluded, when she left her mother and sister at the gravesite to let the driver know they would be leaving shortly. She came around a corner and saw Benno and Jacob talking. She stayed behind a wall to avoid them, hoping they would walk away. She did not want to talk with them. But they remained where they were, and Alice listened in on their conversation. Benno was speaking and appeared animated.

"Jacob, I can't help it. I feel responsible. I can't help but think that if we had just included him in the LLC, he would not have jumped off that roof."

"It is not your fault, it is not my fault. He was having problems long before we set up the LLC. And as I explained to him, the company was hemorrhaging money. We had been able to negotiate a deal with the creditors, but we needed to shut down the second smelter facility and sell the attached house as part of the settlement. We were in danger of losing both office buildings, and that would have been bad for everyone. Most of our income these days is coming from those buildings. For you, me, Adolph and Max. Or now Max's family. My responsibility was to make sure we did not lose the buildings, and I explained that to Max. And if we had brought Max in with us, the LLC would have failed. We didn't tell him that, but you and I both know that. And I could not work with Adolph anymore."

"Jacob, I never challenged you on Adolph. Many of his decisions put the company at risk in the past. I just wish we could have done it differently with Max, or made Max better understand what we were doing."

"I tried to. He just didn't always hear me." Jacob stopped talking, and then let out a loud sigh, and then raised his voice. "It is always my responsibility to do everything in the family. To make sure the business stays solvent, to get us out of the messes caused by others, and now you are telling me I should have made Max better understand the decisions we made. That was not my job! And I don't want to be told that it should have been my job! And I am done talking about this. Besides, we need to get back to Frankfurt. Remember, we have an early morning meeting."

Jacob walked away, and Benno soon followed him. But Alice remained behind the wall, thinking about what she had just heard. She was stunned. When Max told her about the establishment of the LLC, he never told her that the company was facing the possible loss of the office buildings. He may have been too upset about hearing about the new LLC and the fact that he was not in it. Alice now understood why Max was not included in the new venture, but she wished Jacob had been a little more diplomatic in explaining why. Maybe there was no real diplomatic way of explaining that Max was a business failure and might have put the LLC at risk. And given the state of the economy at the time, Jacob's decision was probably the right decision from a business point of view, or at least from the point of view of Jacob, Benno, and their families. Alice just wished that there had been another solution to the company's problems.

And then Alice thought about Max's decision to commit suicide. While the establishment of the LLC may have played a role, so did the four years of fighting in the trenches in the Great War. And if anyone or anything was to blame for Max's death, it really was Hitler and the Nazis. At that moment, Alice decided she needed to leave Germany. That all Jews needed to leave Germany. The question was no longer if, but when.

It was now two months since the funeral, and as Alice opened her eyes again, she could see that Alfred was now reading a book.

"Alfred, the Nuremburg Laws have convinced me we cannot remain in Germany any longer. We need to make plans to leave now."

"I agree, schatzi. But I won't even consider leaving unless you agree to marry me."

Alice blushed, then smiled, then stared into those penetrating blue eyes and said softly, "Yes, I would love to marry you." Alfred kissed the fingers of his right hand and then touched his heart with that hand. And then he drew in Alice and kissed her. Alice knew at that moment that she had loved no one more than she loved Alfred.

•   •   •

The fall of 1935 had been hard for Alice. She was still heartbroken over her brother's suicide, and it had been hard to spend time with her mother. Emma seemed to blame herself for her stepson's death. As much as Alice tried to explain to her mother she could have done nothing to prevent Max from taking his life, Emma continued to wonder aloud to Alice whether she should have been more forceful in how Max had been treated by his older brothers. Alice understood that the relationship between stepsons and stepmothers is complicated, and all the more complicated when one stepson – Max – was essentially raised as his stepmother's natural son. Alice knew that her mother would need time to heal. Still, it was hard for Alice to hear her mother's pain as Alice herself was trying to heal.

And yet, at the same time, good things were also happening for Alice. She was in love, her business was flourishing, and Ruth had been a god-send. Ruth was hardworking and creative. Simply by listening to a few of Alice's instructions, Ruth was able to sketch out a dress. At times, she even suggested some changes to Alice's design. At first, Alice bristled at any suggestions offered by this teenager, until she saw that – at least sometimes – the suggestion made sense. And Alice could tell that Ruth was gaining confidence under Alice's tutelage.

One morning, Ruth came in with the morning paper and showed Alice a notice for a fashion show at the Frankfurt Hof Hotel. "Tante Alice, look at this notice. The Frankfurt Fashion Office is putting on a fashion show of the latest German designs. Do you think we should go?"

"Ruth, I really do love your enthusiasm, but going to a fashion show put on by the Fashion Office is probably not a good idea for us, particularly after the recent enactment of the Nuremberg Laws. I know a lot about the Fashion Office. When it was first established, I was pretty excited about it. After the Frankfurt elections in March 1933, when the Jewish mayor was replaced with the Nazi Frederich Krebs, we were all worried. But one of the first things Mayor Krebs did was establish the Frankfurt Fashion Office and announce that Frankfurt would become the fashion center of the Third Reich. As you can imagine, I was intrigued at the prospect that fashion would be a focus of this new regime and that the focus would be in Frankfurt, even though their focus was also on getting rid of Jews. I naively thought that there might be a place for someone like me in the fashion center."

Ruth was getting excited. "Wow, I never heard about this."

"Well, don't get too excited. Mayor Krebs appointed Margareth Klimt, a known anti-Semite who was a professor in Frankfurt's Arts and Crafts School, as the head of the Fashion Office. After her appointment, Klimt made it her mission to get rid of Jews in all parts of Frankfurt fashion. At the same time, the office was promoting high-end fashion no one could afford. And the designs were hard to replicate into ready-to-wear clothing, which had been one of its missions. That they are holding this fashion show at a fancy hotel says it all."

"I understand your point. We are not designing ready-to-wear fashions, but we are at least designing dresses for the average woman. But aren't you just a little curious about what they are promoting as 'new German fashion?' Maybe we could just sneak in."

"There will be no sneaking in for us. I don't want to give the police any excuse to harass us. Plus, I have seen the "new German fashion" and I am not impressed. I am happy with the 'old German fashion' and so are our customers."

Ruth was quiet for a minute and then asked her aunt, "I understand that the Fashion Office is trying to get rid of Jews in the fashion industry, but how successful do you think they have been? We are still pretty busy."

"So far, not too successful. Their actions remind me of an earlier effort by Krebbs to erase Jews from the city. When he first became Frankfurt's mayor in 1933, Frankfurt was viewed among the National Socialists as 'a city of Jews and Democrats.' To get rid of that image, Krebs received Hitler's blessing to rename Frankfurt 'the City of German Crafts.' When I heard about the idea, I was hopeful. After all, dressmaking is considered a craft. But handicrafts had never been much of a presence among Frankfurt's businesses, and Krebs only wanted to appeal to those Germans who felt left behind by modern technology, and to blame the Jews. But the effort was a failure – have you heard anyone call Frankfurt the city of German crafts?"

"I guess I shouldn't worry. And I better get started on Frau Levy's dress. She is supposed to pick it up tomorrow afternoon and we both know how she will be if the dress is not ready."

"If that dress is not ready, I will need to fire you. I am afraid of Frau Levy, and I will not take the blame." They both laughed, and Alice walked over to her desk to review some invoices. Alice could hear her niece humming a popular tune, and assumed that Ruth was focused on the dress. When the humming stopped, Alice looked up and she saw Ruth staring into the distance.

"Ruth, is everything okay?"

"Yes, Tante Alice. I was just thinking about how I much I love fashion and I was wondering when you first became interested in fashion."

"That is an interesting question, Ruth. I often tell people that I have always been interested in fashion, but I do believe that I can point to a single moment when I decided I wanted my life to be in the fashion world. When I was six years old, my parents decided I could accompany them on a trip to Paris. My older siblings were too involved in their lives, and Selma was too young. As you can imagine, I was very excited about the trip. My first big trip. And to have my parents all to myself. I don't remember the train ride, nor do I remember much about the sightseeing we did in Paris. The one moment that is crystal clear to me was the moment we stepped into Le Bon Marché. At the time, it was the largest department store in the world and had multiple floors of ready-to-wear fashion. The building was huge, with a three-story atrium and a glass dome. I remember standing in the middle of the store, transfixed, and looking around at all the floors. And once I was in the children's clothing department, I had to touch every piece of clothing. I remember my mother bought me a beautiful coat with large brass buttons and a matching hat. I never liked the hat, but I wore that coat until the sleeves were too short for me. From that moment on, I decided fashion would be my life."

"What a great story, Tante Alice. I can almost see you in that coat. I don't think I had a similar moment. I just decided one day that this is what I want to do. But it feels good to know that you and I are doing something we really love. And now I need to get back to Frau Levy's dress." She walked back to the cutting table, and started to hum again.

Alice thought to herself that their conversation must have upset Ruth, and that she needed a little reassurance. But Alice had to admit to herself that she was a little concerned about the Office's efforts to eliminate Jews from the fashion industry. So far, Alice was very busy. And some of her Jewish colleagues were also busy. But others had felt the effects of anti-Semitism and had been forced to close their businesses. She didn't know how much of a role the Fashion Office had played in those closures. She thought the Fashion Office was focusing on the wrong thing – high-priced fashion using strange fabrics – and in ordinary times, this "new German fashion" would have failed. But the Nazi government was promoting the office and this fashion, and Alice knew she could one day find herself out of business. For now, she simply had to focus on the business she had.

CHAPTER 9

Frankfurt, June 1937

Alice looked over at her sister from her desk, annoyed that Selma was distracting Ruth. Selma's apartment was a four-minute walk from Alice's dressmaking studio on Kronberger Strasse, and Selma was spending more and more time away from her own apartment. Alice knew life with Leo had become almost unbearable for her sister, but Selma was a distraction for every one of her workers. She had tried to put Selma to work, answering the telephone or helping with inventory. The one thing Selma would do with any enthusiasm was to cook for Alice and Alfred, and Alice was happy to put her to work in the kitchen. But what Selma seemed to need was company, and more than anything, she just wanted to talk to people who didn't respond with sarcastic comments, like Leo. Selma was just lonely, and Alice didn't have the heart to send her home.

Like most Jewish-owned businesses in Germany, Leo's wholesale coffee business was now just a shell of what it had been. The last of his employees, Semy Katz, was now suing him for commissions he was still owed. Leo had given up his office and the warehouse where he had stored his coffee beans on Gutleutstrasse and rarely left the apartment. At seventy-six years old, Emma was finding it difficult to leave the apartment, but she seemed to be okay spending most of her time in the apartment, generally reading or knitting. Emma also seemed to ignore the fights between Selma and Leo, although Alice suspected it was because her mother was losing her hearing. But Selma found it hard to remain in the apartment.

Alice was thinking to herself that much has changed since she and Alfred had married last year. For one thing, Alfred had virtually stopped working. For years, Alfred had been a top commercial representative for the Robert Kauderer Company, a well-known watch manufacturer in the watch capital of Germany, Pforzheim. Notwithstanding Alfred's great success at selling watches, the company's owner was being pressured to get rid of Jewish employees. Alfred was among the last of the Jews still employed by the company, and was still technically employed, but he was given few opportunities to sell his products. These days, Alfred was mostly home, helping Alice when she needed help with deliveries or unloading supplies. And while Alice's business was still making money, she was no longer making "fine" fashion. Mostly, her clothing was simply functional. She knew her brothers' scrap metal business was making some money, but knew that the business was feeling the effects of anti-Semitism. The Nazi government's decision to rearm its military had resulted in the need for scrap metal, even if the scrap metal came from a Jewish business. However, at this point, Gebrüder Heppenheimer was mostly just selling its remaining inventory, rather than buying and selling scrap.

Alice and Alfred had married in a small ceremony in March of 1936, just before Alfred's mother's death, and then moved together to the apartment on Kronberger Strasse. The new apartment was a one-bedroom apartment, but had a significantly larger living room than Alice's first apartment, with enough space for both a dressmaking studio and for a couch and chairs to relax. The couch and chairs were from Alfred's mother's apartment, covered in a rich maroon pattern that reminded Alfred of happier times every time he sat down. Alice purchased a screen to divide this space from the rest of the room to give Alfred some privacy. The only purchase made by the couple to celebrate their move, Alice splurged on an upholstered screen with an Art Deco design that matched the couch and chairs.

While Alice and Alfred had been talking about emigrating, it was Alfred's mother's funeral that served as the final impetus for their decision to leave Germany. Because of the new rules imposed since passage of the Nuremberg Laws, the burial could not take place until after dark, and only immediate family members could attend. But more troubling was that only family members could dig the grave, although Alfred was able to pay two men to pose as family members to dig the grave. But they all had to walk past Gestapo officers who were monitoring the burial to make sure that Alfred's family was following the rules. Alfred was completely humiliated – and heartbroken – by the experience.

Several weeks after the funeral, Alice and Alfred added their names to the waiting list for visas to the U.S. Alice and Alfred had delayed their decision until they were absolutely ready, since once they made the decision, all of their assets would be placed in a blocked bank account and they would need permission from the German Foreign Exchange Office to withdraw any money, even for business reasons. The Gestapo would also put them under surveillance. They knew that placing their names on the list would make it harder for Alice to keep her business going, or really to live in Germany, but they were ready. They were soon assigned numbers reflecting their places on the waiting list. They didn't understand the significance of the numbers, but were told by friends knowledgeable about the process that the high numbers meant it could be a number of years before they were called by the U.S. consulate for their visas.

Unlike many German Jews, Alice was lucky in one respect. The U.S. had made it difficult for German Jews to obtain visas since the Nazis came to power under the "public charge clause." To prevent immigrants from becoming a public charge, the U.S. required that an applicant have a sponsor who promised to be financially responsible for the immigrant. Because of this requirement, the quota for Germans in the years since Hitler came to power had not even been close to being filled. But the Heppenheimer family had a guardian angel. Alice's Uncle Henry (her father's brother), who had emigrated to America in the 1890s, had a son-in-law, Adolph Keller, who agreed to sponsor anyone who asked. He had sponsored Jacob's son Ernst, he was sponsoring Max's son Kurt, and he had agreed to sponsor Alice and Alfred. As far as Alice could tell, this was the greatest challenge in the process for a U.S. visa, other than their place on the waiting list. They just needed to complete the rest of the paperwork and wait until their numbers came up.

Alice heard Selma and Ruth laughing and was about to tell her sister to let Ruth finish her work when she became distracted again by some papers on her desk relating to Alfred's mother's estate. Alfred was the executor of his mother's estate, and he needed to sell her small four-story apartment building. The building, which was on a tree-lined street across from the zoo in Frankfurt's East End, had been purchased by Alfred's father around 1900, and that building provided his mother with rental income after his father's death in 1920. Both Alfred and his sister Henny had provided their mother with additional financial support, but the depression made it difficult to continue those payments and their mother was forced to take out a RM 15,000 mortgage on the building in the early 1930s. Now Alfred needed to sell the building for enough to pay off the mortgage and to pay any required taxes. The German government had valued the building at RM 27,000, and so anything left following the payoff of the mortgage and taxes could be used by Alfred and his sister (who had also decided to emigrate) to pay for the costs of emigration.

The problem was that Alfred was having trouble finding a buyer. Once potential buyers found out that a Jew had owned the building, they were no longer interested. Or they made an offer so low that Alfred would not be able to pay off the mortgage, and would never receive approval for the sale by the Foreign Exchange Office. And while he was trying to sell the building, he needed to continue the mortgage payments to avoid repossession. So now he was in a financial hole, and it seemed this inheritance was becoming more of a burden than a help.

And then the newlyweds encountered another problem. In order to obtain their passports and permission to leave Germany, Alfred and Alice needed a tax clearance certificate, attesting that they owed no taxes to the German government. In the beginning of 1937, a few months after they had notified the German government of their intent to emigrate, Alfred received a notice from the German tax office that he and Alice both owed back taxes. That made no sense to him. Alice told him she had never had a problem with the tax office, and neither had Alfred. Alice spoke to friends who were also trying to emigrate who told her that mysterious taxes had suddenly appeared that hadn't been there before. Alice and Alfred were struggling financially, and needed every Reichsmark they had. He knew they didn't owe the taxes, and so Alfred filed a complaint with the tax office.

Before he submitted the letter, Alfred spoke with Alice about challenging the tax assessment. Both agreed that it was likely a fool's errand, but both were annoyed with the unfairness of the assessment. Plus, Alfred was frustrated at not having any success at selling the apartment building. And if they could not sell the building, they certainly would not be receiving their tax clearance certificate.

Since they decided to emigrate, things had become more difficult for both Alice and Alfred. It seemed like an edict was being issued every day making it that much harder to live and work in Germany. They had to ask for permission from the Foreign Exchange Office, which monitored their blocked bank account, to pay the rent, to pay their bills, even to help a family member. Leo was never much of a provider, but now was earning virtually no money. Alice was helping her sister pay their bills, but she didn't know how much longer she would be able to help Selma.

Alice heard more giggling and could feel herself getting more annoyed with Selma. But she reminded herself that the annoyance might have more to do with her frustration with her sister over Selma's refusal to even discuss leaving Germany. Selma claimed she needed to remain in Germany because their mother would not leave and Selma was not leaving their mother. Emma was reasonably healthy, but she said that she would not start again in a new country. Plus, Selma said that she could not imagine really bad things happening to any of them. "They are restricting what we can do and where we can live. That happened to Jews in Germany before, and we survived. We will be fine." Whenever Alice heard this from her sister, Alice told her she was wrong, which often led to an argument between the two.

Alice was also finding it harder to visit her sister because of the constant battles between Leo and Selma. In the past, Alice had visited when Leo was at his office, but these days, he was always home. Selma and Leo were sleeping in separate rooms now, so even when he was in the apartment, he often went to his bedroom when Alice was visiting, which made visiting a little more tolerable. He was just as disinterested in seeing Alice as she was in seeing him. Alice couldn't understand how her mother put up with this craziness, but she never asked. Why borrow trouble?

Alice was pleased that she and Alfred were able to convince his sister Henny, husband Sam and daughter Ruth to put their names on the waiting list for U.S. visas. Ruth had become like a daughter to Alice and she felt very protective of her. She had never wanted children with Ludwig. When she and Alfred first started dating, they did discuss children, but they agreed it would be insane to bring children into their crazy world. But having spent time with Ruth over the last two years, she had discovered a maternal part of her she had not known existed. Ruth already had a mother, and Alice had no interest in replacing Henny. But she was happy to be a doting aunt and would do anything for Ruth, and that included making sure that Ruth made it out of Germany.

Finally, Alice walked over to Selma, intending to tell her sister to stop talking to Ruth. But as she listened to what they were saying, she switched from annoyance to concern. When Ruth first began her apprenticeship with Alice, Ruth had spoken about her time at the Philanthropin, the Jewish high school. Ruth had enjoyed her academics, but she really enjoyed her social life. She had a broad circle of friends and attended concerts and parties. Even when the Nazis first took control, Ruth was still able to enjoy her life as a teenager. Alice knew that Ruth's social life had been shrinking, both because some friends had successfully emigrated and because there were fewer opportunities to socialize. Still, when she could, Ruth went out with friends. But where she was going now made Alice nervous. She had begun attending lectures sponsored by the Jewish Lehrhaus.

"Ruth, that is wonderful. I attended several of their classes in the 1920s. The Lehrhaus had shut down at the end of the 20s. I hadn't heard that they had re-opened." Of course, Selma ignored the fact that attending those lectures could be a problem for Ruth.

"My friend Etie heard about the Lehrhaus and she talked me into going. Etie had wanted to be a teacher, and there are classes being taught at the Lehrhaus for Jewish women to become teachers for Jewish children. I am not interested in that, but I have been enjoying the lectures. Martin Buber, the philosopher, has been running the Lehrhaus, and he just brought in this rabbi from Berlin, the brilliant Abraham Joshua Heschel, to help run it. Rabbi Heschel is very interesting and has been lecturing on a variety of topics. There are often receptions after the lectures, and it is a nice way for us to meet others. Mostly, it is a way of getting out and seeing people."

"That sounds like fun. Maybe I could join you and your friends some evening."

"I would love that, Selma. I will let you know when the next lecture will be."

Oh, that's concerning, thought Alice. Sometimes, Selma was clueless about what was appropriate for Jews at this time, especially for someone as young as Ruth. Clearly, Selma didn't appreciate the dangers of attending a lecture like the ones put on by the Lehrhaus. Ruth and her parents are trying to get out of Germany. Ruth needed to avoid any potential problems. Alice knew the Gestapo had put all Jews who had applied to emigrate under surveillance, and that surveillance likely included attending Jewish lectures. Alice couldn't tell Ruth not to attend the lectures – that was not her place. But she needed to speak with her parents about this. Or at least warn them about the potential problems to their emigration status if Ruth continued to attend these lectures.

Alice knew Ruth was spending the evening with friends, and so Alice called Henny to ask if it was okay for her and Alfred to come over that evening. After dinner, Alice and Alfred walked over to Henny and Sam's apartment. They knocked on the door, and Henny invited them in. The apartment was large and well furnished. Sam had been a dentist for many years and had done well. He was still practicing dentistry, but his practice had shrunk in recent years. At least that is what Ruth had told her.

"Alice, Alfred, it is so nice to see you both. Come in and I will make us some coffee." After exchanging some pleasantries, the four sat down and Alice came right to the point of their visit. Sam was not one for small talk and it was often easier not to try.

"Henny, Sam, I wanted to speak with you about Ruth. First, let me just say again what a great job she is doing. If things were different, she really would be a star in the fashion world. Unfortunately, these days, our designs are pretty simple, but she still does great work. But we came over this evening to talk about something else. I am assuming you know that Ruth has been attending lectures at the Jewish Lehrhaus. I think it is great that, even with everything going on, the Jewish community is still working to educate the young people. But I have heard that there might be elements within the Lehrhaus that are openly opposing the Nazi government. I am sure that Ruth is not part of that, but I am concerned that the Gestapo might think that she is. And I am also concerned that this could give them an excuse to make emigration harder for her or for all of you."

Sam was the first to respond. "Alice, we know Ruth has been going to the lectures and we have heard rumors about some rebellious elements within the Lehrhaus. We have spoken with Ruth about this and have told her to be careful. She says she understands, but I am worried that she does not fully understand the danger she may be putting herself in. I really appreciate you coming to us with this. I know how much you care about Ruth."

Henny looked over at her husband and then sighed. "Ruth is only 18 years old. The Nazis have forced her to grow up, but sometimes we forget she is still young. She still wants to go out and have fun, and sometimes she doesn't understand that she needs to be more careful. And between us, I do worry that some of her friends may be involved in things that could get Ruth in trouble. She hasn't told us anything, but I worry."

"Is there any way you could try to speed up the progress of your applications? Of course, I don't know why I am asking this, since things have been so slow for me and Alfred." She looked over at Alfred and gave him a sad smile.

"We are doing the best we can. And now I am dealing with the likelihood that the Nazi government will strip me of my dental license soon. Maybe this year, maybe next year, but I know it will happen, and that will just make it harder for all of us to leave. But Henny and I have been thinking about trying to send Ruth to America first. Or maybe sending her to my cousin in England and then she could try to get a U.S. visa once she is there."

Alfred finally weighed in. "I will miss Ruth coming to our apartment every day – she really is a breath of fresh air. But Alice is right –attending those lectures is dangerous for her. And for the both of you. She is a little headstrong, and probably would not listen to any of us. And she also might not agree to leave Germany on her own. Sam, maybe you could contact your cousin in England and see if you can get her out of Germany. And then only tell Ruth what you have done if you can actually make it happen."

They all agreed that there was no point in getting into an argument with Ruth if they didn't need to. So, Henny and Sam said that they would start the process for Ruth leaving Germany on her own, and the four of them then drank their coffee, mostly in silence.

•   •   •

The one good thing that had happened recently for Alice was that she and Benno had become closer. Following Max's suicide, Alice had wanted to avoid both Jacob and Benno. She was feeling a bit too broken. But when Alice married Alfred, she invited both Jacob and Benno to her very small wedding. Jacob claimed he would be away on business, but Benno came with Margot and their two sons. Alice was happy that they came. With everything going on, she realized it was important to have family around.

Just a few weeks after Alice and Alfred's wedding, Benno and Margot invited Alice and Alfred for dinner. Alice had not been in their apartment since their son Hans' bar mitzvah in 1935. The apartment was in the West End, and a relatively short walk from their place. They had a nice time at dinner, and Alice remarked to Alfred on the walk home that she felt good about renewing her relationship with Benno. Alice knew she could never have much of a relationship with Jacob, but it was nice to be able to spend time with Benno and Margot. Alice and Alfred continued to see

Benno and Margot, usually for dinner, and sometimes included Emma and Selma.

A week after the visit to Henny and Sam's apartment to talk about Ruth, Benno called to see if Alice and Alfred wanted to join them for a concert. Alice had always enjoyed going to concerts, but Benno and Margot had been in a league of their own – they had had season subscriptions to both the symphony and the opera. After 1933, Jews could no longer attend the Frankfurt symphony or the opera, so Benno and Margo were forced to give up their subscriptions. Benno and Margo regularly attended concerts performed by the newly established Jewish Cultural League, which performed in the city's synagogues. While both Benno and Margo acknowledged that the quality was not as good, both still loved going to hear music. Alice was not quite the aficionado that her brother and sister-in-law were, but she loved listening to music and told Benno that she would be happy to go.

The concert was being held at the West End synagogue the following Sunday, the place where Alice and Alfred had had their first date. The West End Synagogue was the newer of the two Reform synagogues in Frankfurt, built in the early part of the century. The synagogue was a bit more modern – in terms of architecture and services – than the Main Synagogue, but Joseph and his children had always attended the Main Synagogue, and Alice always felt a bit like a traitor every time she stepped into the West End Synagogue. Of course, at this point, it didn't much matter. There was now just a single rabbi serving both synagogues, Rabbi Salzberger. And Alice rarely stepped into any synagogue these days, anyway, even for the High Holy days. Alice had agreed that they would meet at the synagogue for the 6 pm concert and then have some dinner after the concert at Benno's apartment.

Alice and Alfred decided to dress up for the concert – it had been some time since they had put on nice clothes. It almost felt like normal times for Alice, picking out a nice dress and matching it with some jewelry and shoes. She decided to wear her green dress, which she had made for herself when she had first opened her dressmaking studio. The dress was silk and she was particularly happy with the design. She sat down on the bed with the dress in hand, thinking about the changes she had made to the initial design, until she had come up with something that would show off her figure. At some point, she became aware that Alfred was sitting next to her.

"Where did you disappear to this time?"

Alice blushed. "I didn't go anywhere. I was just thinking about the work I did to design this dress."

"It always amazes me how you can just disappear into yourself and not even be aware of what is going on around you. I have been sitting next to you for five minutes and you didn't even know I was there. Maybe your sister is right. Maybe you do go into outer space!"

"Ha Ha. Very funny. Although we won't be laughing when Benno yells at us for being late for the concert. Let's finish getting dressed."

Alice and Alfred lived a five-minute walk from the synagogue, but they were enjoying the relatively warm evening and the fact that they were going to a concert, and so walked a bit slower than normal. The anti-Jewish signs and other Nazi propaganda, which had been removed just before the 1936 Olympics, had returned to the lamp posts and the sides of buildings – Jews with larges nose and long beards stepping on the backs of the German people or smiling blond youth wearing Nazi uniforms. Alice and Alfred tried to ignore the posters, holding hands and focusing on their walk and the upcoming concert. When they arrived at the synagogue, they saw Benno and Margot speaking with some people, and they walked up to join them.

One of the men talking seemed especially animated. "What do you mean you haven't put your names on the waiting list for emigration? Are you crazy? You need to do that immediately!"

"Isaac, we are still talking about it. We are still not convinced that this is something we need to do right now."

"Benno, your brother Jacob didn't need any convincing."

"I don't always do what my brother does." Alice could see Benno bristle at that comment. Alice suspected that it wasn't Benno that was hesitant about this decision. She had heard Margot say more than once that in a land that had produced Goethe, Shiller, Mozart and Beethoven, the Nazis could not remain in power. Alice wondered if Benno agreed with her. She had tried to speak with him about this in the past, but he had always stopped the conversation. She was tired of trying to get Selma to apply to leave. She only had so much energy.

When Benno saw Alice, he told his friend he would think about their conversation and said goodbye. "Perfect timing. I was ready to be done arguing with Isaac."

Alice wanted to say that she agreed with this man, but held her tongue. Instead, she said, "Thanks for the invitation. We were so excited to dress up for a concert. It is rare these days that we have an excuse to dress up."

"It was our pleasure. Let's go in and grab our seats. Margot is very particular about where we sit. Something about the acoustics in the room." Benno looked over at Margot and both grinned at each other. Regardless of what happened between Alice and Benno in the past, it was always a pleasure to spend an evening with Benno and Margot. Unlike Selma and Leo, this was a couple who truly liked each other and liked spending time together. That always made it fun for anyone else who spent time with them. Perhaps this was an evening when they could forget about Nazis and tax clearance certificates.

This was to be an all-Mozart concert. The orchestra began to tune up and everyone took their seats. The concert soon began and Alice looked over at Alfred. They both smiled and he squeezed their hand. About thirty minutes into the concert, Alice heard a ping. It sounded like someone had just dropped a glass. Alice heard another ping, and then another, and then felt a piece of glass fall onto her lap. At that moment, someone yelled "They are throwing rocks at the windows." People quickly got up from their seats and some began to run out of the sanctuary. Alice also stood up and looked up to see several broken windows as she was leaving her row of seats. As quickly as it started, the pinging stopped. A few people stopped leaving and began to return to their seats. But the concert was over – the musicians were already packing up to leave. The rock throwers had not done a lot of damage, but they had succeeded in disrupting the concert.

Alice was aware of the silence as she was leaving the synagogue. Only after she had left the building could Alice hear any talking, and then, all at once, she could hear multiple and heated conversations. She was holding Alfred's hand, and the two walked until they found Benno and Margot. Margot was clearly shaken – this was her last refuge from the craziness that was her life. And then she started to cry. Alice could understand why she was upset – and perhaps a little scared. But in all the years she had known her, she had rarely seen Margot cry. Margot was not a crier.

Benno looked at Margot and then at Alice. "We have something to tell you. We were going to tell you over dinner, but now is just as good a time as any. Hans was told yesterday not to come back to his school. We knew it would happen eventually, since there were only two or three Jewish children left in the entire school. As you can imagine, Hans is devastated. He now will need to start an apprenticeship." Hans, the elder of their two sons, was the more academic of the two and the one who was planning to attend a university. When they still lived at the smelter facility, Hans would take the tram daily to the Gymnasium in Frankfurt, studying during the long ride. Like his cousin Kurt, Benno and Margo had decided that their older son would obtain a university degree. Like Kurt, their son would be a professional and would not work in the scrap metal business. And now, all of those plans lay in ruins.

Alice looked at both Benno and Margot and could see that they wanted to be alone. Sometimes, it helped to share pain with other family members, and sometimes it was better to share that pain alone. When Benno suggested they try to attend a concert in the next few weeks, Alice heard the message and agreed that a concert in the near future would be nice. The two couples said their goodbyes and Alice and Alfred walked the short distance to their apartment. Alice wondered if the rock throwing at the synagogue and Hans' expulsion from the Gymnasium would finally convince Margot to put their names on the waiting list for US visas.

•   •   •

The weekend following the incident at the Westend Synagogue was the opening weekend of the summer season for the Frankfurt bath resorts. Frankfurt had a number of public bath resorts along the Main River, but the Heppenheimer family had always gone to the Nierderrad Licht- und Luftbad (Light and Air Bath). Located on a peninsula in the Main River, the bath had a sand beach, a river pool, and a café. When Alice was a child, the facilities were rather primitive. But while she was living in Nuremberg, the city had added changing rooms and showers. And while the consumption of alcohol was forbidden through the 1920s, the café began serving wine and beer in 1933. After Alice returned to Frankfurt, one of her favorite activities in the summer was to spend an entire Sunday at the Nierderrad bath, swimming in the pool and enjoying the afternoon with family or friends.

Unfortunately for Frankfurt's Jews, the enactment of the Nuremberg Laws impacted this coveted summer leisure activity. While Jews could frequent any of the public baths before those laws were passed, beginning in the summer of 1937, Jews in Frankfurt could only visit the Nierderrad Light and Air Bath. As it turned out, this was one of the few new directives that did not affect Alice, since she had always gone to the Nierderrad Bath. And that was Alice's plan for the first Sunday the bath was open.

Alice woke early that Sunday morning and was just too excited to remain in bed. She began packing the wicker basket with enough food for lunch and an afternoon snack, taking her time as she made the sandwiches. Alfred and Alice had planned to pick up Selma and Emma around 10 am, and the four of them would take the tram to the bath. Fortunately for Alice, Leo would not be joining them – he claimed it would be too hot for him. After she finished preparing all of the food for the day, Alice still had an hour before they needed to leave, and so sat down with a cup of coffee and read yesterday's paper. Alice didn't mind the wait -- it was nice to just sit and not have to work.

Just before 10 am, Alice and Alfred left the apartment and walked to Selma's apartment. Of course, when they arrived, Emma was not even close to being ready. But Alice expected that her mother would be late and joined her sister in the kitchen. Selma inspected the food basket, made a face at Alice, and then replaced much of what Alice had packed with food she had prepared. Alice laughed, but did not object. When Emma was finally ready, the four left the apartment and walked to the tram stop. As they boarded the tram, they could see others carrying baskets for a day at the bath. As they continued the ride, Alice could see the car filling with more and more Jews taking the tram to the Niederrad Bath. Alice thought to herself, regardless of all the other challenges in their lives, today, Frankfurt's Jews were going to enjoy a day in the sun. That was certainly the case for Alice.

The tram stopped just outside the gates of the bath, and virtually everyone exited the tram. They all walked up to the ticket booth to pay the small admission fee. The Jewish community had been forced to lease the bath from the city for the 1937 summer season, and the fee was intended to cover the cost of the lease.

After entering the facilities, the ladies went to the right and Alfred went to the left to change into their bathing suits. After they finished changing, Alfred rented four chairs and an umbrella and then the four found a place to settle for the day.

Alice and Selma had taken swimming lessons as children and both immediately went into the pool to swim. Emma did not like the water, but enjoyed watching her daughters swim. Alfred was afraid of the water, but was happy to sit in a chair and read his book. He also enjoyed talking to his mother-in-law. Emma had been raised by a religious scholar and Alfred had attended an orthodox yeshiva. Alfred was no longer religious, but Emma still attended services when she could and liked to discuss the week's Torah portion with Alfred when they were together. Emma's scholarly father believed it was important for all of his children to receive a Jewish education, and Emma was happy to share that knowledge in conversations with her son-in-law. At some point, Alice stopped swimming and looked over at her mother and Alfred. It was clear they were arguing over some point and having fun. Without having to worry about whether Alice or Selma would be bored by the conversation, the two could enjoy challenging each other with various arguments, which they were clearly doing. But it was always in good fun, and neither ever left the discussion with bruised egos, so Alice went back to her swim.

Around noon, Alice opened the food basket. Alfred had already walked to the café for cold drinks. The sun was strong, but the breeze from the river kept everyone comfortable as they ate their lunch. After lunch, Alice decided to take a nap, and was soon sound asleep. Deep into a dream, Alice could hear her name and woke with a start. She stared at Alfred.

"What's wrong? What's happened?"

Alfred smiled at her. "Nothing has happened. I am sorry I startled you. They are about to start the boat races and I thought you would want to watch."

Alice took a deep breath to calm herself. "I was dreaming that you were being chased by Nazis and then I heard you call my name in the dream. I thought something bad had happened. But it was just a dream. Yes, let's go watch the races. Where are Selma and Mama?"

"Your mom was getting a bit warm, so Selma took her to the café for a cold coffee."

The Jewish sports club Schild was on the peninsula next to the Nierderrad bath and had built a boathouse in the 1920s. Following the restriction on Jewish participation in all sporting events, Schild invited other Jewish boat clubs to store their boats at the boathouse and then organized rowing races to run through the summer. The first rowing race was about to start when Alice and Alfred reached the shoreline. There were so many people there to watch the race that Alice and Alfred had trouble seeing the river. Six boats were in the water and then the gun went off to start the race. People started to cheer for their team and Alice and Alfred soon found themselves cheering for Schild. The race lasted about a minute and Schild was victorious. Alice and Alfred hugged each other and then hugged others who had been cheering for Schild.

There were several other boat races, but Alice and Alfred decided to take a walk instead along the path that followed the water. Others were also walking along the path, and Alice and Alfred stopped to chat with several people they knew. Alfred noticed someone selling ices and bought them both ices. They reached their chairs as they were finishing their ices. Selma was reading and Emma was napping.

"Welcome back. How were the races?"

"We only watched the first race. Schild won, which was pretty exciting. Then Alfred and I took a walk along the water. How is Mama doing?"

"I think Mama might be ready to leave."

"I am also ready to leave. Let's pack up everything and then we can wake Mama. We can all change in the changing rooms and then head home."

By the time they left the bath, it was nearly 3 pm. The tram arrived almost immediately after they reached the stop, and it soon filled with other Jews, exhausted from their day at Niederrad Bath. Alfred found a seat for Emma and Selma, but he and Alice were forced to stand. That was okay, Alice thought. The ride would be relatively quick. As the tram started to empty of bathers, Alice could hear several teenage boys in the back bothering an elderly Jewish couple.

Alfred looked at Alice and shook his head. "Alice, say nothing. Just look to the front of the tram. Out stop is next."

As soon as the tram stopped, Alice and Selma helped up their mother and the four quickly left the tram. I hope that couple is okay, Alice thought to herself. But she knew it would not have helped them if she had tried to intervene. What could she or Alfred have been able to do? They actually could have made things worse. She tried not to think about the couple as they walked her sister and mother home.

Alice was singing to herself as she prepared dinner that evening. Nothing fancy, just a cold soup and a cold chicken salad. She could hear Alfred enter the kitchen. Her hugged her from behind and kissed the back of her neck.

"Well, someone is in a particularly good mood."

"I am. It was just a really nice day. The weather was perfect and it was nice not to have to worry about being hassled by people that hate you. The only bad thing that happened to me today was that my shoulders got a little too much sun. But being there today makes me think maybe we can wait out this craziness. Maybe if the Nazis gave us our own space to live, we could be okay."

"I know what you mean about feeling safe in a place. It was really nice to be in a place where it was okay to be Jewish. But that was only because the Nazi won't let Jews visit the other baths.

And we are not safe even in places that are just for Jews. Remember what happened last week at the concert in the synagogue? Today was just a respite from reality. We will never be truly safe as long as we are in Germany. And I believe it will only get worse. We need to leave as soon as we can."

"I agree. Still, it was nice to feel totally safe, at least for a few hours. Hopefully, we will feel that all the time once we are in America."

•   •   •

Alice awoke the next morning with a smile on her face. Yesterday had been a good day, she said to herself. She could smell coffee and toast – Alfred must have gotten up early and started breakfast for the two of them. While Alfred had almost no work to do these days, he was still used to getting up early. And like Alice, he might be feeling good about the wonderful day they had had yesterday. It had certainly been a while since they had been able to truly forget about the daily nightmare of living in Nazi Germany.

Alice got out of bed and put on her bathrobe. She went into the bathroom to perform her morning rituals, and then she walked into the kitchen. She walked up to Alfred, put her arms around him, and gave him a passionate kiss.

"Well, good morning to you, too. You were sound asleep when I got up, and so I thought I would start breakfast. But maybe we should go back to bed."

Alice looked into Alfred's piercing blue eyes and smiled. "If it were any other day, I would say absolutely. But I have an early morning fitting for a bride. Fortunately for me, German Jews are still getting married. How about this evening?"

"It's a date. Why don't you sit down and I will get you your breakfast and coffee."

Alice smiled at her husband. "You're a good man, Alfred Falkenstein."

As Alice was about to sit down, the telephone rang. It was too early for a customer call, but maybe her seamstress Bertha was sick. Following enactment of the Nuremberg Laws, Alice was forced to replace her two non-Jewish seamstresses with two Jewish seamstresses. About six months ago, she had to let one of those workers go. Unlike some of her competitors, who had been forced out of business, Alice still had work, but she had less work. Alice recognized that, in the future, she might also have to let Bertha go. That would leave just her and Ruth.

Alice answered the telephone. It was Hermann Schmidt, her fabric supplier. Since she opened her dressmaking business, Herr Schmidt had been her main fabric supplier. When her other suppliers stopped selling to Jews, Herr Schmidt had become her only supplier. Herr Schmidt was a good and honest man who seemed to have no problem supplying Alice with fabrics. They never spoke about politics – it was dangerous to discuss politics these days with anyone – but Alice had the sense that Herr Schmidt had no love for the Nazi government.

"Good morning, Herr Schmidt. How are you on this warm summer day? And how is that son of yours? Still giving you trouble?"

"Good morning, Frau Falkenstein. Busy as always. Thanks for asking about Rolf. I suspect he will always be an endless source of trouble for me. But he is doing deliveries today, so that should keep him out of trouble, at least for today. He is supposed to deliver fabrics to you today and that is why I am calling you. I received a directive from the government yesterday regarding materials we supply to Jewish businesses. We have been told to reduce those orders by ten percent. We have everything that you have asked for, but unfortunately, I must reduce the order by ten percent. They haven't told me how to reduce your order, so I thought I would ask you what you need now, and what you can put off until next month."

"Herr Schmidt, that is so kind of you to ask. I really need the blue wool and white cotton. I have someone coming in today for a fitting. The rest of the order can wait until next month. I understand the need to follow orders and I really appreciate you trying to help me. What time should I expect Rolf?"

"He should be there around 10 am. And, again, I am so sorry Frau Falkenstein."

"Herr Schmidt, I completely understand. And have a nice day."

Alice sat down at the table and took a sip of her coffee. She looked up at Alfred. He had heard her side of the conversation and understood. She sighed loudly and then said to Alfred, "I have been losing business because of the Nazis. And now they are cutting my supplies. I know Herr Schmidt was trying to be as accommodating as possible, but there is only so much that he can do. My guess is that this will not be the first directive restricting my supplies. They will keep issuing them until I am finally out of business."

Alfred sat down next to Alice, took her hand, and kissed it. He took a sip of his coffee. Alice and Alfred then ate in silence.

CHAPTER 10

Frankfurt, November 1938

November 9th started out cold, typical for a fall day. Alice woke up early and started the coffee. She had not been sleeping well lately and really needed the coffee. Alfred had stopped working – no German seemed to want to buy a watch from a Jew and his company finally had to let him go. Alice's business had also slowed down. She had some work, but could only afford to keep on Ruth. But she could not let Ruth go. Ruth needed the money and Alice needed the companionship. Plus, Ruth was the only member of her immediate family with an income, since the Nazi government had finally taken away Sam's license to practice dentistry.

Like all Jewish enterprises, the Nazi government had been trying to drive Jewish dressmakers out of business. For many years, the clothing and fashion industry in Germany had been dominated by Jews. Much of the leaders in the fashion industry were in Berlin, but even in Frankfurt, Jewish women like Alice were keeping the ladies well-dressed. The Nazis had been trying to close Jewish dressmaking businesses by replacing them with German fashion enterprises supported by the Nazi government. But the Frankfurt Fashion Office had essentially failed in its mission to recreate German high fashion. Now, the Nazis were trying a new approach to replacing Jews in German fashion. The Nazis established the Federation of German-Aryan Manufacturers of the Clothing Industry with the aim of permanently eliminating German Jews from the design, production, and sale of clothing and textiles. The designs were hideous, and only the most fervent of Nazi supporters had been wearing them, at least at the beginning. But Alice was seeing more and more of these designs on women and her non-Jewish customers had mostly disappeared. She wasn't sure how much longer she would be able to keep her business going, and how much longer she could continue to pay Ruth.

At 9 am sharp, Ruth knocked on the apartment door and came right in. Regardless of what was going on in her life or what anti-Jewish propaganda she saw on the way to work, Ruth always arrived with a smile on her face. "Good morning, Tante Alice. Ready to start the day?" For Alice, regardless of how she was feeling, seeing Ruth always made Alice feel better. "Let's first have a little coffee, Ruth. And then we can start on Frau Goldmann's dress." It was nice to still have some work to do.

After they finished their coffee, Ruth went to the table to cut the dress. Alice thought about how Ruth needed to leave Germany as soon as possible. Alice knew Henny had been in contact with the English cousin, but had not shared this news with Ruth. The Jewish Lehrhaus had been shut down by the Nazi government earlier in the year, and so there was less concern with Ruth potentially jeopardizing her emigration application. In fact, as far as Alice could tell, her niece was only working for her and then returning home to her parents.

It was hard, at times, for Alice to remain optimistic, both about her ability to escape from Germany and her ability to survive in Germany. Until 1938, she felt that she and Alfred would be able to handle the various edicts issued by the German government. While Alfred could no longer work as a watch salesman, Alice's dressmaking business was still functioning, and Alfred was keeping busy helping his wife. But things changed dramatically for all German Jews in 1938. For Jews who were lucky enough to obtain a visa, the increases in taxes and the application of other fees now meant that they could take no assets with them when they finally emigrated. And in order to ship goods overseas, Jews now had to obtain approval from the Foreign Exchange Office of all items to be shipped and to pay a tax on any items purchased after January 1, 1933. No jewelry or works of art could be shipped abroad. All Jews – even those who had not applied to emigrate – had to register all of their assets, at the values determined by the Nazi government, and to open a blocked bank account. And all Jews had to seek permission to withdraw any amount from those blocked accounts. The Nazi government now controlled the lives of all German Jews.

German Jews were somewhat encouraged by the announcement in June 1938 that representatives from 32 nations and 40 private aid organizations would be meeting in Evian, France to discuss the current plight of German Jews. While German authorities continued to impose more and more onerous requirements on German Jews, they still seemed committed to forcing Jews to leave Germany. The challenge had been finding a country that would allow all the German Jews to emigrate. The U.S. government had recently eased some of their restrictions for immigration, but it still remained a significant challenge to obtain the coveted U.S. visa. On the other hand, after years of permitting German Jewish emigration, Palestine's borders were now virtually closed to German Jewish immigration. After nine days of discussions, only the Dominican Republic expressed a willingness to take a large number of refugees. Alice was disappointed when she saw the news in the *Frankfurter Zeitung*. And scared – in the same article, German government officials said that they would need to take more drastic actions to make Germany "Judenfrei," or Jew free.

Of course, it didn't help Alice's mood that her brother Jacob and his wife Johanna had just received their U.S. visas, and were leaving for America at the end of the month. Benno had told Alice that Jacob had received the tax clearance certificate from the German finance office at the beginning of the year, which then enabled Jacob and his wife Johanna to obtain their passports to leave Germany. Alice suspected it was Alfred's complaint about those made-up taxes that the tax office claimed they owed that was preventing them from receiving their tax clearances. Maybe Alfred should just pay the taxes and be done with it. And they were still waiting for approval of the contract for the sale of his mother's building. Because they had been having trouble with the sale – no one wanted to buy a building owned by Jews – they finally accepted an offer for RM 24,000. But now the Nazi authorities were reluctant to approve the sale, since it was RM 3,000 less than the assessed value. They really needed to sell that building, to pay their existing taxes and likely future obligations. Alice felt like she was in a hole, which kept getting deeper. It didn't seem fair that Jacob, with his substantial business interests, was able to get a tax clearance certificate. But it was her understanding that Jacob had abandoned all interest in Gebrüder Heppenheimer and was leaving Germany with nothing. In fact, their son Ernst, who had emigrated to America in 1934, was paying for his parents' boat passages to America.

Alice looked over at her niece, who was hard at work, and asked, "Ruth, have you heard anything back from the finance office about your tax clearance certificate?"

"No, Tante Alice. Nothing yet. Mama is getting a little nervous. She knows she needs to wait until the sale of the building has been approved, just like you and Onkel Alfred, but she hoped she could separate me from them for tax purposes. But I told her it didn't matter because I would not leave without them."

Alice knew better than to weigh in on this issue. She was in total agreement with Henny and Sam, but she didn't need to get involved directly. At least, not yet. Regardless of what was going on with the sale of the building, if there was an opportunity for Ruth to leave – like going to England – she needed to take advantage of it. Alice thought of her nephew Kurt, who had escaped alone to America a year ago, when he was scarcely 17 years old. If Kurt could leave on his own at 17, her beloved Ruth could certainly leave on her own at 19.

"Ruth, it really is just so hard to know that all of us want to leave, and need to leave, and we can't make it happen. But I know your mom is doing everything she can." It was really frustrating for Alice that she had been trying for two years to get out of Germany. Other than Selma and Benno, all of her other siblings had been trying to leave. Her oldest sister Bertha was hoping to obtain her tax clearance certificate soon. And her sister Johanna was also trying to obtain a tax clearance certificate and was having trouble. Alice suspected that Johanna's problems had less to do with her and her husband Isadore and more to do with Johanna's son-in-law Franz Neumeier. Franz and Johanna's daughter Martha had just escaped to Switzerland, leaving behind a substantial amount of money in a blocked account, and also likely had a substantial amount of money waiting for them in a Swiss bank account. The Nazis might be punishing Johanna and her husband for Franz's success in escaping Germany with money. And also might be using them to steal all of Franz's money that remained in the blocked account.

Alice joined her niece at the cutting table. She was thinking how nice it was that they still had work. But Alice couldn't help but think about Jacob. It just didn't seem fair. Although she would love to see how he fared in New York, without people to boss around or a car to drive him around. How will a man who was used to having everything do in a foreign country in a foreign language with no money? Well, at least he will be away from this nightmare, she thought.

• • •

After Ruth left for the day, Alfred and Alice had an early dinner and went to bed around 9 pm. Alice was tired from a full day of sewing and Alfred was also tired, having spent most of the day running errands for Alice's business. Alice was sound asleep when she heard a noise. At first, she thought it was the neighbor's cats.

They had been knocking over garbage cans recently and waking up much of the neighborhood. She rolled over, annoyed at having been awakened. And then she heard another noise, much louder this time. She looked at the clock. It was 4:30 am. What was going on?

Alice grabbed her robe, trying not to wake Alfred, and walked into the living room. She looked out the window and saw bands of men with clubs and torches, yelling. The only words she could make out were "Jews out." Now she understood. She went back to the bedroom and woke up Alfred. "Something is going on outside." Alfred looked out the window and said, "Alice, we need to stay inside and away from the windows. For the moment, this is probably the safest place to be." Alice agreed, but neither of them could go back to sleep. Instead, Alice made them coffee and they sat at the dining room table, listening to the yelling and glass breaking, waiting for the sun to rise.

Things grew quiet in the late morning, and so Alfred and Alice left the apartment to see what had happened. Nothing was amiss in front of their apartment, but when they walked to the Zeil, the main shopping street in Frankfurt, there was glass everywhere. "Jew" was written in paint across the doors of Jewish-owned businesses, along with swastikas and Jewish stars. These were stores Alice had gone to for years. Some stores were even owned by her competitors. They ran into an acquaintance as they were walking, Frau Blum, who told them, "The Nazis have broken the windows of all the Jewish businesses they could find. And they even set fire to all the synagogues. What else are they going to do to us?" Alice could see that the woman was distraught, and so she hugged her. Alice and Alfred decided that there was nothing more to see. Plus, they didn't feel safe outside. They walked to Selma's apartment and then to Ruth's place to make sure that everyone was safe. Alice told Ruth not to come to work that day, or the next few days, at least until things quieted down. And then she and Alfred went to one more place.

They walked the few blocks to the West End Synagogue. They stood on the street across from the synagogue with a few others.

The building was on fire and many of the windows were broken. Across the street, young boys were yelling and cheering. Then the boys looked menacingly at Alice and Alfred. Alice said "Let's go," and they both walked home in silence. As she crossed the threshold to her apartment, Alice could feel the first of what she knew would be a flood of tears rolling down her cheeks.

•   •   •

A few days later day – November 13th – there was a knock at the door. It was mid-morning, but a knock at any time of the day made Alice nervous. She answered the door. It was Benno, and he looked ghost-white. He looked past Alice and saw Alfred sitting in a chair. "Oh good, you are still here," he said to Alfred. Alice asked, alarmed, "What do you mean? And what's wrong? But first, come in."

Benno came into the apartment, and Alice got him a glass of water. Benno drank until the glass was empty, and then said, "I was just released by the police. I haven't even been home yet. I had gone to our office building to make sure it was okay – you know it's just a block from the Borneplatz synagogue and I had heard that the synagogue was completely destroyed. Fortunately, nothing happened to our offices. Although I don't know why I care, since the government is pressuring me to sell the building. After I left the building, a Gestapo officer stopped me and asked me my name. Then he asked if I was Jewish. I said yes and he took me down to the police station. They took out my file – I didn't even know I had a file – and saw that I had a hearing loss from the war and released me. But the officer who released me told me they were arresting all Jewish men starting today. I came here to see if Alfred had been arrested."

Alice stared at her brother. "Arresting Jewish men? Why? That's crazy!"

"I don't know why. All I heard from the officer is that they are arresting Jewish men and taking them to police stations. I need to get home. Margot will be crazy with worry if she has heard about the arrests. I am sorry to bring you such news. Hopefully, what the officer told me is wrong. I just wanted to let you know."

"Benno, thank you for coming. I am not sure what we can do, but maybe they won't take Alfred. Maybe they are only arresting men who they see walking outside." Alice hugged her brother tight, and then he left.

Alice turned to Alfred. "What should we do? It probably makes little sense to go down to the police station to ask if this is true. Maybe I will just go outside and walk around and try to find some people to talk to. I should be safe."

"I will go with you."

"Absolutely not. If they are arresting Jewish men, the last place you should be is outside. You wait here. I will be gone no more than an hour. I could also do a little dress shopping and maybe have my hair done while I am out." Alfred smiled weakly and said, "Okay, I will stay inside."

Alice left the apartment and began to walk around the neighborhood. Initially, she didn't see anyone she recognized, but eventually she saw people she knew. But they were only women. The men seemed to be staying inside. She could tell that people wanted to talk, but were a bit reluctant. Or perhaps, shell-shocked. She finally went over to Hannah Feldmann. Hannah always seemed to know what was going on and was always willing to share. Some thought she shared a bit too much.

"Hello, Hannah. How are you?"

"Hello, Alice. What terrible times. Are you and Alfred okay?

"Yes, we are. Hannah, have you heard anything about Jewish men being arrested?"

Hannah was not married, but she knew lots of married couples and would know about such arrests. "I just heard from Frau Rosenbaum that her husband was just arrested as they were walking home from the store, and others have said to me they heard that an edict had been issued by the Nazis to arrest all Jewish men. Someone said that the purpose was to force Jews to leave Germany."

Alice almost wanted to laugh when she heard this last statement. Force us to leave Germany? We have been trying to leave for two years! She said goodbye to her friend and continued to wander around the neighborhood. She needed to get more information.

After speaking with a few other people she knew, Alice thought it was time to go home. She looked down at her watch – she had been gone nearly two hours, longer than she had intended. Alfred might be a little worried, but she needed to try to find out what she could. She learned only a little more than what she had heard from Benno. Perhaps she would learn more later.

She climbed the stairs to her apartment and opened the door. She called out to Alfred, but heard nothing. She called out again, louder, but still nothing. Alfred had promised not to leave the apartment. Alice knew he would not have left on his own. Where was he? And then she knew – they had already come for him.

•   •   •

Alice had to stop at several police stations before she was finally able to find where Alfred had been taken. She spoke with the police officer in charge of arrests. He confirmed for her that Alfred had indeed been arrested and that he was being held in a cell with others. But the officer would not tell her why Alfred was arrested and how long he would be held in jail. Instead, he told her to go home. "I'm sure he will be home soon enough," he said with a sinister smile.

Alice left the police station and walked to Benno's apartment. Margot answered the door and called for Benno. Alice could barely get the words out – "They arrested Alfred. I wasn't even home when they arrested him." And then Alice began to cry. She sobbed uncontrollably. It must have been all the tears held back for the last few years. She was not sure how long she cried, but at some point she was aware that she was sitting on the couch, and both of Benno's sons were staring at her. Her natural inclination would be to tell the boys not to worry, that she was okay. But she was not okay, and everything would not be alright. But she suspected they already knew that.

Benno sat down next to her. "Tell me everything." Alice told him everything she knew.

"Alice, I have learned a little more since I came to your place. They are putting them on a train tonight and taking them to a place call Buchenwald. No one I spoke with knows anything about this place. It is supposed to be close to Weimar. And no one seems to know what they will do with them once they get them there and how long it will be before they can come back. But from what I am hearing, they are arresting Jewish men all over Germany."

"Do you know what time the train is leaving?"

"I heard the train is leaving at 7 pm. But I hope you are not thinking about going to the station. It is too dangerous. There will be Hitler youth all over the place. The SS have practically advertised that Jews will be at the train station this evening. Please don't go."

"I'll have to think about it. I understand what you're saying. If I go – and I haven't decided that I will – I won't draw attention to myself. I will be almost invisible." But she had already decided to go. How could she not?

• • •

Alice walked to the train station in the late afternoon – she had only been back to her apartment long enough to change her shoes and grab a quick bite. It took about 45 minutes to walk there, but she needed the walk to calm her nerves. By the time she arrived at the station, a crowd had already formed. Almost everyone in the crowd was young, and so she was mindful not to stand out. She was there about an hour when someone yell "There they are!" She turned to see a sea of men in coats and hats walking towards the train. The crowd started to jeer and some even threw rocks. None of the police officers and SS were doing anything to control the crowd and the crowd knew it. Alice just hoped that Alfred would be safe.

And then she saw him. He looked a little disheveled and he might have had the beginnings of a black eye, but otherwise he looked okay. He was not limping, like some of the other men. For some reason, Alfred looked up at that moment and then looked over in her direction. He saw her! He placed his fingers on his lips and then touched his heart. And then he looked straight ahead. He did not want Alice to return the gesture. He did not want her to draw attention to herself. Instead, Alice repeated the gesture, but in her mind. It brought her some comfort. The crowd was getting louder and more aggressive with their rock throwing, but she could see, with some relief, that Alfred had boarded the train without being hit.

Alice stayed until the last man boarded the train. She stayed until the train had left the station. She stayed until the last of the Hitler youth and SS had gone home. She stayed until it was completely dark and she was alone on the street, and then she walked home. She entered her quiet apartment and closed the door. She sat on the couch, and for the second time that day, she sobbed. And this time, she sobbed herself to sleep.

•   •   •

Alice was still asleep on the couch – still in her clothes from the night before – when there was a knock at the door. Could it be Alfred? She ran to the door and opened it. It was Ruth. Ruth! She had completely forgotten about Ruth. It occurred to her she hadn't spoken to Ruth since she first checked on her and her parents the morning of the 10th. That morning, she had told Ruth not to come to work until things had quieted down. That was four days ago. She had called a few times since, but no one had answered the telephone. She was about to apologize for not speaking with Ruth about returning to work when she saw Ruth's face. Ruth had been crying.

"Ruth, tell me."

"They came to our apartment yesterday and arrested Papa. We don't know where they took him. Mama went to the police station yesterday, but they told her nothing. We called you yesterday and last night, but no one answered the telephone. Mama went back again this morning. I told her I was coming here, since I was a little worried about you and Uncle Alfred, and Mama will come here after she is finished. By the way, where is Uncle Alfred?"

"They also arrested him yesterday." That statement was too much for Ruth to hear. She started to sob and fell into Alice's arms. Alice told herself to be strong for Ruth, but she too began to sob. Alice took her niece to the dining room table, told her to sit down, and she made them both breakfast. By the time she returned to the table, Ruth had stopped crying.

Drinking their coffee, Alice told Ruth everything she knew. Ruth listened, but said nothing. When Alice was finished, Ruth asked if she should get to work. Alice assumed Ruth didn't know what to do with herself, and so asked about work. Alice really did love this child!

"No, Ruth, today there will be no work. We will wait for your mother and then we will do something. But it won't be work."

Fortunately, they didn't have to wait long. About thirty minutes later, Henny knocked on the door. Henny seemed surprisingly calm, but Alice knew this was her way of not falling apart. The two women shared what information they had, and then the three of them became quiet. Alice was about to suggest that they go outside to try to find out more information when Henny spoke up.

"Ruth, I am going to say something to you and I know that this will be hard for you to hear, but your father and I have spoken about this and we both agree. I don't know how long it will take for us to get our US visas. We still haven't received approval for the sale of your grandmother's building and until then, your father and I cannot get our passports. But I would feel so much better if you were out of Germany. Papa's cousin Dr. Strauss from England said that you could come live with him, and you would be safer there until you can get your US visa. You owe no taxes. We might be able to speed the process for obtaining your tax clearance certificate and get your passport if it is only you applying to emigrate to England. We will still keep our names on the waiting list for the US visas. But Ruth, you need to go."

Ruth looked at her mom and then at Alice. Alice knew what Ruth was thinking – that her mother was right, but also that there was no way of changing her mother's mind. And Alice could also tell that it was breaking Ruth's heart. Ruth took a deep breath and quietly said, "Okay, Mama." And then she broke down crying.

CHAPTER 11

Frankfurt, July 1939

Alice looked down at her watch. It was nearly noon, and she was hungry. She got up from her chair and walked over to Alfred, who was reading the newspaper. She gently touched his arm, and he looked up at her.

"Are you hungry? I thought I would make us some lunch."

He smiled at her. "I am a little hungry, schatzi. Lunch would be nice. Thanks."

She lightly squeezed his shoulder and walked into the kitchen. She didn't know why, but it always made her feel better to touch him. A squeeze of the shoulder or just a pat on his arm. He had returned from Buchenwald over six months ago, and yet she still found the need to touch him. Sometimes it was an almost uncontrollable urge to hug and hold him, but more often it was just a simple touch. Perhaps it was her way of assuring herself that he was actually here, that he had made it home from that horrible camp. Or perhaps it was her fear that he could be taken away again, at any moment.

She hoped he didn't notice the change, that he didn't notice that she was more anxious. And needed the reassurance of a touch. The problem was that they were home on most days, with little to do. Alice had no work and Alfred had no work. And with no work distractions, Alice worried Alfred would notice. But Alice had other worries. The only money coming in was from Alice's sister Johanna, who could provide them with money from the account left behind by her son-in-law Franz; but that wasn't much. The Foreign Exchange Office, which was in charge of the finances of German Jews, only allowed Johanna to give Alice RM 20 per month. Alice and Alfred were both trying to find work, but it wasn't easy. They were now living off of what little was left from their savings, and had actually begun selling furniture and other household items.

Alice had no work since the end of 1938. After Kristallnacht in November 1938, the Nazis issued a number of decrees that made it impossible for Jews to be hired for any work, other than a government-directed forced labor position. And on December 3, 1938, a Decree on the Utilization of Jewish Assets ordered the closure of all remaining Jewish businesses. Alice was forced to liquidate her dressmaking business, which she had begun while Alfred was in Buchenwald.

Alice often thought about that awful day, the day Alfred was taken, as well as the days that followed. After about a week of almost daily efforts to obtain information, she was finally told what she needed to do to get him home – she needed to provide proof that she and Alfred were serious about leaving Germany. Alice was at a loss as to what more she could provide to show that she was serious. They still had the problem with the taxes owed the government, which Alfred had been trying to resolve. She explained that to the officer, but he still wanted more. What more could she give him?

One day at the end of December, while Alice was reviewing some records related to the liquidation of her business, there was a knock at the door. When she opened the door, she saw standing before her a gaunt and sallow-looking man, wearing striped pajamas and an ill-fitting coat. It took her a second to realize that it was Alfred. She dropped the papers she was holding and hugged him tight. She heard a small gasp come from Alfred and she couldn't tell if it was pain or relief. She let him go.

The first thing she could think to ask him was "Why did you knock?" What a stupid question. But he answered, "Because I forgot my key." They both then laughed, mostly from relief. Alfred was home, even if he was a little worse for wear.

Alfred took off his coat and sat on the couch. Alice brought him a cup of coffee and cookies. "Don't worry about the cookies. Selma made them." Alfred smiled, almost to himself, and took a bite.

"This cookie is quite good. Your sister really does have a talent for cooking and baking."

Alice was pacing the room. She wasn't sure what to do or say next. "You look like you need a bath. Let me draw you a bath. It will take just a second."

"Soon, Alice. It has been a long time since I could just sit and drink coffee and eat a cookie. And let me enjoy just being with you. Please sit with me." Alice sat down next to Alfred. They sat in silence for a while, neither ready to discuss the last seven weeks. At some point, they started to hold hands. Finally, Alfred sighed and said, "Alice, I am so glad to be home. And I guess I am ready for that bath now."

While Alfred was imprisoned, Alice had heard troubling things about Buchenwald. Buchenwald had only recently been built and was ill-equipped for the over 10,000 Jewish men sent there. Some of those in Buchenwald were required to work in the quarry. She had hoped that Alfred would avoid the quarry. Alice had been told that the intent of sending the men to Buchenwald was to push them further to emigrate. Alfred was already motivated to emigrate. Sending him to Buchenwald was just plain evil.

In the first week after his return, Alfred had been relatively quiet and spoke little about Buchenwald. But he finally opened up to Alice about his time in the camp. Alfred told her that, during the first few days in Buchenwald, there was little to eat or drink and the men were mostly placed in temporary housing, forced to sleep in the cold on wooden boards. On the third day, Alfred was given army boots and a stripped prisoner's suit and cap, and moved to more permanent housing. There were daily beatings of prisoners, and many suffered from diarrhea. They were awakened at 5 am each morning, forced to stand at roll-call for more than an hour, and then sent to work. There was little to eat in the morning, and dinner generally comprised a small piece of cheese or sausage. Unfortunately for Alfred, he was forced to work in the quarry, and Alice could tell that the work must have been brutal, based on the calluses on his hands and a lingering cough. But Alfred was gaining back the weight he had lost. And his incarceration had also increased Alfred's drive to resolve the tax issues with the finance office, so perhaps the Nazis had succeeded in their goal.

But now the Nazi government placed another roadblock in front of Alfred and Alice. After Kristallnacht, the Nazis imposed a Jewish levy to cover the cost of the damage wreaked by the hooligans, which required that all Jews pay a fine equal to a fifth of their assets. And the levy would be based on the assessed value of the assets as of April 1938, when all Jews had been required to report their assets to the Nazi authorities. At the time, Alfred's mother's building had been assessed by the Nazi government at RM 27,000, but it had been sold for RM 24,000. Still, the Nazi authorities were assessing the levy based on the RM 27,000 figure. So, Alfred and Alice not only owed the taxes from 1937, but now owed the tax authorities new taxes based on the assessed amount of the building. And the sale had still not yet been approved by the Foreign Exchange Office, so Alice and Alfred had no money to pay the taxes.

For two years, Alfred had been trying to resolve the 1937 tax issue. Alice told Alfred that she would try to get money from her sister Johanna to pay the older tax. In terms of the new tax, maybe the Nazi authorities would be reasonable, Alice told Alfred. After all, it wasn't their fault that the only person willing to buy Alfred's mother's building would only offer RM 24,000. They both agreed that they would contact the tax authorities and pay the earlier tax (she was sure Johanna would give them the money), but ask that they be allowed to pay the levy based on the RM 24,000 figure. Even after paying off the RM 15,000 mortgage, Alfred and his sister would still have money left to pay for some of the various expenses to emigrate. With no work, Alice made it her mission after Alfred returned from Buchenwald to resolve all of their tax issues and finally obtain the tax clearance certificate.

•   •   •

After lunch, Alfred took a nap. The day was an unusually hot one, even for the end of July. Alice opened all the windows in the living room, but the effort brought little relief. Alice wished she had some place to go. Unfortunately, no more visits to the Niederrad Light and Air Bath. The Frankfurt government had permitted Jews to visit the Niederrad Bath during the summers of 1937 and 1938, but the Frankfurt mayor revoked the Jewish community's lease after the 1938 season and instead leased the resort to the Nazi SA group of Hesse. The storm troopers were no longer the force they had been in the 1920s, having been eclipsed by the SS. Still, they remained a threat to German Jews. And now they had access to one of the few places where Alice had been able to escape the heat and pretend, at least for a few hours, that life had returned to normal.

Instead, Alice sat at the dining table, drinking a cup of cold ersatz coffee and thinking about all the efforts they had made since Alfred's return from Buchenwald to resolve their tax issues. Johanna had given them money the previous week to pay off the 1937 taxes the finance office claimed they owed (even though both knew that the tax bill was a fabrication). Alfred wrote multiple letters to the finance office trying to resolve the current tax issue caused by the imposition of the Jewish Levy, but so far, the issue had not been resolved, and Alice was worried. Then Alice started thinking about Ruth. She was relieved that their efforts had been a success. Ruth had left for England last month, and was now living with the family's cousin, Dr. Strauss. Henny had worked hard to get Ruth's tax clearance certificate and passport. By the time Sam was released from Buchenwald in December of last year, most of the documents needed for emigration were in place. And then Ruth got lucky. After Kristallnacht, England had eased its immigration regulations for Jewish refugees, and Ruth was able to escape Germany. At least something had worked out.

Ruth had told Alice how torn she was about leaving her parents, particularly her father. Sam's health had been poor since his return from Buchenwald; his high blood pressure, which had been under control, was worse, and now he was suffering from kidney disease. This dentist to the neighborhood had laid mostly in bed since his return.

The day of Ruth's departure was hard for everyone. Ruth was scheduled to leave in the morning, taking the train to Hamburg. The boat from Hamburg to England would be leaving the following day. Ruth had already packed her one suitcase, which had been inspected and approved by a customs officer. She could only take with her RM 10. But she wasn't worried; her cousin would provide her with whatever she needed. She was mostly concerned about how her parents would do after she was gone. And the reality of her father's health had finally hit Ruth – would she ever see him again? Alice and Alfred accompanied Henny and Ruth to the train station; Sam was too ill to leave the apartment, and Ruth had said her goodbyes to him there. The family all hugged Ruth and then she was gone. They all felt like a giant hole had just opened before them.

Henny called Alice a few days later to let her know that Ruth was safely in England. Ruth had telephoned her mother. Long distance! But her cousin had insisted.

Sitting at the dining table and thinking about her niece, Alice was missing their easy banter. It had really been fun working with Ruth. Alice was already missing her more than she could have imagined. She took another sip of her cold coffee and was startled out of her day-dreaming. There were three loud bangs at the door. No friend would knock like that. She had her suspicions of who it was. When she opened the door, she was right – the Gestapo. What could they possibly want now?

The Gestapo knew where every Jew lived, since all German Jews were required to register with the Gestapo at the beginning of the year. And all Jews had to take on new middle names: Sara for women and Israel for men. Because the Gestapo knew where the Jews lived, they would randomly harass Jews in their apartments. Alice had assumed it was their turn for harassment.

"We are here to see Alfred Israel Falkenstein. Where is he?" Their manner seemed more "official" than simple harassment.

"Just a minute. I will get him."

Alice left the living room and went into their bedroom. She gently woke Alfred from his nap. Alfred looked up and asked, "What is it, schatzi?"

"Dear, the Gestapo are here. They want to speak with you."

Alfred quickly got out of bed, and put on a shirt, tie, and jacket. He wanted to be properly dressed when he faced the Gestapo. He entered the living room and asked them what this was all about.

"Alfred Israel Falkenstein, you are being charged with violation of the Nuremberg Laws for Racial Defilement. Please come with us."

Alfred's jaw dropped. "What are you talking about?"

"No questions. Come with us."

With that, they each grabbed an arm and pulled Alfred down the stairs. They pushed him through the building's doors, into the waiting car, and then drove off. Alice had followed them out of the apartment building. She knew better than to say anything to the Gestapo. She now stood in the street in her housedress, staring at the car as it drove off.

What now?!?

•   •   •

Alice dressed quickly, grabbed her purse, and went to the local police station. She had hoped the Gestapo had taken Alfred there and she was right. She had to wait two hours before anyone would speak with her. When an officer finally did, all he would say was that Alfred was being held in a jail cell and that she should find a Jewish lawyer. Alice wanted to say that there were no Jewish "lawyers" left in Germany, but she held her tongue. She merely said "Thank you" and left.

Alice's head was swimming and she was alternating between frustration and anger. What was going on? Racial defilement? She knew that racial defilement under the Nuremberg Laws meant sex between a Jew and a non-Jew, which was now illegal. Could Alfred be having an affair with a non-Jewish woman? Could he be that stupid? And then Alice asked herself, "How well do I really know this man I had married? After all, I have only been married to him for three years. Plus, he had told me he had had extra-marital relations while he was married to Erna. Had he engaged in this same behavior?" But she had to stop thinking about that now. She needed to find a Jewish lawyer. But where was she going to find a Jewish lawyer? And then she remembered – Selma.

Alice knew Selma and Leo were virtually enemies and that Selma had been sleeping in her mother's bedroom. But when Selma and her mother came for dinner last month, Selma surprised Alice by announcing that she had hired Siegfried Popper to help her obtain a divorce from Leo.

"A divorce? Why would you want to obtain a divorce now? With everything that is going on, why do you need a divorce? Why don't you and Mama just leave the apartment? Move in with me and Alfred. Plus, from everything I have heard, it would just make it harder to obtain an American visa." Alice had still not given up trying to get her sister to leave Germany.

"Mama and I are planning to leave the apartment soon. I really can't stand living with that man. But I also can't stand being married to him. Alice, you know what it's like to need to divorce someone." Alice wanted to say that that was a different time, but what was the point?

"Anyway, my lawyer Dr. Popper sent Leo a letter telling him I was contemplating a divorce and you won't believe what Leo said in response. He said he didn't care since he was emigrating to Palestine. Apparently, his five siblings have recently moved to Frankfurt and all of them are going to Palestine. He said that they would be receiving special visas to go through Trieste in Italy, even though the Palestine borders are otherwise closed to Jews. And he specifically said that I could not go with him, like I would ever go with him."

"Wow, Leo is going to Palestine." Alice was a little jealous, not about going to Palestine, but about going anywhere. And then Alice noticed her sister appeared angry. "Selma, are you upset about his leaving?"

"I don't care if he stays or goes, but how are Mama and I going to live? He was never much of a provider, but with him gone, we will have less money." She wanted to tell her sister to drop Dr. Popper and then she would have less financial troubles. But it was clear Selma was intent on the divorce, and Alice knew better than to try to convince her otherwise.

But now Alice needed a lawyer, or whatever he called himself these days. She knew Jewish lawyers could no longer be called lawyers. She believed they were now called "consultants." Her sister had told her that Dr. Popper's office was on Neue Mainserstrasse, and so she walked there, without an appointment. The walk was short and she was still a jumble of emotions when she knocked on the door. A short man with grey hair who appeared to be in his mid-50s answered the door. She assumed this was Dr. Popper.

"May I help you?"

"Dr. Popper, my name is Alice Falkenstein. You are helping my sister Selma Lewin with her divorce. I am hoping you can help me."

Dr. Popper gave her a sympathetic smile and led her into the foyer. They walked down the hallway, through a large space, and into his office. She could tell that, at some point, there had been a receptionist and other lawyers working for Dr. Popper. Now he was the only person working in the space. He left her to get them both some coffee. While he was gone, she looked at his wall. She saw a framed diploma from the University of Frankfurt, his license to practice law, several awards, and pictures of him with who she imagined were important people.

Dr. Popper noticed Alice looking at the wall. "My wife used to call that my 'Wall of Fame.' Of course, that was when I was a lawyer. Now, none of this counts anymore. I suppose I should just take everything down, although I am not quite ready."

"Dr. Popper, I completely understand. Things keep changing so fast and none of us is ever ready."

"Well said, but enough about my problems. Please have a seat and tell me why you are here."

Alice told him everything she knew, which was not much. He had a very sympathetic manner, which made Alice feel better. It was also comforting to have someone who could help her through this mess. At least she hoped he could help.

"As I am sure you can imagine, violation of the Nuremberg Laws is a very serious charge. I will do everything I can to help you, Frau Falkenstein. As I said, I am no longer a lawyer. Most lawyers lost their licenses to practice law in 1933, but a few of us were able to continue practicing until last November, just after Kristallnacht, when a total ban went into effect. But nine of us were granted special permission to practice as Jewish consultants, mostly to help other Jews with emigration issues, but also because non-Jewish lawyers cannot help Jews. So that is where we are now."

"Dr. Popper, before we go any further, I need to tell you I am not sure how much I can pay you. We have been struggling with tax issues, and who knows what Alfred's arrest will do to our current finances."

"Frau Falkenstein, please don't worry about that. Your focus right now needs to be on trying to get your husband out of jail. We will work out a payment arrangement once everything is resolved. Right now, I will go down to the police station and try to obtain the charging document. And I will try to speak with your husband and try to arrange for you to speak with him as well." For the first time since Alfred's arrest, Alice could finally breathe. All she could say was "Thank you," but that said it all.

• • •

Alice had been home about an hour when the telephone rang. It was Dr. Popper.

"I have seen the charging document and I have spoken with your husband. The officers agreed to allow you to speak with your husband at 4 pm today. Meet me at my office at 3:30 pm, and we can walk over together."

Alice was at Dr. Popper's office at 3:30 pm sharp, and they left together.

"Frau Falkenstein, it is a nice day to walk and I often spend too much time inside. Let's walk to the station and I will let you know what I have learned so far. According to the charging document, your husband had an affair in the beginning of 1936 with a Fräulein Betti Herbst, who lives in Nuremberg. Because the Nuremberg Laws were already in effect at the time, that would have been a violation of the law. I asked your husband about the charge. He told me he had dated Fräulein Herbst around 1930, but had stopped seeing her because, and these are your husband's words, the woman was crazy. He said that he saw her again, probably in 1936, when they were both on a train new Nuremberg while he was travelling on business. He said that she was being a little inappropriate with him and she was making him nervous. Nuremberg had grown especially anti-Semitic by that point and he didn't want to draw any attention to himself. Fräulein Herbst looked at his hand and noticed a ring and said that it would be really nice if she had a souvenir from him. He took off the ring and gave it to her. She then said that it would be nice if they could get dinner together. He told her he couldn't because he was moving to Frankfurt and walked away. He changed rail cars, and she didn't follow him. He said that nothing else happened."

Alice listened carefully to everything that Dr. Popper said. 1930 was around the time that Erna and Alfred were getting a divorce. Erna never shared with Alice why they were divorcing. On their first date, Alfred had mentioned that he had had extra-marital relations during his marriage. Alice never asked him about his dating history after Erna, but assumed there had been other women, maybe even non-Jewish women. After all, Erna was not Jewish. What if Fräulein Herbst is telling the truth?

Before she knew it, they were at the police station. They entered the station, and were then led down the hall to a small room with a few chairs. She and Dr. Popper sat down, and in about five minutes, the door opened and Alfred was led into the room. Alfred looked overwhelmed and it took a second for him to realize who was in the room. He walked over to Alice and hugged her. "Alice, I am so sorry this is happening. This is so crazy. Did Dr. Popper tell you what I told him?"

"He did, but I need to hear it from you. Did you have an affair with this woman just before our wedding?"

Alfred looked directly into Alice's eyes. "No, I did not. I barely remember this. When Dr. Popper told me about the charges, I then remembered this woman asking me for the ring. I had dated her for about six months after my divorce from Erna. She was crazy and so I stopped the relationship. When I first saw her on that train, I looked away and hoped that she didn't see me. No such luck. I can't believe I told her I was moving to Frankfurt. I don't know how this all happened, but she must have told someone about the ring and that I was living in Frankfurt. But she is completely lying about us having an affair. Alice, I would never do that to you. I need you to believe me."

Alice stared hard at Alfred. She wanted to believe him. In the three years since they married, he had never given her reason to worry. But she was reminded that she really knew little about why his marriage failed or the years after his divorce. And do you ever really know someone completely? She was starting to make herself a little crazy and she needed to focus on what to do next. And she needed to reassure Alfred, since Alfred would be returning to a jail cell. And she needed to be clear-headed for a different reason -- violation of the Nuremberg Laws could mean a long prison term or even a death sentence.

So she needed to be strong for Alfred – and for herself. Even if she had doubts, she needed to put them aside. "I do believe you Alfred. So, Dr. Popper, what do you need me to do?"

• • •

Since the Nazis came to power in 1933, there had been many bad days for Alice. Max's suicide, Kristallnacht, the forced closure of her business. But as Alice crossed the threshold to her empty apartment, she thought to herself that today was one of the worst.

When Alfred was arrested after Kristallnacht, he was gone for nearly two months. That time felt like forever to Alice. As she put down her purse on the table near the door, she thought, "What if, this time, he never comes home?" She knew about men who had died in Buchenwald. Alfred could have been one of those men. He could be beaten in jail, or could be sent away to one of the camps she had been reading about. But as quickly as she thought of those horrible eventualities, she shook her head and said to herself, "No. I will not dwell on 'ifs' or 'maybes.' It would not help me or Alfred." Instead, Alice went into the kitchen, made herself a quick dinner and then sat down at the dining room table. Yesterday's paper was on the table, and she decided to read it while she was eating. That should calm her down.

The *Frankfurter Zeitung* had been founded by a Jew and had been a great supporter of the Weimar Republic, but was now little more than an arm of the Nazi Ministry of Propaganda. Still, Alfred liked to read the paper, trying to ignore the more troubling articles, and Alice often skimmed the headlines after Alfred was finished. Alice sat down with her dinner at the table, opened the paper, and scanned the articles. Nothing really interested her as she turned one page after another. And then she came to an article titled "Degenerate Art Exhibit Opens Today in Frankfurt." The article included a picture of Government officials attending an exhibit that had been travelling through Germany. Alice had read about this exhibit when it was first announced in 1937. Joseph Goebbels, the Minister of Propaganda, had ordered the confiscation of over twenty thousand works of art from Germany's art museums and had created this exhibit with some of those works. It had taken about two years to reach Frankfurt. According to the article, the exhibit included the "degenerate" paintings of Pablo Picasso, Edvard Munch, Vincent Van Gogh, and the "Jew" Marc Chagall. Alice had seen the works of all of these artists at Frankfurt's Städel Museum. It was actually the first time she had ever seen a work by Chagall. She loved the way he used color and structure in his Jewish-themed paintings. The contemporary art rooms at the Städel Museum had been closed in 1933, but the works had sat in a warehouse until they had been confiscated by Goebbels in 1937. These are the great masters, she thought to herself. Alice wanted to open and window and yell, "There is no such thing as degenerate art!!!" She was so angry that she could no longer sit. She got up from the table and started to pace. Back and forth, back and forth, back and forth. After a few minutes, she could feel herself calming down a little. And then she had an idea.

Alice took out her design folder, the folder where she kept all of her favorite purse and dress designs. She found a few blank sheets of paper. She thought about Chagall's unique images,

Picasso' unusual shapes, Van Gogh's bold textures. And then she thought about dresses she would like to design, incorporating all of those ideas. And then she started to draw those designs. The designs flowed from her pencil. It was as if the designs had been stuck behind a dam and the dam had just burst. She could not stop her pencil from moving. She could not stop herself from drawing. She was barely aware that time was passing. She kept drawing and drawing and drawing until her hand finally cramped and she could no longer draw. She looked up and saw that it was after 1 am. She had been drawing non-stop for five hours. She was exhausted. But she was also feeling calmer. She put down her design book and turned off the lights.

Alice went into the bathroom and reached for her metal curlers. For the past few years, she had put her hair in curlers every night, so that she would have her waves in the morning. Previously, she had gone to a hairdresser, who used a permanent wave machine to give her the waves that were so fashionable. And while she could no longer visit the hairdresser, she was not ready to give up her waves, and so she set her hair every night. But what was the point now? Alfred was not home, and who knew when he would be home? And so, for the first time in a long time, Alice went to bed without her curlers, abandoning yet another part of her life.

•   •   •

Dr. Popper gave Alice a list of places she would need to contact. Alfred tended to stay in the same hotels when he travelled on business, and so Alice wrote to those hotels, asking whether they had proof that Alfred had been there and had checked in alone. She also wrote to Alfred's former employer, Robert Kauderer Company, hoping the company would have his travel schedule from that period. Unfortunately, none of the hotels responded to her request, and Alice was told that Alfred's former boss was on vacation in the Balkans and they did not know when he would return. She was running into one brick wall after another.

Alice was having another problem. With the likely expenses of Dr. Popper and with no income, she could no longer afford to pay rent. She and Alfred were already having financial challenges before his arrest. And with everything so uncertain, she could no longer justify the cost of the apartment. There was really only one place she could move to, at least in the interim, although she dreaded the conversation.

Alice walked to her sister's apartment the next day. She assumed they would all be there. Selma opened the door and smiled when she saw it was Alice.

"Alice, so nice to see you. Any news about Alfred?" It didn't even occur to Selma to wonder why her sister was there, without a prior call.

"Nothing has changed, although it has already been a month since his arrest. I am worried that I will not be able to find anything that would help to prove his innocence. But I am not here to talk about Alfred. Can we sit down?"

"Sure. Should I get Mama?"

"No. I only need to speak with you." They both sat down on the couch, and Alice began. "With Alfred in prison, I can't afford to stay in my place. And I can't really justify it, if it is just me. I was wondering, and this would only be until Alfred gets out of jail, if I could stay here. It would only be temporary. We will find a new apartment as soon as Alfred is released from jail."

"Alice, you don't need to ask. Of course you can stay here. And you can stay for as long as you like."

"But what about Leo?"

"Who cares about Leo? You will sleep in my room with me. Mama can sleep in the living room. Besides, he seems a little happier since he announced he will be leaving for Palestine. We are certainly fighting less. I will tell him you are staying, and he shouldn't care. But just in case, I will tell him about it after you leave. But I won't give him a choice."

"Selma, thank you so much. I will give notice on the apartment. I should be ready to move in about two weeks. Is that okay?"

"As far as I am concerned, you can move in now. And it will be great living with you again, even if it will be for just a short time."

Notwithstanding all the craziness in Selma's life, and all the craziness Selma sometimes imposed on others, Selma could always be relied upon if Alice ever needed a place to stay. "Thanks! I'll let you know when I am ready to move in."

That day was two weeks later. Alice made a few back-and-forth trips with Selma, who seemed to be enjoying herself. Alice also arranged for movers to move her remaining furniture, which they placed in a section of the living room of Selma's apartment. Alice could tell that Selma was really looking forward to having her sister live with her again. Of course, this would differ greatly from the last time the two lived together. Then, Alice was newly single and focused on her new career. And Selma was newly married and optimistic about her future. Now Alice was focused on getting her husband out of jail. And Selma was looking forward to getting rid of her husband for good.

While Alice was moving in, she noticed a large trunk and six large suitcases in the dining room. "Selma, why are a trunk and suitcases in the corner of the dining room?"

"Leo is trying to get customs approval for them to be sent to Trieste, and then to Palestine."

"But why so many suitcases? Leo has that much stuff to send?"

"No, his siblings came over last week with the suitcases and other bags. Apparently, this is all of their things. I heard them talking and they were worried that they were trying to send items they are not allowed to send. Leo told them to just put everything in the trunk and the suitcases and he would take care of it. But that is their issue, and I am staying out of it. I just really want Leo gone."

•   •   •

Alice was not sure how living with Leo, Selma, and her mother again would be. Alice slept in her mother's bed, and they set up Alice's bed in the living room for their mother. Selma was correct that Leo seemed happier, and even spoke with Alice a little about his up-coming emigration to Palestine. Leo and his five siblings all had their passports and they were simply waiting on their visas. Emigration to Palestine was now nearly impossible for German Jews, but Leo explained that he and his siblings had been able to secure special visas. But the trunk and six suitcases remained in the living room, and with each passing day, Leo seemed to get crankier and a little shorter with Selma. Leo had told Selma that he was trying to get a customs official to come and certify the contents, but so far no one had come. And this seemed to make Leo more and more anxious.

Alice was grateful to have a place to live and thought it was important to contribute some to the rent for the apartment. Alice would have offered to help cook, as well, but recognized that Selma was a much better cook. Alice was surprised at how well her sister took to cooking. Alice also knew that her mother did not like eating the non-kosher meat Selma was now cooking, but Emma never complained. Immediately after the Nazis came to power in 1933, ritual slaughter in Germany was banned, but the Jewish communities in Germany were able to negotiate with the Reich to import kosher meat from Denmark. Kosher meat remained available for purchase (at an inflated price) until Kristallnacht in 1938. After the pogrom, kosher meat was banned and could now only be purchased on the black market. After the ban was announced, Emma said that she was comfortable eating non-kosher meat, as long as Selma did not serve any pork. Emma did not want to put her daughter at risk by asking her to find kosher meat. The first time Selma cooked with non-kosher meat,

Alice was over for dinner (Alfred had just been taken to Buchenwald) and Emma complimented her daughter on the delicious stew. Alice wanted to hug her mother after she heard the compliment.

Alice found the main challenge in living in the apartment was finding moments of quiet. Since Kristallnacht, all Jews were banned from the cinema. But the reality was that it had been a number of years since Alice had any interest in going to movies in Germany. Before the Nazis came to power, Alice loved going to the movies with friends, particularly after the advent of sound. But since the Ministry of Propaganda had essentially taken over the German movie industry, the theaters were mostly showing Nazi-sponsored documentaries like "Triumph of the Will" or overtly anti-Semitic dramas, and had banned any of the movies that would have been appealing to Alice. And even if the movie itself was relatively benign, the multiple newsreels shown before the movie would boast about the greatness of the Aryan nation or warn about the evilness of the Jew.

Instead, Alice spent her time mostly trying to obtain evidence of Alfred's innocence, but still without much success. She did find out one interesting piece of information about the woman who had accused Alfred of the affair from an old acquaintance of Alfred's who had worked with Alfred and who had originally introduced the two. He was not willing to put this in writing (he was afraid of the Gestapo), but he told Alice on the telephone that he had heard that Betti Herbst had been in a knife fight with an old boyfriend sometime in the 1920s and the boyfriend had gone to jail. He had also heard that she had a boyfriend who was in the Gestapo or the SS and who was very jealous. He told Alice that if the boyfriend had seen the ring, he might have decided to make trouble for Alfred, especially after finding out that he was Jewish, but that was only a guess. He then said that he was sorry for ever introducing Alfred to Betti, because "that woman was trouble." He told Alice that he always liked Alfred, but that he didn't want to get in trouble with the Gestapo. But he wished her well and hung-up.

Well, that was interesting, Alice thought. It would explain, at least in part, how it came to be that Alfred was charged. Of course, even if Alfred's acquaintance submitted a written statement, it wouldn't prove that Alfred did not have an affair with this woman. And it also did not prove it to Alice. Still, Alice telephoned Dr. Popper and told him about the call.

She was thinking about that call the following morning when the telephone rang. Selma answered and Alice could hear her sister say into the telephone, "Hello Dr. Popper. How are you? Yes, just a moment."

Selma called to her sister. "I thought he was calling me about the divorce." Selma had told Alice that Dr. Popper would file the actual divorce papers after she had left the apartment or Leo had emigrated to Palestine, which ever came first.

Alice took the telephone from Selma. "Hello Dr. Popper. How are you?"

"I am fine, but you will be better. Alfred is being released from jail today. They have dropped the charges. You will need to pay the court costs of RM 155 in the next month, but you can pick him up today at 4 pm."

"Today? Oh, Dr. Popper! Thank you so much! Wow, they actually dropped the charges? You really are a miracle man."

"Frau Falkenstein, I would like to take credit for this, but I really did nothing. If I had to guess, I would say that the charges were never real in the first place. You had told me your husband had filed challenges to the tax office for back taxes twice. The Gestapo has been working closely with the tax office, and this could have been in retaliation for the challenges. Or, as you told me, that woman's boyfriend was jealous. Or it may have been a combination of the two. My advice to you is to pick up your husband at 4 pm and pay the Nazis whatever taxes they say you owe. Hopefully, this will keep the two of you out of jail and on your way to America. I will send you my bill, which will be very small and which you can pay when you are able. And tell your sister I look forward to seeing her soon."

"Thank you again, Dr. Popper. And I will tell my husband to pay the taxes. All of them!" Alice placed the telephone back in its cradle and looked at her sister. "I am picking up Alfred this afternoon."

Alice sat down in the chair next to the telephone. She was so relieved that Alfred was coming home today. And she thought about the last four months. They would not have dropped the charges if Alfred had actually had an affair with the woman. So he was telling the truth – all of her doubts disappeared. But then she got angry. How easy it was for some crazy woman to accuse her husband of an affair. And how easy it was for the Gestapo to arrest her husband based on nothing. And then she looked over at Selma. Alice could see the tears welling up in Selma's eyes. She stood up, walked over to Selma, and gave her a hug. Selma hugged her back. Alice had wanted this hug to mean that Selma was relieved that Alfred was coming home. But Alice knew better. Alice knew Selma was thinking that Alice would soon be moving out and then she would be leaving her and going to America.

CHAPTER 12

Frankfurt, September 1940

Alice was in the middle of making dinner when she heard Alfred open the door. He called out hello to her and went into the bedroom to change. He then went to sit in the small living room to read the paper. When he first moved back to Frankfurt, Alfred had read the *Municipal Gazette of the Jewish Community* every week, enjoying both the feature articles and the local gossip. After Kristallnacht, all the Jewish newspapers were shut down. In their place, the Nazis had ordered the creation of the *Judische Nachrichtenblatt* and the Nazis controlled the content of the paper. There wasn't much to read in the paper, and the only relevant information regarding Jewish Frankfurt was the listing of times for services at the "worship tents" that had sprung up around the city after all four of the synagogues had either been destroyed or damaged. Still, Alfred liked the continuity of sitting down after work to read a Jewish newspaper, and so he read the *Judische Nachrichtenblatt*.

Alice knew her husband would be tired and hungry, and she did her best with the limited food supplies that were available. The Nazis had begun issuing ration cards to Jews in 1939, restricting where Alice could shop and limiting the amount of meat and butter she could buy. More restrictions were imposed in the beginning of the year, so that Alice could no longer buy fruit or legumes, and was restricted to a pound of sugar, half a pound of jam, and three eggs per month. Because Alfred was working as an excavator in a nursery, she could buy 7 ounces of meat a week. She tried to stretch these rations as much as possible, although that usually meant that Alice finished dinner hungry. Alice thought to herself as she was finishing the dinner preparations, "Well, at least I have been able to lose that ten pounds I have been trying to lose for years."

When Alfred and Alice sat down to dinner, Alice asked him about his day. But she could tell that he was struggling to answer. The work was grueling, and there were few breaks in the day. He had received this job assignment in June, a forced labor position. He had no choice but to take it. Plus, they needed the weekly earnings of RM 30. Their money – what little they had – was tied up in a blocked account. Shortly after the Kristallnacht pogrom, the Nazi government had approved a monthly allowance of RM 300 for Alice and Alfred, to be deducted from their bank account. That was enough to cover RM 65 in rent, plus food and other expenses. That monthly amount had recently been reduced to RM 280. Alice's sister Johanna was still helping them with RM 20 a month, and while they had given up the telephone when they moved to the apartment on Oberlindau, they still struggled to pay their bills each month. They finished the meal in silence, and Alice took the plates into the kitchen. Alfred returned to his chair to read the rest of the newspaper. By the time Alice finished washing up and returned to the living room, Alfred was asleep in the chair and the paper had fallen to the floor. This was how it was most nights.

Alice sat in a chair across from Alfred and picked up the paper. This apartment on Oberlindau was small and on the top floor, but they didn't have to share it with others. They found the place soon after Alfred was released from jail and it was just around the corner from their old apartment. Selma and her mother were not so fortunate. They managed to remain in their apartment until April – all three of them. Alice was not sure why Leo had been unable to leave for Palestine, although Selma told her that a customs official did actually come to take away the trunk and suitcases. Alice wondered if Leo's complaints to the tax office was the reason he had never received his visa. Selma told Alice that Leo had filed a complaint with the tax office about the taxes he was told he owed for 1937 and then complained about the taxes for 1938. The tax office even initiated a criminal complaint against Leo in 1938, but that complaint was ultimately dismissed. Alice assumed that the criminal charge was a fabrication, meant to harass Leo because he had the nerve to complain to the tax authorities about taxes he likely did not owe. Just like Alfred. Maybe Leo would have received his visa if he had just paid the damn taxes, Alice thought to herself. Instead, in April, Leo, along with her mother and Selma, were required to leave their apartment and move into Judenhäuser – Jewish houses. The Nazis wanted to move the Jews away from the West End and into the East End, where the Heppenheimer family had lived years earlier. They were trying to create ghettos without the barbed wire, and unfortunately Selma and her mother were among those Jews in Frankfurt who had been forced to move into a "ghetto." They were living at Eschersheimer Landstrasse 39 in the house of a former doctor and his wife. Leo moved into a different Jewish house. While Selma was no longer living in the West End, it was still only a ten-minute walk to Alice's apartment, and Alice encouraged Selma to visit whenever she wished.

As much as she could, Alice continued to sew. She had sold the electric sewing machine and one of the treadle sewing machines, but she kept the third machine. She repaired all of their clothes – Alfred's clothes in particular needed to be constantly mended. She really didn't have a choice. Clothing cards had been issued to all Germans in November 1939, but Jew were then forced to surrender those cards the following month. No new clothes. In January 1940, Jews were banned from receiving voucher cards for textiles, shoes, and leather or rubber materials for shoe soles. Alice was able to pick up small jobs from neighbors and friends, but sewing thread was also being severely rationed for Jews, so Alice was limited in what jobs she could take. She knew she would receive a forced job assignment soon, and hoped it would be a sewing job.

Much had changed in Europe in the last two years. Germany had annexed Austria in March 1938, but this was celebrated by the Austrians. Germany then invaded the Czech provinces of Bohemia and Moravia in March 1939. War began on a large-scale with the invasions of Poland in September 1939, France in May 1940, and Belgium in May 1940. The United Kingdom and France had declared war on Germany in September 1939 and Italy joined the German side in June 1940 by declaring war on France and the United Kingdom. Alice and Alfred had lived through the Great War and Alfred had actually fought for Germany in that war. Now Germany was at war again, but was also at war with its Jews.

More and more of Alice's family had been able to emigrate to America. Max's son Kurt had left in 1937, and Max's widow Recha and his other son Alfred had left in 1939. Alice believed the Nazis had driven Max to suicide and so was happy that his family was actually able to escape. Her oldest sister Bertha, whose husband Marcus had died in 1925, was able to obtain her tax clearance certificate and traveled alone to America in 1939. But her sister Johanna was still in Germany, and she and her husband Isadore were still working to obtain their tax clearance certificate. Alice couldn't figure out why Johanna was having such a problem, since Isadore had essentially stopped working in 1933 when the original Gebrüder Heppenheimer stopped trading scrap metal, and was mostly relying on his son-in-law for support. But, selfishly, Alice was not unhappy about the delay, since Johanna had been so generous in her financial support to Alfred and Alice.

Probably the only good thing to come out of the Kristallnacht pogrom was that it lit a fire under Benno and Margot to leave. They immediately put their names on the waiting list for US visas and began the work of trying to leave. With both Jacob and his cousin Adolph safely in America, Benno was forced to sell Gebrüder Heppenheimer on his own at the end of 1938, and both he and his older son had received forced labor assignments in 1939. The family was also forced to leave their apartment after their landlord told them he didn't want to rent to Jews. Fortunately, the family found another apartment in the West End, at Telemannstrasse 18. It was a smaller place, but at least they had not been forced to move into a Jewish House.

Alice was pleased to see Benno when he dropped by her apartment earlier in the month. He clearly had good news. "I just received word from the American consulate that our quota numbers have come up."

"Oh, Benno, that's great. When do you leave?"

"Well, there is a small wrinkle that I didn't find about until today. The American Vice-Counsel is requiring that we have to have enough in our bank account to satisfy a funding requirement to live in America and he has set a pretty high amount."

"What does that mean? Doesn't he know you can't take any money with you to America except the RM 10 that you can carry? That all of your money is in a blocked account that will never leave Germany?"

"Yes, I tried to explain that to him. He didn't want to listen. I had the sense that he really doesn't want us to get the visas. It is hard enough to deal with anti-Semitic Nazis. But to have to deal with anti-Semitic officials from America? I did the calculations and I should be able to meet the funding requirement by the early part of next year. It will be okay. Just getting to this step is a big deal."

"I agree. I wish we could help you, but we are struggling just to pay for rent and food."

"Don't worry, Alice. I have faith that we will all make it out of this hellhole." And with that, he left.

Alice was hoping Benno was right. It took some time before the sale of her mother-in-law's building was finally approved and the money deposited into their blocked account at Deutsche Bank. Payment of the Jewish Levy and all remaining taxes had been paid.

Finally! But they were still waiting for their tax clearance certificate, and Alice did not know what was holding it up. But even with the tax clearance certificate, Alice and Alfred would still need to wait, since it would be some time before their numbers would be called from the waiting list for U.S. visas.

Alice had visited her sister Johanna recently, and Johanna was discussing her own struggles to emigrate. While Johanna's daughter and son-in-law were safe in Switzerland, Johanna and her husband Isadore were still waiting on their tax clearance certificate, which Johanna thought would be issued any day. But Johanna, like Alice, had an unfavorable number for a U.S. visa. Johanna had been speaking with her daughter and all four decided to try to obtain visas for Haiti. Johanna's son-in-law Franz thought that, if they could get to Portugal, they could try to obtain U.S. visas there. Alice thought the plan sounded a bit dubious, but didn't share that thought with her sister. Alice was also a little jealous of her sister's excitement. Alice wished she had some glimmer of hope that she would soon be able to escape the madness, but these days hope was scarce.

Around 10 pm, Alice put down the paper and shook Alfred awake from his chair. "Dear, it's time for bed." Alfred looked up at Alice. He was too tired to say anything, but he had enough energy to give Alice a weak smile. Then the two walked to the bedroom and went to bed.

•   •   •

The next morning, Alice was making Alfred breakfast when there was a knock at the door. Alice's first thought was "the Gestapo." Since Alfred was released from jail, they had periodically come to the apartment, asking rude questions and clearly trying to intimidate both of them. Or worse. The previous week, the Gestapo had banged on their door at 6 am. The two officers went into the living room and threw the chair's cushions on the floor. They knocked over tables. They went into the bedroom and opened the drawers and threw the clothes on the floor. They then insisted that Alfred and Alice turn over the jewelry that they were hiding in the apartment.

Alice said, "You know we turned over all of our jewelry already. There is nothing in the apartment."

One of the officers looked over at the nightstand and saw Alice's watch. She saw him looking and said, "We were told that we could keep our watches. This watch has no value."

"Well, you can keep the watch, but we will continue to look until we find the jewelry." Alfred looked at Alice and nodded. Alice reached over to the nightstand and picked up the watch. It was a relatively cheap watch, but Alfred had given it to her early in their relationship, and she treasured it, especially now that everything else he had given her was gone. She handed the officer the watch and the two left.

There was a second knock and Alice grabbed her housecoat and answered the door, hoping for just another round of annoying questions and not something worse. She was relieved to see that it was not the Gestapo, but Selma. But then she worried for a different reason. Selma seemed angry.

No time for small talk. "Selma, what's wrong?"

"Frau Wallach, who lives in the apartment where Leo is living, just came to my place. Leo has been arrested, and she hoped that I would be able to help. I had the sense that Leo hadn't told her about the divorce, since she asked me if I could find Leo a lawyer. I told her that Leo already had a lawyer, and I gave her the name. She asked me if I would call the lawyer, and I told her it probably wasn't a good idea. I didn't tell her he was Leo's divorce lawyer. I don't know why Leo didn't just tell her to call his lawyer. It's just like him!"

As was typical of Selma, she seemed to focus on the wrong thing. "Selma, why was Leo arrested?"

"Do you remember when that customs official came to our old apartment last year and then took the trunk and suitcases away?" With everything else going on, Alice had forgotten that Leo's belongings had been taken away to be shipped abroad. However, neither Leo nor his siblings had ever received their visas to Palestine, and all were still living in Frankfurt. "Apparently, it has something to do with that. I don't know more than what I just told you. But I am assuming it's pretty serious."

"I assume so too. You should probably let Dr. Popper know about Leo's arrest. He will need to know that anyway. He probably will also give Leo's lawyer a call."

"That's a good idea. I was planning on seeing Dr. Popper today anyway. I know I am being a little selfish, but I can't help but be angry at Leo. How could he put himself in that situation? And his arrest will just make it harder for me to live. The RM 5 he sends me each month is not much, but it helps. I have almost nothing left to sell and Dr. Marx and his wife have been very nice to me and Mama, but they are struggling as well."

"I am sure Dr. Marx will understand. Do you want to sit down for some breakfast? It's not much, but it will give you a chance to catch your breath."

"You know I can never say no to a home-cooked meal. Except perhaps when you make it. How about if I see what you have and I can make us something good. And I will bring what is left back for Mama."

Alice gave her sister a hug and sat down at the table, happy to be served breakfast.

·   ·   ·

The charges against Leo were even more serious than Alice imagined. Selma had heard from Dr. Popper, who had called Leo's lawyer Sigmund Kaiser. Leo was being charged with foreign exchange offenses and with bribing a government official. According to the charging document, Leo had loaded multiple jewels and other valuables into the trunk and suitcases, along with RM 5,700, and paid the official RM 250 to provide the necessary seals. Even though everything was supposed to go to Trieste in Italy, Dr. Popper thought that the trunk and suitcases had likely remained in Hamburg and were finally opened by the Gestapo. Dr. Popper told Selma that cases like this usually resulted in several years in prison even before the Nazi era. But given the times, Selma should expect that Leo will not be getting out of jail for quite some time.

Alice knew her sister was thinking about the loss of the money, and Alice was thinking about this as well. Alice knew that, given what Leo was facing, she (and her sister) were being rather petty. But she didn't care. Leo had been a terrible provider and had made Selma miserable. And while Alice would never have expected Selma to go with Leo to Palestine (or anywhere else), his decision to leave Selma with no resources was heartless. And where did he get the RM 5,700 from? Had he been hoarding money all this time, not providing for Selma and claiming poverty?

A week after Leo's arrest, Selma came to Alice's apartment. The two were sitting at Alice's kitchen table, enjoying some coffee and the delicious cookies Selma had baked, even with the ersatz ingredients. Dr. Popper had told Selma that Leo's trial would probably occur in the middle of 1941. In the meantime, Leo would remain in jail.

"With everything going on with Leo, I am assuming you are going to delay the divorce?"

"Why would I do that?"

"Selma, you know I am not a big fan of Leo, but do you think this is the right time to pursue this? Maybe you could wait until after his trial."

"Alice, I can't and I won't. I don't want to be married to him any longer. Finding out that he was planning to take all of that money and jewels with him to Palestine and leaving me with nothing just reminded me how selfish he is. I need to be free of him. There is not much within my power right now. I can't go to concerts, I can't go to the movies. Mama and I are forced to live with complete strangers. I need to be able to have one thing go my way. It's his fault that he is in jail, not mine. He can handle the divorce."

Alice sometimes thought that her sister was a bit unfocused and, at times, spoiled. Perhaps that comes from being the youngest child of older parents. But she had a good heart, and her marriage had been a disappointment. Alice had always hoped that Selma would find someone who saw her strengths, but that person was not Leo. Alice did understand why Selma wanted to be free of him. She had wanted to be free of Ludwig, although for different reasons. And Alice also understood the need to have at least some part of your life within your control.

"Selma, I understand the need to move forward with the divorce. Let me know what help you need from me."

Selma gave Alice that winning smile. "You know I will."

CHAPTER 13

Frankfurt, February 1941

The last of Joseph Heppenheimer's children still in Germany sat down to lunch, knowing that this might be the last time they would all be together. There had been seven of them: Bertha, Johanna, Jacob, Benno, Max, Alice and Selma. Bertha and Jacob had already emigrated. Max was dead. The four remaining siblings, their spouses, and Emma decided to have a celebratory lunch for Johanna and Isadore. They were leaving Germany in a week and it had been a while since the family had been together. A dinner was out of the question – the 8 pm curfew imposed on Jews since September 1939 made that impossible. Everyone used some of their rations, and they decided to have the lunch at Benno's apartment, since it was the largest. They also brought some of their limited coal rations, so that everyone would enjoy a warm apartment.

That Johanna and Isadore were able to leave was something of a miracle. They had finally received their tax clearance certificate in November, but they would not obtain their US visas until at least 1942 because of their place on the waiting list. They had been talking about trying to use Haitian visas to leave, but they could not obtain train passage. The Joint Distribution Committee, the Jewish relief organization helping Jews escape from Germany, had negotiated with the Nazi government for sealed trains that would leave from Berlin, but they were only for those with U.S. visas. But fortunately for Johanna and Isadore, their son-in-law had been very wealthy. And he was living in Switzerland. And he had a Swiss bank account.

When Franz Neumeier married Johanna's only child Martha, he was part owner of a pharmaceutical manufacturing company, with facilities in Germany and Switzerland. The company made an assortment of medicines, but was best known for its cough drops. After Isadore was forced to leave Gebrüder Heppenheimer, Franz essentially supported his in-laws. Just before Kristallnacht, Franz was forced to sell his company to I.G. Farben for a fraction of its value, and then was required to put the proceeds in a blocked account. But he had a Swiss bank account, which he used to help himself and his wife cross the Swiss border just after the sale of his company. And he was able to continue to support his in-laws through the blocked German account while he was living in Switzerland.

Johanna and Isadore were able to pay their living expenses, as well as the Haitian visas, through this account. Johanna was also able to provide some financial support to both Alice and Selma. And Franz was able to help his in-laws get out of Germany through his Swiss bank account. While Franz could not use the money in his blocked German account, he was able to wire money from his Swiss account to Lufthansa to buy his in-laws airplane tickets to Lisbon.

The family members showed up around noon. Food was in short supply, but each of the women did their best to make the event festive. Their favorite foods were missing, but that was okay. It was wonderful just to be together.

The rest of the family were already in the apartment when Alice and Alfred arrived with Selma and Emma. Benno's younger son Werner was home, although eighteen-year-old Hans was away working at a brick factory – a forced labor assignment.

Everyone exchanged greetings and sat in the small living room. Alice could not remember the last time this many members of the family had been together.

Benno was the first to speak and asked the questions everyone else wanted to ask. "So, Franz has a Swiss bank account? Who knew he even had a Swiss bank account? Did you know Johanna? And who knew you could use a Swiss bank account to buy Lufthansa airplane tickets?"

Johanna smiled and decided to answer only the questions she wanted to answer. "I didn't know buying plane tickets was even a possibility for us. But Franz called me and told me he had been able to buy two plane tickets. Since then, we have been racing around, getting the visas for Portugal. And who knows how long we will be there? Franz spoke with a friend of his, who said that it could take months for us to get our U.S. visas."

"Well, at least you will be out of here." Alice could hear a bit of an edge in her voice. But she thought to herself, "Why are you complaining about having to be in Lisbon for months? You will be out of here. Alfred and I need someone who would buy us airplane tickets." Alice was wondering if Benno was having the same thoughts.

Alice then thought it would be good to lower the temperature in the room, at least metaphorically. "Johanna, we are so excited for you. None of us has ever been on a plane. What a great way to leave this place! And the weather is supposed to be better in Portugal."

"Thanks, Alice. We are really happy to be leaving, and to be leaving on a plane. The weather in Portugal could be snowy and freezing and I wouldn't care. Just as long as I am out of Germany." Just as she said it, she realized that the comment was a bit thoughtless, given that Alice was nowhere near being able to leave. She looked over at Alice, who was looking down at the moment. "Don't worry, Alice. I know that your time will come. I just know it."

"Thanks, Johanna. I just have to hope." But Alice remembered Johanna telling her that a cousin living in Mannheim, Sally Heppenheimer, had been recently deported, along with all the Jews living in Mannheim, to Camp der Gurs, an internment camp in the south of France. As far as anyone knew, Sally and his wife were still there. And another cousin, who had married into the Heppenheimer family but who was born in Poland, had been sent to the Polish border in October 1938. While she had been allowed to return to Frankfurt, other Jews sent to the border were forced to remain in Poland. Alice was wondering whether all of Frankfurt's Jews would one day be forced out of the city. She hoped she would be safe in America before that could happen to her and Alfred.

Alice was aware that both her mother and Selma had been quiet throughout the conversation. Her mother had made the decision to stay put, and Selma would not leave her mother behind. Or at least, that was what Selma said. Alice sensed that there was also a reluctance on Selma's part to leave Germany, but, as close as they were, they didn't discuss it. She wondered if Selma's position had changed in any way, given recent events. But Selma said nothing and Alice didn't pry. And she certainly would not bring it up today. So she played the peace-maker, as she often did. "Anyone hungry? The dishes all looks great. How about if we sit down to eat?" Whatever else was going on in the world, the Heppenheimer family did love to eat. And so they sat down to enjoy their last meal with Johanna and Isadore.

•   •   •

Alice was happy for her sister, but Johanna's leaving was going to be hard for Alice. They had never been close, but it had brought Alice some comfort knowing that Johanna was near. Plus, Johanna had been helping Alice and Alfred for the last few years, providing then with RM 20 every month. That had been important when the Foreign Exchange Office had restricted them to RM 280. But their allowance was now being reduced to RM 100, so Alice expected that the loss of her sister's support would hit them especially hard.

Moreover, Alice and Alfred had virtually run out of things to sell. Hardest for Alice was the recent sale of her prized gramophone. She had had the gramophone for more than twenty years. It had travelled with her to Nuremberg and kept her sane during some of the more troubling times with Ludwig. She had brought it with her to Frankfurt and still played it, even after Alfred had bought her a more modern radio/phonograph combination. She sold that phonograph first, after Jews were required to give up their radios in September 1939. She rarely listened to the radio, anyway, since most programs were spewing anti-Semitic nonsense, when they weren't promoting Germany as the greatest nation ever. But Alice was ultimately forced to sell the gramophone. She felt rather ridiculous when she realized the gramophone was probably the thing she missed the most of all of the things she had been forced to sell.

With the loss of her sister's financial support, Alice knew she needed to secure a forced labor job soon. The few small sewing jobs she picked up were not enough, and often paid next to nothing. She needed something more substantial.

Alice had recently submitted a request to the city government to allow her to work as a ladies' tailor. She had also recently visited the Dressmakers Guild to ask whether they would support her request. She had been an active member of the Guild until she was forced to close her business, and she felt she had had a good relationship with the leadership. She was not naïve – she knew she was a Jew and that the Guild had been active supporters of the Nazi government. But she had hoped that there would be some goodwill left.

She had made an appointment just after the new year with the vice-president of the Guild, whom she had had a good relationship with. Albert Schmidt had been a master tailor for years and had been in a leadership position with the Guild since Alice had joined the Guild in 1933. Alice had always felt that Herr Schmidt judged her based on the quality of her work. And Alice knew she did good work, or at least she had done good work when she could work.

When Alice arrived at the Guild offices, she told the receptionist she had an appointment with Albert Schmidt. Herr Schmidt came immediately to the receptionist's desk and told Alice to follow him to his office. As he reached his office, Herr Schmidt said, "Frau Falkenstein, it is so nice to see you again. Why don't we sit in my office and catch up." He then quickly shut the door. Alice suspected that, as much as Herr Schmidt might have liked Alice, he was a realist and had to work with the rest of the Guild. He clearly didn't want people to know that he was meeting with a Jewish woman.

"Herr Schmidt, I want to first thank you so much for seeing me. I know you must be really busy and it was so nice of you to take time out of your schedule to meet with me." She didn't need to add "And thanks for agreeing to meet with a Jew." They both understood what his meeting with her meant.

"How are things with you, Frau Falkenstein?"

"To be honest Herr Schmidt, things have been hard since I had to close my shop. You know how much I love to design and sew dresses and I really miss the work. I came to see you because I was hoping that the Guild would send a letter to support my request to work as a ladies' tailor. I sent a letter to the Ministry last month and they are considering my request. Any word of support from the Guild would be great."

"Frau Falkenstein, I have always liked you and your work was second to none. Let me see what I can do." He didn't have to say that this would be an uphill battle. Both of them knew it. But Alice believed that, if there was a way Herr Schmidt could get the Guild to provide support for Alice's request, and not create trouble for himself or the Guild, he would do it.

"Herr Schmidt, I can't tell you how much I appreciate anything you can do to help. I know you are really busy, so I will let you get back to your work. I can see myself out." They shook hands, and Alice left his office. She walked as quickly as possible, trying not to draw attention to herself. Well, she tried, she thought, as she left the building. It seemed more likely than not that the Guild would not provide that letter of support. She should have left the building feeling dejected, but she actually felt the opposite. Perhaps it was that she at least attempted to get back to something that she loved. Or perhaps it was hearing from someone that she respected that she did good work. In fighting each day just to survive, it was really nice to hear something positive.

.   .   .

Several days after her sister Johanna flew to Portugal, Selma stopped by Alice's apartment. Because Alice no longer had a telephone in her apartment, there were more unannounced visits. Generally, Alice was okay with this, although every knock raised the possibility of another visit from the Gestapo.

Selma seemed a bit more pre-occupied than normal and seemed to want to get right to the point about her visit, so Alice made it easy. "So, what do I owe the honor of your visit today?"

"Frau Marx is a little worried about Mama getting around their house. Our bedroom is on the second floor, and it is getting harder and harder for her to climb the stairs. I have to admit that I am also concerned. Frau Marx suggested Mama may do better at the old age home attached to the Jewish hospital. Dr. Marx still has connections there, and told me he could get Mama a room there. What do you think?"

"I also have to admit that I have been worried about Mama climbing those stairs. I sometimes forget that she is nearly 80 years old. But what do you think Mama's reaction will be to living someplace away from her children? And being moved to an old age home? She always talked about how she would rather die than be moved into one of those places. She always talked about how it was up to her children to take care of her in her old age. How would we be able to convince her it would be in her best interests to move to the home?"

"Good question. I have been asking myself that all the way over here. But understand that I also have mixed feelings about this. I decided not to try to emigrate because I couldn't leave Mama behind. And now I am thinking about trying to put her in an old age home. So does that mean I am leaving her? And then I think of all the support she had given me – especially through all my challenges with Leo – and I wonder how I can put her in a home. But then I watch her every night when she climbs up the stairs and every morning when she climbs down the stairs."

"Is there any way you and Mama could move someplace else?"

"I tried. But they keep moving more and more Jews out of the West End and into these Jewish Houses. There are already ten of us living in the Marx's house. There are not enough houses and apartments for the ones they are moving. I am actually surprised that they have not tried to move you and Alfred out." Alice was surprised, as well, since she had seen others in the neighborhood evicted from their apartments and moved to Jewish Houses. Just one more thing to worry about, but not right now.

"Well, it sounds like Mama can't stay in the Marx's house. I know she doesn't want to leave you and you don't want to leave her, but I guess you really don't have a choice. I also worry that things will get worse for all of us, and maybe she will have access to more food and be safer at the home."

"I think you're right about both things. And now I have a huge favor to ask. Will you come back to the Marx's house with me and help me talk Mama into the move?"

"Sure. Let me get my coat."

• • •

Convincing their mother to move into the old age home turned out to be easier than either had expected. Climbing the stairs in the Marx home had been harder on Emma than she had been willing to admit to her daughters. Emma also worried that things would continue to get worse, and she actually wanted Selma think about leaving Germany. As long as they lived together, Selma would never leave – she would feel responsible for her mother. But with Emma living in the old age home, there was no reason for Selma to remain, and Emma told her so.

Selma did not want to discuss leaving Germany. "Mama, let's get you moved first. Then we can talk about me leaving Germany, okay?"

Emma smiled and nodded her head. "Okay, my darling. But we will discuss it soon. You need to put your name on the waiting list as soon as I move into the home. Promise me you will."

"Mama, let's get you moved in first and then we will discuss my leaving, okay?"

It took Dr. Marx only two weeks to find a place for Emma in the home. Alice arrived at the Marx house the morning of the move to help her mother finish packing, but Emma was nearly finished by the time Alice arrived. Alice realized that there was really very little to move. When Joseph was alive, he had bought Emma a number of beautiful pieces of jewelry and expensive dresses and furs. He was not an extravagant man, but he liked to treat Emma well. After the Kristallnacht pogrom, all Jews were required to deliver their valuables to pawn shops set up by the Reich. Emma could keep only a few items, but those had been sold in the last year, along with the rest of their furniture. Emma closed her one suitcase, and Selma took the suitcase down the stairs. Emma said that she was happy that this was the last time she needed to go down those stairs. Me too, thought Alice.

Selma and Alice splurged on a taxi to take their mother to the old age home on Gagernstrasse 36. The home was part of the Jewish center complex, which also included a Jewish hospital. Once one of the city's best hospitals, the Jewish community was forced to sell the entire complex to the city of Frankfurt in 1939, although the community was permitted to continue to use the hospital and the Jewish center, which included the old age home, although they had to pay the city rent for the privilege.

As the taxi pulled up to the home, Emma grabbed Alice's hand. Alice was sure that her mother would tell her that this was a big mistake and that they should immediately return to the Marx's house. But Emma said nothing. A tear was falling down her cheek, and Alice couldn't tell if that was sadness or resignation, or perhaps a little of both. If she was being honest with herself, Alice had to admit that she had never wanted her mother living with her. She loved her mother, but it had been Selma who had promised their mother that she would always have a home with Selma, and Alice had been happy to cede that responsibility to her sister. But now Alice felt some guilt as they were now moving their mother into an old age home. Emma left the car and Selma grabbed the suitcase. Alice quickly wiped the tears from her eyes so that her mother would not see them. As the three entered the building, Alice thought that this was one more step toward the total destruction of their lives.

CHAPTER 14

Frankfurt, July 1941

Growing up, Alice and Benno had never been close. Benno was 14 years old when Alice was born, and Alice often felt like a child around him, even when she herself was an adult. She had been close to Max, and harbored some resentment towards Benno at how Max had been treated following the failure of the Mannheim smelter facility. While she now knew the factors that went into the decision of Jacob and Benno to start the new scrap metal trading business at the end of 1933, she still struggled not to blame Benno, at least in part, for Max's suicide. But since Max's death, Alice and Benno had become closer. This was especially the case after the Kristallnacht pogrom, when Benno and Margot finally decided to emigrate to America. The two shared their various efforts and frustrations at trying to secure those coveted visas. And now Benno had succeeded. He was going to America. But at a great cost. As had been typical of their lives since the Nazis took control, every time they thought they could take a breath and enjoy a moment, something terrible would happen. Alice had succeeded in her dressmaking business, but then had been forced to close her business. Alice had reconnected with and then had married Alfred, but then Alfred had been arrested. Twice. Selma and Emma had finally moved away from Leo and his temper, but her mother was then forced to move into an old age home. And now, Benno would finally be leaving Germany and taking his sons to America, but he would be going without Margot.

Benno had come to see Alice earlier in the day. Alice had been expecting this visit since she had read yesterday's newspaper. Benno had kept Alice abreast of all of their struggles over the past six months to secure their visas. When she opened the door, she could tell that her brother was upset. She told him to sit down at the dining table and she went into the kitchen to get them coffee. When she returned, Benno started to talk. Alice could tell that he needed to review all that had happened, to see if there was something that he missed, something that he could have done differently, something that he could still do. She knew it was best to let him talk.

"Alice, I am assuming you saw the headlines. Despite all of our best efforts, Margot cannot obtain her U.S. visa. Remember how excited I was last month, when I had finally met the funding amount imposed by the American Vice-Consul, and had called the Consulate in Stuttgart to schedule an appointment for all of us. We knew about the medical exam, but thought nothing about it. And then that Vice-Consul told us he would need to reject Margot's application because there was a spot on her lung x-ray. That made no sense to either of us – Margot felt fine. She asked that they re-do the x-ray, or at least be allowed to speak to the person who took the x-rays. The Vice-Consul refused both requests. And then he said something that made it clear to me that his decision was likely based on other factors. He said, 'Herr Heppenheimer, there is nothing to require that you and your sons go to America. Perhaps it is best that you not leave your wife, particularly if she is sick. Your sons would certainly not want to leave their mother behind.'"

Alice took Benno's hand. "I remember you telling me that the Consulate had used a Germany company to perform the x-ray, and you thought that maybe the problem was with that company."

Benno's face became dark. "I think the reason that Margot's visa had been denied was that Vice-Consul Jenson hoped that I would decline the visas for me and the boys to stay with Margot. I doubt there really had been anything on the lung x-ray, especially after we found out that she was fine. I remember hearing from others that this particular Vice-Consul was anti-Semitic and used his position to limit the number of Jews entering the U.S. It was Jensen who set the high funding amount, even knowing that we would not be able to take any of that money with us when we finally emigrated. It simply delayed our emigration, and that was likely Jensen's intent. And then the x-ray. But before I could even respond, Margot told Jensen that the boys and I would take the visas. Margot calmly told him, "Mr. Jensen, don't worry about me. I am sure I am fine. I will just find another way to leave Germany. But it is most important that Benno and my boys get to America." That is just like her! And so we took the three visas and left the Consulate."

Alice refilled their coffee cups. "And then you discovered Margot had no lung problem."

"Yes, the next morning, Margot walked to Selma's apartment to ask Dr. Marx how to get an x-ray. She knew doctors could no longer practice medicine, but also knew that Dr. Marx still treated anyone who needed medical help. And he knew nearly everyone still working in the Jewish hospital. Dr. Marx listened to Margot's story and then told her who to see at the hospital. He even wrote a note, which he gave to Margot. What a great man he is! She went straight to the hospital. What was the point of delay? The worst thing they could say to her was to come back another day."

Alice smiled. "That is just like Margot, taking charge of the situation."

Benno nodded in agreement. "Yes, when Margot decides to do something, nothing is going to stop her. She arrived at the hospital and asked to see Dr. Friedland. Dr. Marx had explained to Margot that Dr. Friedland had been a pulmonologist before the Nazis had revoked his license, and was now an x-ray technician. So he would be able to take the x-ray, but he would also be able to read the x-ray and, hopefully, determine if there was a problem. Dr. Friedland came out to the reception area, and Margot handed him the note. After he was finished reading the note, he took Margot to get x-rayed and soon returned with the x-ray in a folder. He handed Margot the folder and said, 'Frau Heppenheimer, you are perfectly fine. There is no spot on your lung. I don't know what happened in Stuttgart. Perhaps there had been a fly that landed on you just as the x-ray was being taken. But your name and today's date are on the x-ray film, and I am listed as the x-ray technician, in case there are any questions. Good luck with this.' He shook her hand and left the room. When Margot came home and told me this, I was so angry."

Alice shared in his anger. "I can just imagine how angry you were when you heard."

"Vice-Consul Jensen could have allowed Margot to be x-rayed again, but he wouldn't. And he wouldn't because he knew nothing was wrong with her. This was a ploy to get us to stay in Germany. First the high funding requirement and then the mistake with the x-ray – if it even was a mistake. But I tried not to show Margot my anger and told her it was May 21st, and she just needed to contact the American Consulate to schedule another appointment. Because all Jews have been forced to give up our telephones, Margot raced to the telegraph office to send them a telegram. She seemed so happy when she left!" Alice could see tears forming, but Benno shook his head to stop himself from crying. He needed to keep talking.

"The following day, Margot received a response from the consulate. They said in the telegram that they were extremely busy and could not see her until July 10th at 11 am. I was annoyed, but she calmed me down. She said that that would be fine. She had waited this long – she could wait a little longer. And we would all still be able to take the sealed train from Berlin to Portugal together, which was not scheduled to leave until July 30th. All our plans were in place until yesterday's headlines in the *Frankfurter Zeitung*. June 30th. The worst day of my life."

"Alfred and I saw the headlines yesterday, that the German government has ordered that all the American consulates be closed. We didn't know what it meant for Margot and decided to wait for you to come to tell us. So, Benno, what does it mean?"

"I immediately sent a telegram to the American consulate to ask them, since we also didn't know what it meant for Margot. We received the response this morning and I came right over. There will be no new U.S. visas issued." And then Benno broke down. Alice hugged her brother, and she sobbed, as well.

•   •   •

Alice felt a little guilty that she was jealous when she heard that Benno had obtained visas for himself and his sons. She felt badly about Margot's situation, but was confident – at least in May when Benno and his sons received their visas – that Margot would be able to obtain her own visa and leave Germany with her family. Still, it was hard for Alice every time a family member or friend received a visa, because it was yet another reminder of her own challenges in trying to flee Germany. But it was especially hard when Alfred's sister Henny stopped by their apartment in the early part of June to tell them she had just been told to come to the American Consulate in Stuttgart to receive her US visa. Fortunately for Henny, her appointment had been a few days before the US consulates were all closed.

Although Alice adored Ruth, she never felt particularly close to her sister-in-law Henny. When the three were together, Alice spoke mostly to Ruth. There was something a bit flat about Henny's affect that made Alice a little uncomfortable. Henny had been a teacher, but lost her position just after the Nazis came to power. Alice thought that the loss of her job might have affected Henny. Alice once asked Alfred about his sister's demeanor, but he didn't seem to want to talk about it, and Alice never pursued it again. Just before Ruth left, she asked Alice to check on her parents, particularly her father, who was mostly bed-ridden by the time Ruth left. Alice promised she would.

Sam had passed away in December 1939, shortly after Ruth finally obtained her US visa and sailed from England to America. Henny was relieved that her daughter was finally in America, but devastated that she had lost her husband. She was more withdrawn after Sam died, so it was even more of a struggle to talk with Henny when Alice visited. She was always happier when Alfred joined her for the visit.

Because Henny had inherited half of her mother's estate, she had also inherited the same problems Alfred had relating to the sale of their mother's home. Henny was also struggling to obtain her tax clearance certificate, but unlike Alfred, she had never filed a complaint with the tax office. Alice thought that this might be why Henny was able to obtain her tax clearance certificate before Alice and Alfred. She only needed to wait until her number came up on the waitlist, which it obviously did. And now Henny was one more family member who would be leaving Alice and Alfred behind. While Alice told herself that she needed to be gracious, it just didn't seem fair.

And so Alice had invited Henny over for lunch to celebrate a week after her appointment in Stuttgart. This was just a few days after Benno came over with the bad news about Margot, and Alice was feeling rather emotionally exhausted. Alfred was also feeling bad about Benno's situation, but was also working hard not to be jealous of his sister. Alice knew Alfred was thinking about his mother's building and how it would have been better for all of them if the building had simply burned up in a fire. But he rallied and shared in the good news. And both Alice and Alfred were happy that Ruth would be able to see her mother again. Henny was scheduled to leave on the same sealed train taking Benno and the boys to Portugal.

•   •   •

Alfred and Alice went to Benno's apartment on Telemannstrasse 18 on July 27th to say goodbye. The mood was somber – no one wanted Benno to leave without Margot, but everyone agreed Benno needed to go with the boys while they still could get out of Germany. They would take the train tonight for Berlin, and then, while in Berlin, they would work with the Joint Distribution Committee to obtain the necessary visas for France, Spain and Portugal. The sealed train would then leave Berlin on July 30th and would remain sealed – with them in it – until it crossed the border into Spain. Benno had learned that they would be travelling in third-class carriages, with bathrooms, but no food service. They would need to bring their own food, and there was no telling how long the trip would take.

Benno invited his sister and brother-in-law into the apartment. The place was a bit of a mess, with papers strewn around the living room. Alice could see two large steamer trunks in the corner of the living room. The trucks had the official seal from the customs office.

"Benno, I see that the customs official has already been here."

"Yes, he came yesterday. He compared everything in the trunks to the list I had provided to the Foreign Exchange Office. I had to itemize everything – shirts, pants, shoes, even socks. And it made me so angry that I had to pay a tax on everything we purchased after the Nazis came to power. We didn't want to have a fight with the office, so we decided to pay a tax on almost everything on the list. What does it matter, anyway? We will never see any of the money in our blocked account. The freight forwarding company is coming tomorrow to send the trunks to Hamburg for shipment to New York."

Alice looked at her brother and smiled. "I hope there is nothing valuable in those trunks."

Benno winked at his sister. "I think I told you about Margot's cousin. That was the only smart thing we did before Kristallnacht. He had a visa for Switzerland and so we gave him all of Margot's best jewelry. When the Nazis required us to turn over all of our jewelry in the beginning of 1939, we had almost nothing left to turn over. The cousin is now in New York and he will give us everything once we land."

"Very smart, Benno."

"Thanks, but let's not talk about such things. Margot has just made some coffee. Please sit down with us." Margot's mother, Johanna Lebrecht, was also there. She would be living with Margot after Benno left. "Margot and her mother are going to try to get passage to Cuba, and then get their U.S. visas there. Hopefully, this will go quickly and we can all meet up in New York soon. Alice, I want you and Alfred to try getting Cuban visas so that you both can go with Margot." Alice didn't have the strength to remind him they had no money for Cuban visas. But now was not the time. Instead, Alice said, "Yes, Benno, we will try."

When Margot walked over to spend some additional time with the boys, Benno asked Alice to join him in the bedroom.

"Alice, I am a little worried about Margot. She has been really strong for the boys, but I am worried that she will fall apart after we leave. Could you please stop in from time to time to make sure that she and her mom are doing okay?"

"Benno, you know I will."

"I know that. I guess I just needed to hear you say it. Of course, I am worried that I will fall apart once we leave. Margot and I have never really been apart. We have always vacationed together, we have always done everything together. Remember the vacation we took to Norderney? You were still married to Ludwig and this was when Hans was just a baby, so it must have been in 1923. It was a really hot summer, but swimming in the sea was great. And boy did we eat well. And we were all so relaxed. We really did have a wonderful time."

"I remember. It was a great vacation. We have had a lot of great times together. And we will have great times together in the future."

"Alice, I did want to tell you how sorry I am ..." Alice put up her hand to stop her brother from saying any more. The two had made their way past the issues with Max and she was happy with their relationship. If this was the last time they were ever going to see each other, she did not want them to have this painful issue as one of the last things they discussed. And if they were to see each other again, they could then resolve whatever needed to be resolved.

Alice simply said, "It's okay, Benno."

•   •   •

Alice woke early the next day for her job at Carl Winnen's work wear factory, a forced labor job. Albert Schmidt had been true to his word and was actually able to convince the Guild to send a letter in June in support of Alice's request. Unfortunately, just after the letter was submitted, Alice was informed that she would be working at the factory, making RM 10 a week. She wouldn't be designing dresses, but at least she would be sewing. But the work was exhausting, sitting at the sewing machine and sewing 10 hours a day. These days, Alice and Alfred both came home from work with just enough energy to eat and read a little before bed.

But Alice had made a promise to Benno, and so Alice stopped after work to see how Margot was coping the day after her family left. Margot's face was drawn and her eyes were red. It looked like she had been crying. But Margot rallied when she saw Alice and invited her in. Margot's mother was sitting in a chair in the corner knitting and the three ladies shared some ersatz coffee. They spoke about some neighborhood gossip and then Margot encouraged Alice to go home to Alfred. She could see how tired Alice was, and she also didn't want to talk about Benno and the boys. For the moment, it was just too painful.

· · ·

A few days later, Margot came to Alice's apartment. It was just before curfew, but Margot wanted to share her news. She had just received a telegram from Benno. They had arrived in Lisbon, and everyone was well. They were very excited to share that, when they had crossed the border into Portugal, the Joint Distribution Committee had arranged a feast that included food they hadn't had for years, including white bread. When Alice heard the words "white bread," she started to laugh. Maybe it was the relief in hearing that they had made it or that they were so excited about having something as ordinary as white bread, or how happy she would be to have just a slice of white bread herself. Perhaps Margot was thinking the same thing, because she started to laugh. They both laughed, and then they hugged. Margot said goodbye and walked back down the stairs. Alice remained at the threshold to her apartment, watching her sister-in-law leave. She was not a religious person, but she whispered a prayer for her brother and nephews. And for Margot.

CHAPTER 15

Frankfurt, October 1941

Alice was finally beginning to get the hang of the large industrial sewing machine. Her first forced labor position – at the work wear factory – had not lasted long. Since the end of August, she had been working in a saddle making factory, operating one of the sewing machines. Alice thought it was odd that a portion of the German military was still using horses, but she never questioned the decisions of the Nazi government – at least, not out loud. She did not love this job – sewing was just a small part of the process of making a saddle. And sewing leather was more difficult than sewing cloth. Plus, the machines themselves were much larger and more difficult to handle. But sewing machines are sewing machines, and she was learning how to use the larger machines. And, so far, she had avoided any injuries.

She was at her machine focusing on a particularly tricky stitch when she noticed that a few of her fellow workers had stopped working and were gathered in a circle. Alice recognized them as some of the Jewish workers. It was easy to identify the Jewish workers, now that all Jews were required to wear yellow Stars of David on their outer clothing. Becoming alarmed, Alice stopped working and joined the circle. One of her co-workers, Sarah, said that she had arrived at work late because the Gestapo had stopped her to check her name against a list. Apparently, officers were rounding up Jews and marching them through the city.

Someone asked, "Where are they taking them?"

Sarah said that she heard someone say that they were being marched to the Grossmarkthalle, the city's wholesale fruit and vegetable market in the East End. She also heard that they were being deported, but she didn't know where.

Another asked "Are they arresting them all over the city?"

Sarah said that she lives in the West End, and she thought the arrests were just in the West End. At least that was what she saw as she walked to work. All the people that she saw were carrying luggage and had cardboard signs around their neck, listing their names and other information.

At that moment, the foreman came over and asked why they had left their machines. Sarah tried to explain, but the foreman didn't care. Instead, he smacked her face and said, "Shut up and get back to work or I will have all of you Jewish swine arrested."

Alice did the best she could to concentrate on her sewing. The last thing she needed was to get hurt. Sarah said the West End. She lived in the West End. She left before Alfred this morning. What if he had been arrested? Margot and her mother also lived in the West End. Selma was in the North End and her mother was in the East End, so she assumed they were okay. But who knows? She told herself not to worry, since there was nothing she could do.

When her shift ended at 6 pm, she immediately grabbed her things and ran out of the factory. She wished she could take one of the trams home, but Jews were now forbidden from taking the tram. Selma's Jewish House on Eschersheimer Landstrasse was literally on the way home, so she stopped there first. The house was not in the West End, but Sarah might have been wrong. Plus, Selma had been a bit down recently, and the news of deportations was bound to upset her.

Most people – including Alice – would think that pursing a divorce while everyone else was trying to get out of Germany was a bit crazy. But the effort had actually been a help to Selma. For a while, it was all Selma could talk about, but Alice knew it helped to distract Selma from all the bad things happening to Jews, and it also helped to distract her from the absence of her mother. There had been a surprising number of filings made to the court through 1940 and this year, and even Alice had to submit an affidavit describing how bad the marriage had been. Leo had been convicted of his crimes in June of this year and was sentenced to over two years in prison. Still, while Leo was serving his sentence in Prison Diez, his lawyer continued to respond to the filings made by Dr. Popper regarding the divorce. Finally, in the beginning of September, Selma received the divorce decree. But instead of making her happy, it seemed to take all the air out of Selma. And Alice understood why. Now there would be no more distractions.

Alice reached the Marx's home around 6:15 pm. She didn't need to knock – it was as if Selma had been expecting her. "Hi Alice. I assume you heard? Dr. Marx was out visiting a patient, even though he is not supposed to do that, and found out about the deportations, and came right home. As soon as I heard, I went over to your apartment, and your neighbor told me he saw both you and Alfred leave for work, so I knew both of you were okay. And then I walked over to the old age home. Mama was worried, but she is fine. Do you know if Margot is okay?"

Well, that was a relief about Alfred, thought Alice. "I don't know about Margot. I wanted to make sure Alfred was okay, but it sounds like he is, unless they picked people up from their work places."

"Oh, I hadn't thought of that. You should probably check right now." Now Alice was worried again about Alfred.

"I will. I am glad you are okay." Alice was anxious to get home, and she hadn't been sure how long she would have to indulge her sister. So it was good that Selma was thinking about what Alice needed, and didn't make Alice stay longer. Alice left immediately, almost without saying goodbye.

It normally took her 15 minutes to walk home, but today it took just 5 minutes – she nearly sprinted the whole way home. She raced up the three flights to find Alfred standing in the living room. He was okay! She was pretty sure he would be, but it was a relief to know. She grabbed him and hugged him hard. He hugged her back.

Alfred was the first to speak. "As soon as I could get away, I came straight home. I knew you went to work, but I wanted to make sure no one came to your factory to get you. They were already in the neighborhood knocking on doors as I was leaving. They stopped me because they saw the yellow star on my coat. They checked my identity card, saw that I was not on the list, and let me go." Since January 1939, all Jews were required to obtain and carry an identity card, with a "J" for Juden (Jewish) prominently displayed. Alfred continued, "I guessed that if I was not on the list, you were also not on the list. But I just needed to make sure."

Alice smiled with relief. "I am just so glad to see you. I checked on Selma on my way home from work and she is fine. And so is Mama. I am so glad that Henny is finally in America with Ruth. One less person to worry about." It took Henny nearly two months to secure boat passage in Lisbon, but she finally arrived in New York last month. She sent a telegram as soon as she arrived.

But then Alice thought about Margot. She also lived in the West End with her mother. "I need to check on Margot."

"I will go with you. I am not letting you out of my sight." Alice gave Alfred a small smile and squeezed his hand, and then they both left.

As they were leaving the apartment building, Alice asked Alfred about what he knew.

"I heard they had a list of people who were being walked to the Grossmarkthalle. I also heard that the list was only Jews who live in the West End. They were told to pack some clothing, and then someone else told me they had heard from one of the Jewish Community officials that the Jews were being taken by train to Lodz in Poland."

"Poland? Why?"

"I don't know. But hopefully we will find out soon. The other thing I heard was that it was pretty chaotic, with people going into the apartments after the Jews left to steal things."

They were at Margot's building within minutes. After Benno had left, Margot and her mother had moved to a smaller apartment on Schumannstrasse, but it was still an easy walk from Alice's apartment. They knocked on the door, but no one answered. They knocked again, but still no answer. After the third knock, a neighbor opened his door. "They came for them this morning. All I can say is good riddance. Now get out of here before I have you arrested." He then slammed his door.

Alice and Alfred stood in front of the door, stunned. Then, thinking that the neighbor's threat was not an idle one, they left. They walked back slowly to their apartment. They ate their dinner in silence, and then they went to bed. They had no energy to process what had just happened to Margot. That would need to wait until the morning. Alice wondered what she should tell Benno. But she knew she needed to write him right away, although she wasn't sure the letter would ever reach him. Margot had told Alice that Benno had finally obtained boat passage from Lisbon in August and was now living with his sons in New York. She had even given Alice the address. Alice knew Benno was trying to get his wife and mother-in-law to Cuba, and so would need to know that they had been deported.

Alice went to work in the morning and heard more about what had happened from co-workers. Between 6 and 7 am, various sorts of German officials had knocked on the doors of Jews living in the West End, who were told they had two hours to get ready to leave. They could pack very little and had to write their personal information on cardboard signs that would hang around their necks. They were marched to the Grossmarkthalle and taken to the basement. In the middle of the night, they were put on train cars and taken to Lodz. Apparently, the Germans had turned part of this Polish city into a ghetto and the Jews on the train would be living in the ghetto.

"Deported. This is unthinkable." Alice was speaking with the woman next to her at the factory. Martha was Jewish and had been a seamstress, working for her brother-in-law. He had been forced to close his business after Kristallnacht, and he was one of those who had just been deported. "Why do you think they decided to deport these people?" Alice asked. Martha did not respond, but Alice had her answer a few days later when she saw men in various Nazi uniforms moving into those "Jewish" apartments with their families. She said to Alfred during dinner, "I guess they found a new way to evict Jews. First, they moved them into Jewish Houses. Now they are deporting them. What's next?" She didn't expect Alfred to answer. But she was worried. Would they be next? Had the Nazis found a new way to get rid of German Jews?

Alfred and Alice had finally received their tax clearance certificate the previous month. But instead of feeling relief at having obtained the coveted certificate after years of struggle, both were surprised to find that they actually felt nothing when they opened the envelope. Alfred continued to inform the Foreign Exchange Office every time there was a change in Alice's employment, to ensure that their taxes were paid and there would be no taxes owed. But they were not going anywhere. It was too late to try to obtain a U.S. visa, since the American Consulates were closed. They could try to get Cuban visas, but they had no money to spare. Plus, the Cuban visas hadn't done Margot and her mother much good. Even with those visas, Margot and her mother couldn't find a way to get out of Germany, since they couldn't obtain passages on a sealed train without U.S. visas. And Alice didn't know anyone with a Swiss bank account to buy them seats on a Lufthansa flight like her sister Johanna. Despite all of their efforts, it looked like, at least for the moment, they were stuck in Germany. Now they just had to hope that there would be no more deportations. Maybe they had not been so fortunate to remain in the West End.

•   •   •

The Sunday after the deportations, Alice woke early. Alfred was still sleeping, and she often let him sleep in on Sunday. It was their only day off, and Alfred needed the rest. Plus, their limited coal rations would mean that the apartment would remain cold for most of the day, so the warmest place in the apartment was under the covers, in bed. But Alice was feeling restless, and she needed to leave the apartment. Both of them needed to leave the apartment.

"Alfred, wake up. I really need to get out of this apartment. Let's walk to the zoo."

"The zoo? Are you crazy? It's cold outside. And it is cold out of bed." Alfred turned over, prepared to fall back asleep.

"No, Alfred, I'm serious. It actually looks like a nice day today. I really cannot stay in this apartment one more minute. Let's get dressed quickly, pack up something to eat, and walk to the zoo."

Alfred knew better than to argue with Alice once she had made up her mind about something. He got out of bed, put on some warm clothing, and joined his wife in the kitchen, watching as she made two sandwiches with the leftovers from the night before. "Nothing fancy, but it will do," said Alice. She then smiled at Alfred and he smiled back.

When Alice was a child, one of her favorite activities was to walk to the zoo on a Saturday morning in the summer. The zoo was in the East End, always just a few blocks from their various apartments. There was always a band or two playing in one of the bandstands, and there were always snacks to purchase. Even though it was a Sabbath morning, her mother allowed her to spend her money, although Emma never purchased anything on the Sabbath. Alice liked making faces at the animals, and walking around the lake. Alice knew she needed to try to recapture some of that joy. Especially now.

Alice and Alfred grabbed their coats with the Jewish stars prominently displayed and left their apartment. The weather was rather nice for a late October morning and they decided to walk along the Zeil, the main shopping street in the downtown section. Before the Nazis came to power, many of the stores on the street were owned by Jews, including most of the larger department stores. Now, some of those stores had been replaced by "Aryan" stores, while other storefronts were simply closed. Alice and Alfred were aware that people were glaring at them as they walked by, but they didn't care. They were actually enjoying the stroll.

They walked past a large department store that stretched an entire block. The name of the store was Hansa, but Alice remembered when this store had been owned by a Jewish family.

"Alfred, do you remember when this was Kaufhaus Wronker? It was owned by Hermann and Ida Wronker. My parents knew them a little, through their charity work. My mother once told me Herr Wronker fed needy children during the Great War in the store's cafeteria and his wife worked for the Red Cross during the war. They even lost a son in the war. I used to love coming here with my mother as a child. It was always an event and we always dressed up. First, we would shop, starting on the top floor and working our way down. Then we would go to one of the cafes for lunch. If we were lucky, my father would join us for lunch, but only if he was having a meeting with clients in one of the other rooms in the café. Of course, when I moved back to Frankfurt and they were selling ready-to-wear clothing, the department store was a competitor. But I still loved walking through all the departments, and seeing all the goods they were selling. But now Jews are not allowed inside. How things have changed in just a short period of time!" But Alice stopped herself from thinking about their troubles and tried to enjoy their walk. She even started to window-shop, joking with Alfred about items that she thought would look great on him. They both purposely ignored the "No Jews Allowed" signs prominently displayed in the windows of each of the stores. At some point, they were both smiling at the silliness of this exercise.

"Alice, I didn't want to do this, but you were right. Getting out of that apartment was the right this to do this morning. I actually almost feel normal. Although I would probably feel more normal if these people would stop staring and pointing at us."

"Just ignore them. Let's just enjoy our morning stroll." Which they both did.

By the time they reached the zoo, both were ready to rest up on one of the benches. They picked a bench away from other people – no need to encourage trouble. Alice took out some of the cookies she had packed, and they ate their snack in silence. Alice looked over and saw Alfred making a face after he bit into the cookie. She still struggled to make palatable cookies with the ersatz butter she was permitted to buy, but at least they did look like cookies this time. At some point Alice became aware that Alfred was speaking to her, but she hadn't heard what he had said.

"It has been a while since you have disappeared on me. I was talking to you, and at some point realized that you hadn't heard a word I said. Where did you go this time?"

"I saw this couple walk by and she was wearing this lovely coat and then all of a sudden I started designing a new outfit for her. And then for him. I am so sorry I disappeared on you."

"Actually, schatzi, I am happy you disappeared on me. It is the most normal thing you have done in months."

Alice and Alfred then got up from the bench and walked around the zoo, holding hands. At some point, they sat down to eat their lunch. It was the best day they had had in a very long time.

CHAPTER 16

Frankfurt, November 1941

Winter had come early. It hadn't yet snowed, but the morning temperatures were below freezing, and the skies were grey. But winter was also in the hearts and minds of all of Frankfurt's Jews. The deportation of the West End Jews in October had been a shock to every Jew left in Frankfurt. Life in Frankfurt had already become intolerable for Jews, with shortages of food and coal and almost daily harassments from the Gestapo. And then the October deportation.

Alfred had heard that the Association of Jews in Germany, which had been established by the Nazis in 1939 but employed only Jews, knew about the October deportation before it occurred and even supplied the Gestapo with names, although the Gestapo had told them what neighborhoods they were targeting. But the Gestapo wanted to keep it a secret and directed that no one be told. It made Alfred angry that Jews were helping the Nazis deport Jews. Alice agreed, but wondered to herself what she would have done if she had been working for the Association.

Alice went to work early, hoping that she might be able to leave a little early. Jews could only shop at 4 pm for an hour, and the stores were often out of most foods by then; she was hoping to get there exactly at 4 to have the greatest chance of finding at least some decent produce. As she sat down, she noticed that Sarah, who today was operating the sewing machine next to hers, was particularly quiet. She knew better than to ask a direct question, and so just commented on the cold weather. Sarah didn't look up, but simply said, "We just received a notice. We are on the next transport. We are leaving on November 12th. In two days, we will be gone."

"A notice? What do you mean you received a notice?"

"They brought it last night. A Gestapo officer knocked on our door and handed us a piece of paper. He made us read it first and then he left. Me, my husband and our two children are being deported. He wouldn't tell us where. They are coming to our apartment on the morning of the 12th, they will check to make sure we are not taking anything of value, and then they will escort us to the Grossmarkthalle. We are supposed to bring RM 50 each to pay for the train. Can you believe they are going to make us pay for our own deportation?"

Alice immediately felt relief. If no one had come to her apartment last night, then she was hoping they had avoided this second transport. And then she felt a little guilty, because Sarah and her family had not. "Sarah, I am so sorry. Is there anything I can do?"

"Alice, thank you for asking, but there is nothing anyone can do. We had been trying for years to leave, but that door officially closed at the end of last month, when Germany announced that the borders were closed to all emigration. Once that happened, we expected something bad would happen to us. Particularly after the first transport. I guess it is only a matter of time before all the Jews are taken away."

A pretty harsh statement, and she could understand why Sarah would make it. But Alice also wondered how long she and Alfred would be able to remain in Frankfurt.

After a few minutes, Sarah added, "I didn't know whether I should continue to show up for work, but there really isn't anyone to ask. Plus, I don't want to get arrested and then be separated from my family. So I guess I will continue to work until we have to leave." Alice didn't know what else to say to Sarah, and Sarah added nothing else. And so they focused on their work.

•   •   •

Alice had been able to leave work in time to make it to the market, although there was little left. Her rations card had already limited what she could purchase. But she was able to purchase some very bruised onions, some fatty meat, and a few moldy potatoes. Of course, the ersatz coffee was always available, and she purchased some of that, although Alfred always made a face when he drank it.

Alice was already making dinner when Alfred came home. She could tell from his face that he had already heard about the upcoming transport. She went up to him and they hugged. They remained hugging for a few minutes and then Alfred went to change. There was time to discuss this, but for now, let Alfred rest up. As hard as Alice's days were, she mostly sat. Alfred, on the other hand, digs most of the day. His hands had become calloused and he had actually gained some muscle. He is hungry all the time and even with the extra rations, Alice often did not have enough food for both of them, and so went without. But Alfred never complained. Perhaps this was from being in a second marriage. Or perhaps it was because Alfred is just a decent person and understands that they have to be easy on each other in order to survive the madness.

When it was time to eat dinner, Alice had to wake Alfred in his chair and they both went to the table. She placed the stew on the table. Alfred looked down at this plate. "Wow, there is meat in the stew!"

"It is not the best cut of meat, but I was able to leave work just a little early and make it to the market before they ran out of everything. Of course, it helped that we are allowed extra rations. Good thing you have the excavator job!" Alice could tell that Alfred was struggling just to smile – was he just tired from work or was it the news about the upcoming deportations? She decided to let him raise the subject. She didn't have to wait long.

"A couple of men I work with received notices about the upcoming transport. I am assuming you heard at work."

"I did. This woman at work, Sarah, received a notice. It looks like they are now giving people a few days to prepare for the transport. Maybe they learned their lesson from the first transport, when no notice was given and things were pretty chaotic. Sarah told me they are limited in what they can bring and they can't bring any valuables. Like any of us have any valuables left."

Alfred then looked at Alice with alarm. "I just thought about Selma and your mother. I can't believe I forgot about them!"

"Oh, I forgot to tell you. When Sarah first told me about the notice, I immediately thought about my mother and Selma. But I wasn't thinking that Selma might have worried about me. I couldn't believe that Selma actually showed up around 10 am to check on me. One of the advantages in her not having a forced labor job yet. And one of the advantages in having a sister like Selma, who would ignore my directive that she never come to my work. Still, I was happy that she showed up, so at least my mother wouldn't worry." Alfred shook his head and smiled. That was Selma!

"But I thought I would stop at my sister's house on the way home from work tomorrow. I am sure the latest deportation notice has her worried. I had been meaning to visit her anyway. I will certainly be home before curfew."

"Selma will like that. We can eat when you get home." Alice and Alfred were quiet through the rest of dinner. The combination of work and the stresses from this new deportation had worn them both out. But there was a comfort in just being together and being momentarily safe.

·   ·   ·

Frau Marx answered the door when Alice knocked the next day. She was a short stocky woman who had a rather brusque manner, but she had kind eyes and, based on how she had treated both her mother and Selma, a heart of gold. "Good evening, Frau Marx. I hope you and Herr Doktor are well."

"We are, Frau Falkenstein. And I hope you and Herr Falkenstein are also well. Please come in. Let me get your sister."

"Thank you, Frau Marx."

Selma had appeared while Alice and Frau Marx were talking. The Marx home often felt like a train station, particularly during the early morning or early evening hours, with people going to or coming from work. Since her mother had moved out of the house, another family had been forced to move into the Marx house. Selma often complained to Alice about how crowded the house had become. Alice and Selma found a quiet corner and both sat down.

"If you have come here to yell at me about coming to the factory yesterday, don't bother. I would do it again. I just needed to know that you were safe and that you knew that me and Mama were safe."

"I am not going to yell at you. I am actually grateful that you came. It was a relief to know that you and Mama were not on the list. Although I did get some grief from the foreman. But if it wasn't this, it would be something else."

"Well, I am glad that you understood why I needed to come. And I am glad you came today. Everyone in the house is talking about this upcoming transport. No one from the house was on the list, but I am still going a little stir crazy. Can we take a walk, just around the neighborhood? I will make sure you get home before curfew."

"Sure." Alice could tell that her sister needed to get out of the Marx's house. If they stayed within a block of the house, they should be fine.

"Alice, I am really starting to worry about these deportations. It can't be good that these people are being sent to ghettos. Do you think they might stop with this deportation?"

"I really don't know. Alfred is worried that they will keep deporting Jews until there are no more Jews left in Germany. But I can't imagine how they could move all of those people. And where will they live? How will they be fed? It all sounds a little insane to me. They should have just let us leave when we wanted to leave." Alice wasn't thinking when she made this last statement. Even if she had been able to leave, Selma wasn't leaving. And Alice knew that if she had received her U.S. visa, Selma would have been devastated. She wondered how her sister would be coping now if Alfred and Alice were safely in America.

"But what if there are more transports?" Selma was clearly worried. Alice tried to calm her sister down.

"Alfred told me he thought both transports amounted to over 2,000 Jews. He said that still leaves about 8,000 Jews in Frankfurt. That is a lot of people. I can't imagine they will try to get rid of all of us. Plus, who will do their forced labor jobs?" Alice tried to believe what she was telling her sister. But she was not so sure. The Germans could get others to work in their factories, or could move the factories to the countries they had invaded. There was no way of knowing what was to come. And she worried about what had happened to those on the October transport. She had not heard from Margot and no one at work had heard from anyone who had been deported. And although she had written Benno, unsurprisingly, she had heard nothing from him.

•   •   •

Frankfurt's Jewish community had mostly been stunned by the first transport of the city's Jews. They had also hoped that this would be a one-time event, driven by the desire of Nazi officials to obtained coveted apartments and avoid finding more Jewish houses. The second transport made it clear that this was just wishful thinking. Now, many were wondering when the next transport would occur. Friends and family were sharing any information they heard, even if its reliability was questionable. Those with connections to anyone working for the Association of Jews in Germany were encouraged to find out what they could.

The Association of Jews in Germany's mission had initially been to facilitate the emigration of Germany's Jews. The Association grew out of the Reich Representation of German Jews, which had been created in 1933 by Rabbi Leo Baeck and other important Jewish officials to support German Jews during the Nazi period. After its creation in 1939, the Association of Jews in Germany (the name change reflecting the Nazi position that there were no longer any "German Jews") was also tasked with developing files for all German Jews, with each person's information on an index card. After Jews could no longer leave Germany, the Association's focus changed to now helping the Gestapo identify where the Jews lived. The Association did not prepare the actual transport lists for the two deportations in Frankfurt, but they provided the names based on what neighborhoods in the city the Gestapo had decided to target. So far, neither Alice nor Alfred had heard anything that would be considered reliable. And so they went about their days, going to work and trying to live as best as they could. And Alice was also doing her best to keep up her sister's spirits.

Without a job, Selma had little to do during the day, and that was not helping her mental state. While Selma helped Frau Marx with the cooking for everyone living in the house, she also spent a lot of time with her mother in the old age home, and those visits were also not helping. Selma had told Alice that their mother spoke about just two things. Either she expressed frustration that she had to live in the old age home, away from her children. "Parents should not be separated from their children." She seemed to have forgotten that she was moved only because she could no longer live in the Marx's house. And then she expressed remorse at having encouraged Selma to stay in Germany. "I should never have encouraged you to stay. I should have made you apply for a U.S. visa like your sister." But Selma didn't argue with her mother, telling Alice, "She has just turned 80 years old. She is safe in the home and is eating well. If these are the two conversations she wants to have, I am going to let her. Look at me, being sensitive to Mama's needs."

A week after the second deportation, Alfred heard rumors at work about a third transport. He decided not to share this information with Alice – why worry her if the rumors turned out to be false. But the next day, Alice heard the same rumors and shared them with Alfred when she came home from work.

"Alice, I heard the same rumors, but who knows what to believe? My guess is that we will continue to hear rumors. I think we need to try to ignore them or we will all go crazy."

"I agree. Let me start dinner and you rest on the chair. Let's promise that we won't say a word about deportations tonight." Alfred nodded and then walked over to the chair to rest.

Alice had just begun slicing some onions when there was a knock at the door. She wiped her hands and went to the door. It was a Gestapo officer. Alfred got up from his chair and joined her at the door. The officer read from a piece of paper, announcing that Alice and Alfred would be on the next transport, leaving on November 22nd. He handed them the deportation order, as well as an asset declaration form. He told them to fill out the form. They would need to hand the form to the officer who will come to their apartment on the morning of the 22nd. He told them to read the deportation order carefully. And then he left. The entire conversation lasted less than five minutes. Five minutes and their whole world had turned upside down.

Alfred closed the door, stunned. In his hand were the two pieces of paper. The first paper was titled "Document:

Deportation Notification Form." He read the instructions out loud: "(1) list all assets on the asset declaration form; (2) leave behind all valuables other than a wedding ring; (3) take no more than RM 50, which would be used to pay for the transport; (4) pack a small suitcase with warm clothes; and (5) pack a handbag with food for three days."

Alice was not listening to the instructions. She had stopped listening after she heard the Gestapo officer utter the word "transport." And then she yelled out loud – "Transport?" The notice had finally come and she was now having trouble breathing. Alfred grabbed both of her hands and looked into her eyes. He breathed slowly, and then she began to slow down her breathing. Still, she thought she was going to faint. Alfred took her hand and walked her over to the two chairs they sat in at night to read. So much for trying to ignore the rumors and have a nice dinner, Alice thought.

The notice said that they were leaving on November 22nd, in three days. They needed to go to Deutsche Bank for the RM 100, although they would need to receive permission to withdraw the money from the Foreign Exchange Office. Alfred said, "I assume paying for our deportation is a good enough excuse for the withdrawal." Alfred's sense of humor could be heard, but there was also a bitterness in his tone, which Alice shared. Paying for the "honor" of being deported.

Alice said, "I will go to the market and buy what I can for the three days-worth of food we need to bring. It won't be fancy, but I will make sure we don't go hungry. Perhaps four days-worth would be better. Once we are on the train, who knows when we will eat again, so it is better to be on the safe side."

"Alice, if you go to the market, I will take care of the bank withdrawal."

"We also need to figure out what to bring. But we don't even know where we are going." They knew the first transport went to

Lodz in Poland and there were rumors that the second transport went to Minsk in the Soviet Union.

"I think we can assume that the place we will be going to will be colder than here. We need to make sure we have enough warm clothes. If we can only bring a small suitcase each, we should probably wear as much clothing as we can. We need to assume that, wherever we end up, we may not be able to buy any clothes, even if somehow we are able to get money."

"I wonder if we will be able to work. Maybe they will put me to work as a seamstress. I imagine wherever we end up, they will need tailors."

Alfred took both of Alice's hands. "Schazi, I know this will be hard, but we will be together. And I can't imagine it will be much harder than the last year, and we have managed to survive the many food shortages and anti-Semitic edicts. But you will have the hardest task now. You will need to tell you mother and sister. Telling Selma may be worse than any transport." Alice couldn't help herself – she laughed and shook her head yes.

· · ·

Not having a clear direction on what they should do, both Alfred and Alice reported to work the next day. When she arrived at work, Alice walked over to the foreman to tell him she was being deported in two days. "That's in two days. In the meantime, I expect you to work. That means today and tomorrow. Now go to your machine." And then he added, "No big loss for us. They are bringing in workers from the East to replace you Jews, anyway." Well, I guess that answered my question about how they will get along without Jews, Alice thought. But Alice was distracted all day and nearly put a needle through her finger. How was she going to tell her sister that she was being deported? Interestingly, she wasn't as worried about her mother.

Alfred and Alice agreed that Alice would visit her sister after work, and that Alfred and Alice and Selma would go to see her mother the following day – the day before they would be leaving on the transport. The rumor was that the deportation was still targeting Jews living in the West End. Both Alfred and Alice therefore assumed that neither Emma nor Selma had received a deportation notice, since neither lived in the West End, although Alice still needed to make sure. It was a cold day, but Alice hardly felt the weather as she walked to the Marx home after work. She was worried about how her sister would react to the news. Alice had always been the stronger one, the responsible one, the one in charge of handling problems. Selma had always relished her position as the baby of the family, sometimes a little too much. Alice was hoping her sister would rise to the occasion, particularly because Alice herself was anxious about being deported.

Alice knocked on the Marx's door, aware that this was probably the last time she would visit this house. Selma actually answered the door. She looked at Alice and she knew. She grabbed Alice and then they both hugged. Selma pulled her sister into the house and closed the door.

"I heard about the notices this morning and was worried all day. I decided not to go to your workplace since your foreman gave you such a hard time the last time and assumed you would stop by on the way home from work. But it has been a long day, and now I know." Alice looked at her sister, and could see a few tears falling.

"I had considered coming here first on the way to work, but I had to be at work early and didn't want to wake the Doktor and Frau Marx." Alice was also thinking that, depending on how the visit had gone, she might not have been able to make it through the work day. Seeing her sister after work was the better plan.

"I understand. I am just happy to have you here. I told myself all day that when you came, I would be brave. And I am trying to be brave. But I am so afraid for you – and for myself. I was thinking today about how hard it was for me when you were living in Nuremberg. But at least, I could visit and you could visit. And we could write letters. And now you are going someplace – we don't even know where – and I don't know when I will be able to see you and talk with you again. I don't even know if we will be able to send each other letters. You are also not going to believe that I finally received a forced labor position. It starts in two days, the same day you and Alfred are leaving."

"A forced labor job. Where will you be working?"

"In a laundry. But at least I will be making a little money. That will help me and Mama. But I would rather not think about that now."

"I agree. We have two days before I have to leave. Let's make the most of it. Why don't you come back with me. Stay at our place tonight. We can put the two chairs together for a bed. It will not be the most comfortable, but we can stay up late and talk. I don't care about being tired at work. I will be done with that place soon enough."

At hearing that she would be going home with Alice for the night, Selma's face brightened. "It would be like a sleep-over. Yes, let's do this. I want to spend as much time with you as I can. But when are you going to tell Mama?"

"Alfred and I thought that the three of us would see Mama after work tomorrow. We could all meet at the old age home. Alfred also wants to say goodbye to Mama, and having the three of us together with her might distract her enough so that she wouldn't fall apart. Plus, if I had to see her alone, I might fall apart."

Alice and Selma walked into Selma's room to pack a bag. Alice then thanked Frau Marx for her kindness, and the two left for Alice's apartment. They walked arm-in-arm in silence, each trying to find the words to express how they felt. They finally gave up and just enjoyed their time together, knowing that the future was uncertain for both of them.

Alfred was home by the time they arrived at the apartment. Because Alice was stopping to see her sister, Alfred volunteered to go to both the bank and the store after work – he was able to leave work early only because he agreed to make up the time the following day. Alfred had also started dinner, although Alfred was even less of a cook than Alice, and Alice took over. Alice could hear her sister and husband talking from the kitchen, although she could not make out what they were saying. She liked that her husband and sister got along. She remembered how much of a struggle it was to talk to Leo, but that was likely because he was angry most of the time with Selma.

The three had a pleasant dinner, talking about old times. Selma and Alice spoke about vacations they had taken. Alice and Alfred spoke about their time in Nuremberg and the shows Alice had in her arts and crafts studio. Selma said that she wished she had been able to attend more of those shows. Alice talked about starting the dressmaking business and Alfred pursuing her in Frankfurt. And then Selma and Alice talked about growing up in Frankfurt.

"Alice, do you remember the time you convinced me to go with you to a fashion show at the Kaufhaus Wronker? I was probably 11 years old, so it would have been in 1911, just before the war. We had not yet moved to the apartment on Roderberg Weg, so we were living in that apartment closer to the zoo. You had asked Mama if you could go to a fashion show on a Saturday and Mama told you it would not be appropriate because it was the Sabbath. Mama and Papa were going to a bar mitzvah. Mama always gave the help the morning off on Saturday and she asked you to watch me while they were out. After they left, you asked me if I wanted to go with you on an adventure."

"Oh Alice, you were such a bad girl!"

"Alfred, I was actually a very good girl and never disobeyed my mother. But this was a special event, the very first fashion show in Frankfurt, and there would be fashions coming from both Paris and Berlin. As I recall, they were showing the new hobble skirts, which were wide at the hips and narrow at the ankles, and I really wanted to see them in person. It might seem a little old-fashioned now, but they were all the rage then. They were also showing all the new styles for the season, styles I had only seen in magazines. It was going to be a very important show. And I felt like I just had to go and that it would be the end of my life if I didn't go."

Alfred laughed. Alice gave him a nudge and said, "Remember, I was 15 years old, so any disappointment would have seemed like the end of the world for me. And I didn't want Selma to tattle on me if I left her alone, so I enticed her to join me."

"Well, I wouldn't say you enticed me. You tricked me. You told me we would be going on a special adventure, but that it was a secret. We boarded the tram, and then we got off at the Kaufhaus. It wasn't until we were in this large room with rows of chairs that you told me we were seeing a fashion show. It was probably good that you didn't tell me, because I never would have gone with you."

"Why do you think I didn't tell you? We found two empty seats in the back of the room, the show started, and I was totally mesmerized. The fashions were amazing. I had my notebook with me and I started to take notes. Selma was also enjoying the show – admit it, Selma, you were enjoying the show – and during the intermission, I bought us lemonade and cookies. The second half of the show started, and I stopped paying attention to the time. Selma was sitting to my left, and at some point the person sitting to my right left, and so the seat was empty. A woman soon asked me if the seat was free. I wasn't really paying attention to her and was about to say yes when I looked up and saw that it was Mama!"

Alfred was laughing out loud. "Oh no. How did she find out that you were at the show?"

"It wasn't hard to figure out. My mother had come home from the bar mitzvah early, saw that no one was home, noticed that we had both taken our fancy coats, and assumed that I had disobeyed her and had taken Selma to the fashion show. I was fully expecting her to tell me to stand up and walk out of the show. But, instead, my mother sat down and stayed until the show was over. She even saw some of the hobble skirts on the models. As we stood up to leave, my mother asked Selma if she liked the show."

Selma smiled and said, "I remember exactly what I said to her. I told her that the fashion show was okay, but I mostly liked that Alice would get into trouble."

Alfred laughed and looked over at his wife. "And did you get into trouble?"

"No. In fact, my mother bought me a hobble skirt, but one of the ready-to-wear ones they were selling. She knew one of the saleswomen and arranged for her to send us the skirt with the bill after the Sabbath. She never said a word to me about disobeying her, and when Selma was about to tell her how I had tricked her into going, my mother told her it was not a good practice to tattle, especially on a sister."

At that, they all laughed.

The three continued to tell stories, mostly funny stories that had them laughing until they cried. They avoided talking about any of the sad moments in their lives – their three failed marriages, the recent struggles just to live, the friends and family who had been able to leave Germany – or those who had already been deported and had not been heard from since. After a while, Alfred stood up from the table and added extra coal to the stove. No need to worry about using up their allotment. He then left the sisters and went into the bedroom.

Alice and Selma sat in the two chairs and talked into the night. At some point, Selma looked over at her sister and took one of her hands. "Alice, I want to tell you why I told the story about you and the fashion show earlier. I didn't want you to think that I told it because I thought Mama had been too easy on you or a bit too hard on me, although I have to admit that sometimes I did think that. I wanted to tell the story for two reasons. First, I wanted you to know that I was always happy when you included me in your fashion adventures, even when I complained about it at the time. I loved to see the excitement in your eyes every time you saw something that was beautiful or exotic or even shocking. And second, I told the story because I loved that Mama always wanted us to be close, to look out for one another. I tried to look out for you, as best as I could, but I know you always looked out for me. Alice, before they send you away, I wanted you to know that you have been the best sister I could have asked for!" Selma was choking up, and there were tears in her eyes. Alice squeezed her sister's hand, and then hugged Selma, so hard that she thought she might break her sister.

When Alice decided it was time to sleep, she pushed the chairs together to make a bed for Selma. She then spread a blanket on the rug to make a bed for herself. When they were children and shared a bedroom, Alice always found it comforting to listen to her sister snore when she was having trouble sleeping. She remembered that time as she laid next to her sister. After a while, Alice fell asleep to the soft snores of her sister.

•   •   •

The only good thing about her work day was that it was her last day at the factory. The foreman was the same brutish man he had been since Alice started. And once her non-Jewish co-workers found out that she was being deported, they spent the day taunting her. She had made no real friends at the factory – even the Jewish forced laborers kept their distance, since each wanted to avoid being a target of taunts. Plus, no one wanted to get close to someone who would soon be deported. Alice took a last long breath as she crossed the threshold at the end of her shift. She was done with this place!

The old age home was about a 30-minute walk from Alice's factory, but in the opposite direction from home. That meant that the walk home would take about 45 minutes. She always had to keep the times in mind in order to avoid missing curfew, since Jews could not take the tram. Alice and Selma agreed to meet at the home at 6 pm. Alfred needed to work an extra hour, for leaving early the previous day to go to the bank and to the store, so he would not get there until 6:30 pm. They would all need to leave her mother no later than 7:15 pm to make it home by the 8 pm curfew.

Selma was waiting outside the Jewish center when Alice arrived. The old age home was on the second and third floors of the center. They both hugged, and Selma handed her a bag. Alice opened the bag and saw her favorite cookies from when they were children – shortbread cookies.

"I haven't had these cookies in years. Selma, where did you get the ingredients for shortbread cookies?"

"I found a way to get some of the ingredients, although I had to adjust the recipe a bit. No butter. I hope you are not too disappointed. They probably don't taste the same as the cookies that Sarah used to make. I just didn't want you to go hungry on your trip, given the cookies you make."

Alice could feel the tears coming, and fought hard to block them. "Selma, I'm sure they are perfect. Thank you so much." And then they hugged again.

Alice and Selma opened the doors of the center and walked down the hall to the elevators. On the way, they passed two long lines of people – one for used clothing (since Jews could no longer buy or make new clothes) and one for the soup kitchen. Alice thought that, in the nine months since Emma had moved to the home, both lines had gotten longer and longer. Alice and Selma took the elevator to the third floor and walked down the hall. Since their mother had moved here in the spring, more residents had moved in – or been forced to move in. Everyone shared a room, but some rooms had to accommodate three or more women. Emma was lucky – she only had a single roommate, Frau Levy. When they reached her mother's room, Emma was sitting in a chair beside the bed. They said hello to Frau Levy, who then excused herself and left the room. She could tell they needed privacy.

Emma looked at her daughters and knew why they were there. At least one of them would be on that third transport she had heard about. But she would let them tell her. "Alice, Selma, it is so nice of the two of you to stop by to see me."

Alice spoke. "Mama, you know curfew is at 8 pm, so we don't have much time. Alfred and I will be on the next transport. They didn't tell us where we are going, but we are leaving tomorrow morning. They gave us a list of what we can and should take. They are also making us pay to take the train. Can you believe that? Like this is some vacation for us. Maybe we should just say, no thanks, we would rather just stay home." Alice had intended to stay calm and measured for this visit. After all, she was here to try to keep her mother calm and hopeful. She hadn't intended to get upset. But she was speaking rapidly and, despite her best efforts, she had started to cry.

Emma got up from her chair and went to her daughter and hugged her. When Alice was seven years old and was playing with friends outside, she had fallen and scraped her knee. Alice started to cry and one of her friends called her a baby, which made her cry even harder. She ran inside and called for her mother. Her mother came right to her and hugged her and asked very gently what was wrong. She then told Alice that it was okay to cry and that she was not a baby. Alice was remembering that moment and felt safe in her mother's arms. She wanted to stay in her mother's arms forever. But at that moment, she heard Alfred and was brought back to the room and the point of her visit.

"Mama, I want you to know that Alfred and I have everything we need. We are both healthy and strong and we will do whatever we need to do. And we will all see each other again, when this madness ends."

"Alice, my darling, I have faith that we will all be together again. I have always been so proud of you. You were my brave child, going out into the world. To go to that art school, to open your own studio, to start you own dressmaking business. You found love again and both of you make each other happy. I love you and will miss you, but we will see each other again."

Alice always worried a little when her mother spoke to her about her successes in front of her sister. Alice knew Selma sometimes felt judged by their mother and didn't always like it when Alice was praised and Selma was not. Alice glanced over at her sister, but Selma was smiling at Alice. In what Alice understood might be Selma's last act of generosity towards her sister, Selma was going to let Alice bask in the glow of Emma's pride toward her elder daughter. Then the three shared a hug, a hug that seemed to last forever.

•   •   •

That night, Alfred and Alice began to complete the asset form. They put all of their valuables on the kitchen table. Not much was left – most had already been turned over to Nazi authorities and other items had been sold. The order allowed them to keep their wedding rings and Alfred's inexpensive watch. Alice was thinking about her own watch as she read over the form again, the watch that had been taken by the Gestapo. Everything else had to be noted on the asset form and left for the Gestapo – the Sabbath candlesticks, the remaining silverware, the few pieces of china.

Alfred took out the two small suitcases they could use and Alice and Alfred began to inventory all of their clothing. They would take warm clothes, undergarments, socks, sweaters. And Alice had one more thing that she wanted to take with her. Beginning with her purse designs, every design that she thought was special was placed in a folder. That continued when she began designing dresses. The folder was always with her, even after she was forced to close her business. Even during the last two years, she continued to create new dress designs and placed those designs in the folder. She had assumed that, at some point, she would be able to return to dress designing and wanted to be ready. The folder was like an appendage, and she couldn't imagine leaving it behind. If she had to sacrifice a sweater to include the folder in the suitcase, so be it. Alfred understood and said nothing when she put it in her suitcase.

They gathered the clothes they would wear tomorrow on the walk to the Grossmarkthalle. They closed the suitcases and placed them on the floor. Alice packed the food – four days' worth. The Nazis wouldn't know the difference between three-days and four-days' worth of food. And then they were done. It was late, but they weren't tired. What would they do until morning?

Intimacy had been hard for the two of them over the last few months. Between their efforts to leave Nazi Germany and the requirements of their forced labor jobs, neither had felt the desire. But for some strange reason, at the moment when Alice had assumed the two would just break down and cry, they felt drawn to one another. And so they followed their passions and went to the bedroom for their last night together in Frankfurt.

•   •   •

At precisely 7 am, there was a knock at the door. It was a Gestapo officer. He announced who he was, why he was there and asked for the asset declaration form. He reviewed the form, examining all the items that had been left on the dining room table. Alice and Alfred had just finished breakfast, but their coffee cups (for their ersatz coffee) were still on the table. Alfred placed all valuables and other assets in an envelope and handed the envelop to the officer. The officer examined the contents of each suitcase and then sealed the suitcases. Alice and Alfred were instructed to take one blanket each. The Gestapo officer then announced that it was time to leave. Alice forgot she hadn't washed the coffee cups, and asked if she could wash them before they left. The officer said no, and instead handed them two pieces of cardboard with string. He instructed them to write their names, birthdates, and identification numbers on the cardboard. He told them to put the cardboard signs around their necks. They then left the apartment, and Alfred handed the keys to the apartment to the officer. Alfred and Alice were told to join the line of people walking to the Grossmarkthalle. All along the way, their numbers grew, as more Jews joined the procession. They were subjected to jeers and taunts along the way.

The Gestapo had leased the basement of the Grossmarkthalle as an assembly for the deportations from Frankfurt, since it was easy to load the Jews onto the trains from the basement. The walk to the market would normally have taken an hour for Alfred and Alice, but with all the starting and stopping, it took over two hours. By the time they reached the market, having carried their luggage and blankets through the Frankfurt streets, they were exhausted. But there was no time to rest. They were forced to walk across the massive hall to the stairs leading to the basement. Alice looked around at the many people buying and selling fruit and vegetables, who were purposefully ignoring the Jews being marched past them. Alice loved this building, which had been built in 1928 and reflected the modern feel of the period, with curved structures and high ceilings. It was the largest building in Frankfurt and had been nicknamed the "vegetable church." But she was not feeling any love for the building now, and wished she could just go back to her apartment with her husband.

Instead, Alice and Alfred were forced down the stairs to the basement and then made to stand in a line to be processed. When they reached the first table, they were registered and their names were checked against the deportation list. At the next table, their luggage was checked and they were each physically searched to make sure they weren't taking anything they were not supposed to take. The officer took from Alice's suitcase a bar of soap and a hair brush Alice's mother had given to her for one of her birthdays. He also took out the folder with all of Alice's designs. "Not appropriate," the officer said, and threw it in the trash. Alice was about to say something, but Alfred squeezed her hand and shook his head. And just like that, her life's work was gone. At the third table, manned by the tax office, they were told to sign a document that turned over to the German government all of their remaining assets, including the money still in their blocked account at the Deutsche Bank, to pay any outstanding taxes. Alfred audibly grunted when he signed the form, and Alice shushed him. At the fourth table, they paid the "travel costs" of RM 50 each. Their names were check for a second time against a list, and they were told to show their ID cards, which were then stamped "evacuated."

By the time Alice and Alfred had finished with the last table, it was around noon. They were told to wait in a large adjacent room. They walked in and saw a sea of people. There were mattresses and straw mats on the floor. Alfred saw an open space and pointed. In normal times, Alice would never have thought to sit on a straw mat. But these were not normal times. They walked over to the mat and sat down. Alice took out two of Selma's cookies for them, and they ate in silence. In fact, there was very little talking in the room. As the day went on, the room continued to fill. No one came in to speak with them about when they would be leaving. Alfred and Alice only knew that time was passing because Alfred still had his watch.

At some point, Alice and Alfred had dozed off and were awakened when all the lights were turned on and Gestapo officers began to yell that everyone needed to get up and move to the large doors. The doors were then opened and everyone walked onto the station platform. It was nighttime, and Alfred looked at his watch.

It was 3 am. Once everyone was on the platform, one of the Gestapo officers announced that the luggage would be placed in the luggage car and everyone would get their luggage back when they had arrived at the Kaunas train station. They were then instructed to form lines and to board the train cars.

Alfred had used trains for years, and was familiar with this type of train. He told Alice that the cars were third-class passenger cars, the only type of train cars Jews could now take in Germany. Inside, there would be benches and a single toilet in the rear of the car. Alfred could see that there would be too many passengers for everyone to have a seat, and so he did his best to push Alice closer to the front of the line. Once they were on the train, he and Alice sat down on one of the benches closer to the front of the car. They could see that all the windows were nailed shut, but that was fine given that it was freezing outside. The car was also cold – they were clearly not wasting coal to heat the cars. The train car continued to fill, and people found places in the aisle to sit. It took only an hour to get everyone on board. There was no way of telling how many people were on the train, but Alfred told Alice he thought at least 100 were in this car. The doors were then locked and the train started to move. Alice looked to the end of the car and saw a Gestapo officer with a gun.

Once the train started moving, Alice thought it was safe to talk to Alfred. "So we are going to Kaunas. That is in Lithuania, right? We have never been to Lithuania. Do you know anything about this place? What do you think we are going to do there?"

"I have no idea."

The person to Alice's left heard them talking and said, "I heard someone ask an officer. He told her we would be working in a work camp. I don't know what that means. My guess is that we will be living behind barbed wire."

Someone else heard the conversation and whispered, "I have family in Kaunas. It is a beautiful city. Or at least it was until the Nazis came. The Jews now live in a ghetto there."

The first person then said, "But I don't think we are going to the ghetto. I think we are going to a separate work camp."

It was clear to Alice that no one really knew. She decided not to speculate where they were being taken. She thought it best to try to get some sleep, since she didn't know what awaited her and Alfred tomorrow. So, she rested her head against Alfred's shoulder and, surprisingly, fell into a deep sleep.

CHAPTER 17

Kaunas, November 1941

Alice awoke with the train jostling back and forth. She looked out of the window. It was light out, but she could not tell if it was morning or afternoon. Alfred was awake and saw her confusion. "It's 10 am. You slept like the dead. How are you feeling, schatzi?"

"My neck is a bit stiff, but I feel surprisingly well-rested, given the circumstances. Did you get any sleep?"

"I dozed a bit. I have been listening to some of the conversation. Based on the signs I have seen and what others have said, it looks like we have crossed the border into Poland. People think that we will probably be in Kaunas by tomorrow morning. The train has not been moving particularly fast and has been stopping a lot. You should probably get on the line for the toilet. I will go after you. Take your blanket – it is pretty cold in here."

It was only then that Alice realized how cold it was in the car. Fortunately, they had on several layers of warm clothes, as well as their blankets. Alice had to step around all the people sitting or sleeping in the aisle. As she made her way to the back of the train, she saw the line – not too bad – but she also experienced the smell. She was grateful that Alfred had picked seats in the front of the train. Still, she guessed that the smell would reach them before they reached Kaunas.

When Alfred returned from the toilet, the two had breakfast from the food they had brought and then just sat. This was going to be a long day. Nothing to do but look out the window. No one near them seemed to want to talk, and Alfred and Alice were not really in the mood to talk. Mostly, they dozed when they could and sometimes just stared off into space. And they waited for noon, when they ate their lunch, and for 5 pm, when they gave themselves permission to have an early dinner. Anything to break up the monotony. It got dark early, but they decided to stay awake until 9 pm. At 9 pm, Alice closed her eyes, but sleep did not come. Perhaps it was the long sleep she had had the night before, or the naps she had taken during the day. But Alfred had fallen asleep and she decided not to move so that he would get some needed sleep.

Alice must have fallen asleep herself, since the next thing she knew, the train was stopping, and Gestapo officers were yelling for everyone to get up. Alice and Alfred grabbed their blankets and moved toward to door. She looked out the door and noticed German SS officers and officers with a different uniform. The person who had family in Kaunas said that they were Lithuanians who were now working for the Nazis. He called them a word Alice did not recognize (but thought it might be Yiddish) and then spat on the floor after he said it. Alfred and Alice got off the train as quickly as possible.

Once they were on the platform of the Kaunas station, Alice could see that the SS officers had rubber clubs and were waiving the clubs at those who were not getting off the train fast enough. Once everyone was off the train, one of the SS officers announced that all the Jews from the train would walk to the work camp and would receive their luggage once they arrived at the camp. They were also instructed to drop their baskets of food. "You will be fed once you arrive at the work camp." The Lithuanian solders and the SS soldiers then ordered the Jews to begin walking toward the camp. The weather was colder than Frankfurt, and Alice and Alfred wrapped their blankets around themselves for warmth.

Alfred looked ahead and behind him and tried to count the number of people. He told Alice that he thought that there might be a thousand of them walking to the camp. Alice looked ahead and behind and was amazed at this sea of humanity. Most were wrapped in blankets, but she could see women dressed in fur coats. She wondered how long those fur coats would last in the work camp.

After about an hour of walking, some people started to lag behind, and the soldiers began to use their clubs to keep everyone moving. The Jews from the train were soon walking alongside a fence with barbed wire, and someone ahead of Alice said that the Kaunas ghetto was on the other side of the fence. Alice looked beyond the fence and could see people in the ghetto staring at them. Someone behind Alice asked a group of women in the ghetto whether the women knew where they were going. No one in the ghetto answered back. The group of women actually turned and disappeared down a street. Alice thought they looked afraid to engage with the Jews from the transport.

Alice soon noticed a structure at the top of a hill. It looked like a fort. Alice assumed that this was where the work camp was. They walked up the hill, and when they reached the top, one of the soldiers announced that this was the Ninth Fort and that they were to go inside the gates. Once inside the gates, they were told to stand in a large courtyard. Alice and Alfred looked around. They didn't see any housing structures for workers. They didn't see any factories. They only saw what looked like barracks for soldiers.

After standing in the courtyard for what seemed like hours, the Jews were told to walk down some stairs, and then walk down a long corridor. They could see large cell blocks, and the doors were soon opened. The Jews from Frankfurt joined people who were already in the cells. Alfred held Alice's hand and they both walked into a cell. More people entered the cell and the door was soon closed. A man who had already been in the cell asked where they were from. Alice heard someone say that they were from Frankfurt, and the man then said, "We are from Munich. We arrived on November 22nd, but I am not sure what day it is."

Alfred spoke. "It is the 24th. How long have you been in this cell?"

"Since we arrived. So that would be two days. We have been given no food or water. Everyone has been using a bucket in the corner of the cell for a toilet. They come by periodically to empty the bucket. We have asked them what is going to happen to us. They have been ignoring us."

Alfred then asked, "But what about the work camp? And our luggage? And they told us we would be fed once we arrived at the work camp."

"They told us the same thing. So far, we have seen no luggage, no food, no work camp. We have just been here, in the freezing cold with no food or water. Maybe they are just trying to kill us."

That last statement sent a shiver down Alice's spine. Maybe this man is right. Maybe they are leaving everyone down in the basement of this fort to die.

Alice and Alfred found a spot to sit. They placed part of one of the blankets on the floor and then wrapped themselves with the rest of the blanket and the second blanket. They looked around the cell. It was dank and the walls were shimmering – they could see ice crystals. Not a good sign. Alice said to Alfred, "If they have been kept here two days without food or water, the same fate could await us." Alfred gave her a hug and said, "We need to conserve our strength. We need to remain seated and use as little energy as possible. And Alice, you will need to use the bucket soon."

"I know I do. And I know I am being silly, but I really hate the idea of people seeing me go to the bathroom. You know I always insisted that my apartments have a private bathroom, even when I couldn't afford it. I hated the idea of sharing a bathroom. And now sharing a bucket!"

"Alice, you don't have a choice. Just use that imagination of yours and create walls and a flush toilet."

"Okay. I'll try." Alfred helped her up and gave her a kiss on the cheek, and Alice walked over to the bucket.

At different points during the day, Alice could hear crying or moaning. Sometimes, someone would shout out something. Mostly, the cries were ignored by the guards, but sometimes the guards yelled back a threatening warning. The day passed slowly. Periodically, Alfred would glance at his watch. Alice decided to ask the time every fourth time he looked. The last time, it was 6 pm. Alice was wondering how they would sleep in this cold cell. Alice thought to herself that she could not remember ever being this cold. Still, at some point, she managed to doze off. She was awakened by someone yelling about the cold. Alfred also must have dozed, since he looked annoyed. He glanced at his watch. 5 am. They would probably not be going back to sleep. They took turns visiting the "toilet."

But they were relieved when, at 7 am, the guards appeared and opened their cell door. The guards announced they would be opening all the cells throughout the morning and everyone would be leaving. The guards yelled that everyone should take whatever they had with them. Of course, no one had anything except their blankets. Alice looked over at the man from Munich. He looked exhausted, but relieved. Alice could not imagine how anyone could have survived three days in this freezing cell.

The guards ordered everyone out of the cell. They yelled, "eyes forward." As she was walking out, Alice noticed that not everyone had gotten up, and she wondered if they were okay. But she knew not to try to find out. She needed to keep her "eyes forward." Given that all the soldiers had guns, she needed to follow their directives. They walked up the stairs and went into the courtyard.

Alfred said to her, "I am so glad we only had to stay in that cell a day. At some point, I counted and there were about three hundred people in our cell. It would have been pretty bad if we had been there a second night. I wonder if we are being walked to the work camp."

One of the guards divided their group into three groups of around one hundred each. Alice and Alfred were in the second group. The guard announced that the first group was to follow him. About five minutes later, they could hear the loud engines of a number of trucks outside the walls of the fort. Alfred said to Alice, "Sounds like they are going to drive us to the camp." Alice was relieved – she did not relish the idea of another long hike.

Thirty minutes after they first heard the truck engines, the guards returned for Alice's group. She thought it was strange that she could still hear the engines. Maybe the trucks had not left yet, or they had brought other trucks for them. Alfred and Alice walked through the gates and the officers directed them to turn right and walk towards what looked, in the distance, like large pits. The officers then told them to stop. They were directed to take off all of their clothes. Everyone just stood there and stared at the guards. "I said to take off all of your clothes. You will get new work clothes." A woman yelled out, "I cannot undress in front of men." Another yelled, "It is too cold to take off our clothes." One of the officers yelled back, "Take off your clothes now or you will be shot. And make it fast." And so the one hundred people in Alice's group took off their clothes in the freezing weather.

Alice had only undressed in front of two men. And now she was naked in front of all these other men. She thought she was being stupid, considering everything that had happened in the last few days, but Alice was embarrassed. She looked around, and she could tell that almost everyone was feeling the same. They were using their hands to try to cover up what they could.

The group was then ordered to walk towards the pit. As they got closer, the front people in the group could see what looked like naked people at the bottom on the pit. When they were about 20 feet away, it was clear the people in the pit were naked and dead. The soldiers then ordered everyone into the pit. No one moved. The soldiers said it again, this time with guns pointed at the Jews. A few ran towards the soldiers and were shot dead, although some managed to scratch a few of the soldiers' faces. Others ran towards the woods and were shot. At that moment, Alice understood why the truck's engines were running – to drown out the noise of the shooting.

The soldiers pushed everyone into the pit and told them to lie down. Those who would not lie down were shot. Alfred turned his head to face Alice, grabbed her hand, and said "Schatzi, I love you more than life itself." And then he said, "Disappear." And Alice knew exactly what he meant.

Alice had never consciously disappeared. She only knew that she had disappeared after the fact. But she now closed her eyes, heard Alfred say "Disappear" one more time, and when she opened her eyes, she was aware that time had stopped. She looked around and no one was moving. The soldiers were standing with their guns drawn, but no one was firing. The soldiers with the machine guns were aiming the guns at the Jews in the pit, but were frozen in place. Alice looked over at the rest of the Jews in the pit, who were lying flat but still alive. Alice stood up, walked out of the pit, and sat down on a nearby bench. She hadn't noticed the bench before, but the bench looked exactly like the bench Alice and Alfred had sat on the last time they went to the zoo, on that last good day together. She looked down and she was wearing her favorite dress, the blue one, the one she had made for her wedding to Alfred. She loved its clean lines and the beaded shoulders, with the dress reaching to just below her knees. She thought it best reflected her skills as both a handbag designer and a dressmaker. She even had on the blue hat with the side bow. She remembered how Alfred had made fun of her for needing to purchase the "perfect" hat to match the dress, but then told her it was one of the things that he loved about her.

Her blue dress had short sleeves, but, remarkably, she was not cold. She smoothed out the folds in her dress and thought about her life. Overall, at 45 years old, she felt she had a good life. She had a talent and a vocation that she was able to pursue, even if her father was not always supportive. But her mother was and had convinced her father to let her attend the Nuremberg art school. Her first marriage did not work, although she didn't blame Ludwig. They were just not well-suited for each other. Alfred was a much better fit. She did wonder if she should have had children. She wasn't sure she would have made a very good mother. But she did feel like she had enjoyed some of the benefits of motherhood with Ruth. Thankfully, Ruth was safe in America. She was happy she was able to play a small part in making that happen.

Alice was mostly sad that she would not be able to grow old with Alfred. They shared a sense of humor and laughed a lot during the happy times. There just were not enough happy times for them. But even during the hard times, Alfred was a rock, giving her the support that she needed. He was a good man. The world will miss him. "I will miss him," she thought. More than anything else, it seemed unfair that someone would kill her, just because hers was a different religion. When her dressmaking shop was open, non-Jews frequented her shop and loved her designs. When she opened her arts and crafts studio and then her purse factory, no one asked if she was Jewish when they bought a purse or a scarf. What had she done that made these people hate her so? And if they hated her so much, why didn't they just let her and Alfred leave?

And then she thought about her mother and her sister. She hoped they would never know what had happened to Alice, but the reality was that, assuming they survived this insanity, they would find out that she and Alfred were dead. She hoped Selma would be able to get over the loss. And she also hoped that Selma would find someone who would treat her well. Alice felt Selma had grown as a person and was ready to find someone who would appreciate her. At least, that is what she hoped. "Mama and Selma, be well. Alice loves you."

She looked to her right and there was Alfred, sitting next to her on the bench and wearing the blue pinstripe suit. This was her favorite suit of his, and he always looked so dapper in it – and he knew it. He even had the watch fob in the vest pocket, the same fob he had been forced to turn over to the Nazis. He had loved that fob. It had been presented to him by his company after he had sold 10,000 watches. Alfred looked at Alice and gave her that smile that always made her melt. And then he touched his fingers to his lips and touched his fingers to his heart. She did the same. He then took her hand and kissed it. She felt warm all over. Alice said to him, "Schatzi, I will love you forever." Then she smiled and closed her eyes.

EPILOGUE

We were back in Frankfurt. But unlike the unexpected stopover a few years ago, this time the return was purposeful. We arrived in the morning and went to the hotel to check in. Wanting to get on Frankfurt time as quickly as possible, we decided to walk around the city and try to stay up until at least 9 pm. We had plenty of places to see, and so we got started immediately.

We walked over to Roderbergweg 30 to where Emma had lived until 1930. We then crossed the Main River and walked to the apartment building on Schaumainkai where Alice lived when she had returned to Frankfurt from Nuremberg in 1930. We walked to the building Selma, Leo, and Emma moved to at Boermerstarasse 60 (and where their Stumbling Stones are) in 1933, and to Alice and Alfred's last apartment on Oberlindau. And then we walked to the Marx's house, the last place where Selma lived before she was deported.

Standing in front of the Marx's house, I was trying to imagine how Selma reacted when she received the news about Alice's death. German soldiers returning from Poland at the end of 1941 brought back reports about the massacre at Kaunas, so there is little doubt that both Selma and Emma knew that Alice had died at Kaunas – and how she had died. Both Selma and their mother must have been devastated when they heard the news. But Selma and Emma would not have to wait long for their own fates. Selma was deported to the Sobibor death camp in May 1942 and Emma was deported to the Theresienstadt ghetto in August 1942, and then to the Treblinka death camp in October 1942. Both would perish on the day each arrived at their respective death camps. As for Leo, after his two-year prison sentence ended at the end of 1942, he was immediately deported to Auschwitz. Leo was selected for slave labor after he arrived at the death camp, but died of heart failure a month after his selection. Those who had helped the Heppenheimer family during their darkest hours – Dr. Marx and Dr. Popper – were deported to Theresienstadt, along with their wives, and all perished in Auschwitz.

The Heppenheimers who made it to America also suffered. Benno never really recovered from the heartbreak of losing his beloved wife. Margot, who was deported to Lodz, likely died in the Chelmno death camp, along with her mother, in May 1942. A part-owner of one of the larger scrap metal dealers in southern Germany, Benno could only find part-time work in a warehouse in New York, and was forced to stop working completely in 1946 because of arthritis. He died on November 9, 1953 at 71. And Jacob Heppenheimer, once the owner of a large and fancy villa in Frankfurt, was forced to live in a small apartment with his son Ernst in Queens, New York once he and his wife emigrated. Jacob never working again and died in 1950 at 71.

Bruce and I went to a nice restaurant for dinner, going over what he would say at the ceremony tomorrow. I had done the research on Alice's life, but this was Bruce's great-aunt and it seemed more appropriate for him to speak. Still, Bruce knew how connected I had become to Alice through my research. I felt more and more of a connection as I learned about her life in Nuremberg and Frankfurt, about her love of fashion, about her drive to open her various businesses, about her two marriages, and about her death at the Ninth Fort. Learning about her death was particularly hard – for some reason, I was hoping to learn that she had somehow emigrated to America, living with Alfred on a vineyard in California. Instead, she perished in the first mass slaughter of German Jews during the war, killed by the Einsatzgruppen, Germany's special mobile killing unit. After the Einsatzgruppen mowed down the nearly 3,000 German Jews with machine guns that day, thirty Jewish prisoners were ordered to cover the pits with dirt. Then these prisoners were shot and left unburied on the Ninth Fort grounds.

The injustices done to Alice and Alfred continued after their deaths. On January 1, 1942, pursuant to the recently issued Eleventh Decree, the German government took official possession of all the assets of Alfred and Alice Falkenstein (as they would the assets of all deported Jews), including their account at the Deutsche Bank. The justification for taking these assets was that Alice and Alfred had "emigrated" when they were deported. Soon after the seizure, an auctioneer was dispatched to the Falkenstein's apartment to sell what was left in the home – the Gestapo had already taken the valuables placed in the envelope by Alfred. There wasn't much left to auction. But there were the two dirty coffee cups, still on the table, left in the Gestapo's haste to bring Alfred and Alice to the Grossmarkthalle. The cups were the last sign the Falkensteins had once lived in Frankfurt.

And now there would be a permanent testament that Alice and Alfred had lived in Frankfurt, had led rich and fulfilling lives. and were loved by family and friends. Like Selma and Emma, Alice and Alfred would now have Stumbling Stones placed in the last place they had lived before they were deported. The Stumbling Stones would be placed at Oberlindau 108. Every person who walks by will now "stumble" across the brass plates. Hopefully, they will look down to see the names of the two people who had lived in the building. They will never know the full story of these people, but they will see their names, and maybe they will say out loud. "Alice Falkenstein, nee Heppenheimer, Born 1896, Deported to Kaunas 1941, Murdered Nov. 25, 1941; Alfred Falkenstein, Born 1896, Deported to Kaunas 1941, Murdered Nov. 25, 1941." And then Alice and Alfred will be remembered.

AUTHOR'S NOTE AND ACKNOWLEDGEMENTS

In 2021, after more than three years of research, I published a book about my husband Bruce's German Jewish family, *Broken Promises: The Story of a Jewish Family in Germany*. Through my research, I was able to discover family members previously lost to the Holocaust. Among the family members unknown to my husband were Emma, Alice and Selma. I continued in my research after the book was published and among the documents I received were the records of Alice's two forced labor positions in 1941. Staring at those documents, I realized I was not finished telling Alice's story.

The challenge for me in telling Alice's story was the problem I identified in *Broken Promises*: that no one knew anything about Alice the person. I knew where she lived, who she married, and how she earned a living. I have most of her business records, several personal letters written by her, and a few photos. But I don't know whether she was funny, or clever, or kind. The Holocaust had robbed her family not just of her name, but also of who she was as a person. In writing *Broken Promises*, I only included in the book what I could prove through documentation. To tell more of Alice's story, I tried to imagine who she was as a person. Based on the documentation I found, which was rather extensive, I imagined Alice as an ambitious, brave, talented, hopeful, and loving woman. Only an ambitious and brave woman would have left her family to pursue her art in Nuremberg, would have opened an art studio and purse factory, and would have divorced her first husband. Only a hopeful woman would have asked the Dressmakers Guild to support her request to operate as a ladies' dressmaker in 1941, and only a very skilled artisan would have actually received that support. And only a woman who believed in love would have remarried at a time when most Jews would have been focused on escaping.

In researching *Broken Promises*, I discovered the Stolpersteine (Stumbling Stones) project and the Stumbling Stones of Emma and Selma. My husband and his two siblings Marc and Rachel requested that stones be placed in Mannheim to remember their family, and on October 12, 2021, stumbling stones were installed at the former home of Max and Recha Heppenheimer to remember them and their two sons Kurt (my father-in-law) and Alfred. My husband Bruce and I have submitted a request for Stolpersteine for Alice and Alfred. Because of the pandemic, the project has been delayed, and the stones might not be installed until 2026. I intend this novel to serve as another stumbling stone for Alice and Alfred.

I have several people to thank for their support and suggestions as I wrote the book. I must start with my golfing friends Laura Manning Johnson and Julie Isaac, who listened to my many musings about Alice and encouraged me to write this novel. Suggestions from my great friend and walking buddy Jill Pargament helped me to make important changes to a number of the chapters. Recommendation from family members Carol Reynolds and Lisa Hack helped me to make the book better and more nuanced. My sister-in-law Rachel Heppen, who feels like a sister to me, read several versions of the book and provided me with useful suggestions on the historical periods and Alice's art. My children Emily and Jonathan provided me with continued support as I wrote the book. And I cannot understate the role my husband Bruce played in this book. He read multiple versions of each chapter and provided important suggestions and edits. He deserves more thanks than is possible.

ABOUT THE AUTHOR

Bonnie Suchman is an attorney who has been practicing law for forty years. Using her legal skills, she researched her husband's family's 250-year history in Germany, and published a non-fiction book about the family, *Broken Promises: The Story of a Jewish Family* in Germany. One member of the family, Alice Heppenheimert, was particularly compelling for the author. This novel is her story. Bonnie lives with her husband Bruce in Maryland.

NOTE FROM BONNIE SUCHMAN

Word-of-mouth is crucial for any author to succeed. If you enjoyed *Stumbling Stones*, please leave a review online—anywhere you are able. Even if it's just a sentence or two. It would make all the difference and would be very much appreciated.

Thanks!
Bonnie Suchman

We hope you enjoyed reading this title from:

www.blackrosewriting.com

Subscribe to our mailing list – *The Rosevine* – and receive **FREE** books, daily deals, and stay current with news about upcoming releases and our hottest authors.
Scan the QR code below to sign up.

Already a subscriber? Please accept a sincere thank you for being a fan of Black Rose Writing authors.

View other Black Rose Writing titles at
www.blackrosewriting.com/books and use promo code
PRINT to receive a **20% discount** when purchasing.

Made in United States
Orlando, FL
13 March 2025

59412112R00166